SINS IN BLACK

DITA DOW

ALSO BY DITA DOW

The Haunting Feast of All Hallows Eve

Mirror of the Damned

The Legend of Thornewood Manor

The Legend of Whispering Pines Inn

The Deceiver's Casket

Cave of Terror

ThrillHers: Thrilling Tales in Isolated Locations

Carnival of the Dead

27 Elmwood Drive

TABLE OF CONTENTS

*Black is not the
absence of light,
but the memory of
sins never confessed.*

Sins in Black

Chapter One

The rain in Sinister Falls never stopped—it just changed its rhythm. This morning, it fell soft and steady, blurring the edges of the towering firs outside my mother's house.

I stood in the doorway, coffee mug in hand, staring out at the familiar stretch of dense forest that had surrounded me for the first eighteen years of my life. I hated it. I hated the trees, the rain, the goddamned mist that made the air heavy and the world feel small.

I took a sip of coffee, enjoying the warmth as it cut the chill creeping in through the open door. The chipped mug was an old souvenir from a trip to Portland my parents had taken decades ago. Frank and Mabel's Pacific Northwest Adventure, it read in faded block letters. It was one of the few things my mom still used from back then.

I glanced over my shoulder into the living room. Mom was fast asleep in her recliner, wrapped in her favorite quilt, the one with the faded red and yellow patches. The one my dad had bought her the year I turned ten. Her gray hair was pulled back into a loose braid, and her face looked peaceful.

The TV was on low, casting faint light and muffled voices across the room. I'd turned it on to drown out the silence of the house, but it hadn't helped much.

She looked so small in that chair, the frailty of her frame a sharp contrast to the woman I remembered from my childhood. Mabel Whitlock had been tough—sharp-tongued, quick with a comeback, and confident enough to intimidate most of the people in this town. But age and rheumatoid arthritis had a way of wearing a body down.

I took another sip of coffee, my gaze lingering on her before I turned back to the rain. I had sworn I'd never come back to Sinister Falls.

When I turned eighteen, I left this place behind without a second glance, swearing to myself I'd never set foot in it again. It was right after Dad died—after the heart attack took him, leaving Mom and me with nothing but grief and a pile of paperwork from the City of Sinister Falls. He'd been the town's accountant for almost twenty-five years, and the stress of keeping the books balanced in a place that thrived on shady deals had worn him down. Or did him in.

I could still see him, sitting at the kitchen table late at night, his glasses perched on the tip of his nose, a calculator in one hand and a whiskey in the other. He used to say he kept the town running, and maybe he had.

I packed my bags two weeks after his funeral. Told Mom I was going to Dallas for college and that I wouldn't be back. She'd nodded, her expression hard to read, and I'd taken it as permission. Back then, I thought leaving was the only way to survive.

But life has a way of pulling you back to the places you thought you'd left behind.

When Mom's health deteriorated last year, there hadn't been a question. I left Dallas—left my job, my apartment, and everything else that was falling apart there—and came back to care for her. It wasn't about guilt or obligation. It was about her.

I'd been standing in this very doorway staring out at the rain, hating it. I'd told myself that if Mom ever needed me, I'd be there. That no matter how far I ran, I wouldn't turn my back on her. And now, six months into my new life back in my old home, I was doing my best to keep that promise.

But God, it was hard.

Sinister Falls had a way of suffocating you, of wrapping its damp fingers around your throat and squeezing until you forgot how to breathe.

I'd spent years pretending this place didn't exist, and now it felt like it was swallowing me whole.

The rain picked up, tapping against the metal roof in a steady staccato that matched the anxiety stabbing my chest. My coffee had gone cold, but I didn't move to refill it. Instead, I watched the rain and wondered if I'd ever get used to the way time stretched here—turning days into weeks and weeks into something unbearable.

Mom shifted in her chair, letting out a soft sigh. I turned to look at her again, her face still relaxed in sleep. She deserved better than this. Better than this town, better than the life she'd been handed after Dad died.

I set the mug down on the windowsill next to the door and traced my fingers along the worn edge of the wood. No matter how much I hated Sinister Falls, no matter how much I wanted to run again, I couldn't leave her. Not again.

The buzz of my phone on the kitchen counter startled me—a reminder that the world hadn't stopped just because I had.

I crossed the room, careful not to wake Mom, and picked it up.

"Whitlock," I said.

"You up?" Chief Nolan rasped through the line, his voice rough from a lifetime of cigarettes and booze.

"Unfortunately," I replied.

"Got a body," Nolan said, like he was reading off the weather report. "Up by the old power station. Walsh is securing the scene."

The way he said it—no emotion, no shock, no humanity—hit me harder than the words themselves. It wasn't indifference; I could have tolerated indifference. It was the ease with which he let those words slide off his tongue, like finding a body in Sinister Falls was just another Tuesday. And maybe, to him, it was.

"I'm on my way."

"Good," Nolan said, his tone as flat as ever. Then, just as I was about to hang up, he added, "Try and wrap this one up quickly, you understand? No need to drag it out."

I paused for a beat, gripping the phone tighter. "Yeah. I understand."

But I didn't. Not really. And I doubted I ever would.

INTERVIEW WITH DETECTIVE HARLIE WHITLOCK

INTERVIEWER: You look a little tense after that call.
Everything okay?

WHITLOCK: Yeah. I mean — no. It's just... it's still weird being
back. I left Sinister Falls when I was eighteen, went to college
in Dallas, and then joined the Dallas Police Department. I never
thought I'd come back, let alone end up working for Nolan.

WHITLOCK: What about you? I remember seeing you around
when I was in high school.

INTERVIEWER: I used to spend summers here when I was
a kid — my aunt lived just outside town. I'm working on a
series about how small towns handle power, policing, and
accountability. Mayor Jenkins invited me out, hoping I'd
highlight some of Sinister Falls' better qualities.

INTERVIEWER: What brought you back?

WHITLOCK: My mom. She needed me. So I came home. Chief
Nolan offered me a job, and I took it. But I don't think he
actually cares if I do it well. That's been... frustrating, to say the
least.

INTERVIEWER: How so?

WHITLOCK: The way he runs things — it's so lax. Cases get
brushed off, details overlooked. It's like he's content to let

things slide as long as they don't make too much noise. That doesn't sit well with me. I spent years in the DPD where we took our work seriously. Here, it feels like I'm the only one who gives a damn.

INTERVIEWER: Do you think he regrets hiring you?

WHITLOCK: Probably. I'm not exactly great at letting things go when I know something's off. I think he expected me to just fall in line, but that's not who I am.

INTERVIEWER: So what are you going to do?

WHITLOCK: Keep doing the job the way it should be done. Whether Nolan likes it or not.

Chapter Two

I tightened my grip on the steering wheel as I navigated the winding road to the power station. The trees pressed in from both sides, forming a tunnel of dense trunks and tangled branches. Fog drifted off the river and swirled over the asphalt, making me feel like the entire world had shrunk down to the size of Sinister Falls. And that's just how this town liked it—closed off from outsiders, refusing to let in the light.

"God, why did I ever come back?" I muttered under my breath.

It wasn't just that I hated the place; it was that I knew better now. After going away to college, after spending time in Dallas working narcotics and homicide, I now knew there were places where the air didn't always feel so heavy. Places that felt big, open, bright. Places where people looked each other in the eye without hesitation.

Here, everyone was too busy looking over their shoulder to notice anything and anyone else.

When I finally pulled up to the scene, I spotted the old power station silhouetted against the gray sky. It reminded me of an abandoned sentinel, its tall towers standing guard over the town. A single patrol car sat with its lights flashing, painting the early morning in strokes of red and blue. I parked behind it and stepped out, tugging my jacket tight to ward off the chill seeping into my bones.

Officer Amy Walsh stood behind the yellow crime scene tape, clipboard in hand, pacing in a tight circle. I remembered feeling that same drive in my early days in the DPD. Eager, ready to take on the world before the world took too much from me.

"Detective Whitlock," she called, her voice carrying a slight quiver that might've been from the cold or from nerves.

I stepped under the tape and joined her. "Walsh," I said. "What do we have?"

"Female victim, mid-twenties, best we can tell," she explained, flipping through her notes. "No ID on her."

I nodded. "All right. Show me."

She led me along a narrow trail that branched off from the cracked asphalt. The power station's metal skeleton loomed behind us, the wind passing through its rusted beams with a low hollow moan. Like it was warning us to turn back. We pushed on until we reached a small clearing shrouded by thick brush.

I've seen dozens of bodies in my career, but something about this one made the hairs on the back of my neck stand on end. The body lay sprawled on the damp ground, torn clothes soaked through. Her arms were stretched above her head, fingers contorted, as though she was clawing at the air itself. Her eyes were wide open, frozen in sheer terror.

A strip of black fabric—satin, maybe silk—was tied tightly around her neck. There weren't any bruises or scratches that I could see, just that pale skin and those horrified eyes. The scene looked staged.

I crouched beside her. "Jesus."

Amy cleared her throat and lowered her voice. "The jogger who found her called it in. He's over there." She gestured with her pen to a trembling man, standing a few feet away near a cluster of trees.

I stood up and wiped my hands on my jacket, even though they were clean. "Thanks, Walsh."

I studied the man for a moment. He was tall and lanky, wearing a soaked windbreaker and running pants caked with mud around the ankles. His face was ashen, and he was staring hard at the ground, perhaps trying to blot out the memory of what he'd seen.

I approached him slowly. "Sir? I'm Detective Harlie Whitlock. You mind if I ask you a few questions?"

He jerked his head up, eyes darting around before settling on me. "Y-Yeah," he managed. "Sure."

"What's your name?"

"Scott," he whispered. "Scott Fletcher."

"Scott, can you tell me what happened?" I kept my tone gentle, hoping to put him at ease.

He inhaled a shaky breath. "I, uh, I come this way almost every morning, around four or four-thirty. Just a short run before work. I—God, I thought it was trash, you know? A pile of clothes someone dumped." He swallowed hard. "Then I got closer and realized... it was her."

"Did you touch anything? Move anything?"

"No. I, uh, I freaked out. Ran back to the road and called 911."

For a moment, he said nothing. "I've never seen anything like that. The way she... she was just staring."

"You did the right thing, Scott. Do you remember seeing anyone else around? Any cars on the road?"

He hesitated. "No, not really. It was pretty dark, foggy... I don't think I saw any headlights. Just my own breath in the cold."

I gave him a reassuring nod. "All right, Scott. You did the right thing. I'd like you to come down to the station later to give a full statement—does that work for you? You need to get into some dry clothes before you catch your death out here."

He nodded and took another shaky breath. "Yeah. Okay. One dead body is enough for me."

I winced, regretting my choice of words. I cleared my throat then said, "I just mean you don't want to be out here soaked for too long. We'll get this sorted."

I watched Scott walk back toward the road then returned to the body, where Amy waited.

"Any idea who she is?" I asked, though I knew the answer already.

"No ID on her."

The cold fog pressed against my chest, as if it were trying to compress my lungs. I could almost feel the secrets of Sinister Falls swirling around me, ready to close in the moment I let my guard down.

Amy's voice pulled me back. "Detective? You okay?"

I forced a tight smile. "Yeah. I'm fine." I wasn't, but I doubted she needed to hear the messy truth.

"So, what now?" she asked, her gaze fixated on the body.

I glanced over my shoulder at the victim, then moved into Amy's line of vision, forcing her eyes on me. "We document everything. Every piece of evidence. We do our jobs. And we get ready, because something tells me this is only the beginning."

She nodded. "I'll grab the camera, start photographing the scene. The coroner's on the way."

"Good," I said, my voice taut with an edge I couldn't hide. "Let's keep this as tight as possible. No leaks. I don't want the whole town in a panic before we have facts."

Amy started back toward the patrol car, leaving me alone with the fog, the secrets, and the dead body.

INTERVIEW WITH DETECTIVE HARLIE WHITLOCK

INTERVIEWER: You're a seasoned detective, but you looked pretty shaken back there. That girl... she's bothering you more than you want to admit.

WHITLOCK: It's not just her. It's what she represents. I can guarantee no one was looking for her. And Nolan won't want to waste resources on a case like this.

INTERVIEWER: Why not?

WHITLOCK: Because to him, she's just another 'nobody.' No family raising hell, no political pressure. Easier to let it fade into the background than actually do the work.

INTERVIEWER: And you're not okay with that.

WHITLOCK: No, I'm not. But around here, what I want doesn't count for much.

INTERVIEWER: You looked... physically disturbed by the body. What's that about?

WHITLOCK: I've seen it before.

I stepped inside the freezer-cold morgue, shoving my hands deeper into my jacket pockets. The antiseptic smell hit me immediately—sharp and clinical, trying but failing to cover up the undeniable scent of death. Dr. Lionel March stood by the autopsy table, dictating notes into his recorder. He'd been here long enough to stop reacting to the cold, but he never stopped looking tired.

"Detective Whitlock," he greeted me, snapping off his gloves. "Right on time."

"March." I walked up to him and looked down at the sheet-covered body on the table. "What do we have?"

"Female. Unidentified," he began, tossing his gloves into the bin and grabbing a towel. "Strangulation. The black ribbon found on her neck? Added after she was already dead. Whoever did this used a thinner wire or ligature. More precise."

I leaned over the body, peering at her neck and trying not to look at her blue lips. "So, not quick," I muttered. "And they wanted to send a message. Figures."

March nodded. "Exactly. The marks around her neck suggest control. The killer knew what they were doing. It wasn't impulsive."

"What about a struggle? Did she fight?"

"Oh, she fought." He gestured at her hands. "Defensive wounds here, bruising on her fingers. Some nails chipped, like she tried to grab at whatever was choking her. But she didn't stand a chance."

I grimaced. "What's the timeline?"

"Time of death? About eight hours ago. Puts it somewhere between midnight and three o'clock in the morning."

"Perfect time to dump a body," I said. "No one on the streets, storm washing away any evidence."

March leaned against the counter, fiddling with the buttons on his lab coat, avoiding eye contact.

"What?" I asked.

"There's more," he admitted, walking back over to the table and pulling the sheet down. "Take a look here."

My eyes followed where he was pointing. There, on her lower abdomen, was a small tattoo—an intricate design of a star with a swirling pattern around it.

"That might help identify her," I said, leaning in closer. "Not exactly a generic design. Can you tell if it's recent?"

"It's healed over, so no. But it's detailed. Someone in town might recognize it," he said.

I took a mental note. "Anything else about the body? Anything… uh, sexual?"

March shook his head. "No evidence of sexual assault. No fluids, no injuries consistent with that. This was about control, not gratification. Strangulation was the purpose."

I straightened, relieved but no less angry. "What the hell's the motive, then? Just domination? Revenge?"

"Could be either," March said, crossing his arms. "But this wasn't random. I'd bet anything that she knew her killer."

"Thanks," I said, moving toward the door. I stopped just short of the hallway and glanced back. "You're one of the only people in this town I actually trust, you know that?"

"That's why you'll figure this out, Detective. You care more than anyone else in this place does."

INTERVIEW WITH DR. LIONEL MARCH

INTERVIEWER: Dr. March, you've been in Sinister Falls for a while now, haven't you?

MARCH: Twelve years. Long enough to know where the skeletons are buried — sometimes literally.

INTERVIEWER: And before that?

MARCH: Seattle. Worked as a medical examiner there for a while. Big city, big crimes, big messes. Thought a smaller town might be a change of pace. Turns out, Sinister Falls has its own kind of mess — just quieter about it.

INTERVIEWER: So, no regrets about the move?

MARCH: Some days, sure. Seattle had its problems, but at least the crimes made sense. Here, it's like a game where only half the players know the rules. But I like my work, no matter where I am.

INTERVIEWER: What is it you like about being a coroner?

MARCH: The dead don't lie. They don't change their stories, don't try to spin a narrative. They tell you exactly what happened, if you know how to listen. And I like the puzzle of it. Putting the pieces together, figuring out what went wrong — it's like solving a mystery where the dead can speak for themselves.

INTERVIEWER: And in a place like Sinister Falls, I imagine there are a lot of stories hidden beneath the surface.

MARCH: More than people want to admit. This town has a long memory but a short attention span. Things get buried — sometimes in the ground, sometimes in paperwork.

INTERVIEWER: What do you think of the police here?

MARCH: Depends on who you're talking about. Some of them want to do good, but they're fighting against a system that's been broken for a long time. Others? They're just here for a paycheck, maybe a little power.

INTERVIEWER: And Detective Whitlock?

MARCH: She's not like the rest of them. The detective actually cares. That's dangerous in a place like this.

INTERVIEWER: Dangerous how?

MARCH: Because when you start pulling at the loose threads, you don't always like what unravels. Sinister Falls is full of people who prefer things stay exactly as they are. The detective? She doesn't let things go. That makes her a problem for some very powerful people.

INTERVIEWER: You think she's in over her head?

MARCH: Maybe. But that's what makes her different. Most people get scared off before they get too deep. She keeps pushing.

INTERVIEWER: What about the politicians in this town? What's your take on them?

MARCH: You mean the ones who pretend they don't know what's happening in their own backyard? They're part of the machine, just like everyone else with power here. Some of them just grease the wheels while others steer the whole damn thing.

Either way, they don't like change, and they don't like questions.

INTERVIEWER: Have you ever had run-ins with them?

MARCH: Let's just say I've been 'advised' more than once to keep my findings quiet. Not that I ever listen.

INTERVIEWER: You don't seem like someone who backs down easily.

MARCH: Comes with the job. I deal with facts, with bodies, not people and their lies. Doesn't matter how much someone wants a truth buried — it always has a way of surfacing eventually.

INTERVIEWER: And when it does?

MARCH: That's when people like Detective Whitlock must decide what they're willing to do with it. Because the truth? It always comes with a price.

INTERVIEWER: Do you think she's ready for that?

MARCH: I think she's already paid more than she realizes. The real question is whether she's willing to keep paying.

INTERVIEWER: And you? You keep looking at the truth, even when it puts you in danger.

MARCH: Someone has to. The dead don't have voices anymore. But I can still speak for them.

Chapter Four

I stood at the cliff's edge, staring down at the dark water. Devil's Backbone jutted out in craggy formations, overlooking a canyon carved by the relentless river below.

From up here, the river looked deceptively calm, but I knew better—its currents were vicious, a twisting path of churning whitecaps that cut through the gorge like a wound. The sheer drop from where I stood made my stomach tighten, but I forced myself not to step back.

I remembered coming up here as a teenager with Shelby Wainswright. She'd bring the cheap beer, the cigarettes she'd swiped from her older brother's dresser. We'd sit on the rocks, legs dangling over the edge, passing a cigarette between us, our whispered dreams mixing with the smoke that curled into the night.

We swore we'd leave Sinister Falls, run away to a big city where no one knew our names. We even made a plan, a real one, down to the bus tickets.

Shelby's unused bus ticket was found on her body.

The officials said she jumped. Said she threw herself off this very cliff over some lovesick crush on Scotty Tremlin, the golden-boy quarterback. But Shelby wasn't like that. She wasn't reckless with her heart, and she sure as hell would've told me if she was hurting. No, Shelby didn't jump. And no matter how many years passed, I'd never believed she had.

A voice cut through the wind. "Harlie."

I turned to see Officer Jordan Reyes standing a few feet away, hands shoved in his jacket pockets, his officer's uniform crisp despite the hike up here. His dark eyes studied me, searching for something, maybe an explanation.

He shifted his weight like he wasn't sure if he should step closer or keep his distance. Then, he pulled something from his jacket pocket and tossed it to me. I caught it instinctively.

A bag of peanut M&M's.

I raised an eyebrow. "You bribing me with candy now?"

He smirked but didn't answer, just walked over and took a seat on a fallen log near me. "Dispatch got a call," he said. "Suspicious person up here. Figured it was you."

"Nice to know I'm so predictable."

"Well, you didn't come back to the station after the morning's homicide." His voice softened. "Been looking for you."

I let out a slow breath, my gaze drifting back to the river below. "Needed to clear my head."

He didn't press, but I felt his presence near me, solid and grounding. After a beat, he said, "I think I know who she is. The vic from this morning."

I turned sharply. "Who?"

"Leah Emerson. Waitress at Harlan's out by the highway. Reported missing two weeks ago by her ex." His jaw tightened. "Dylan Cross."

I swore under my breath. "Cross?"

"Yeah." Jordan's expression darkened. "Told us she ran off. Said she had a habit of disappearing. But something about it never sat right with me."

"And now she turns up dead in the woods near the power plant?" I shook my head.

Jordan nodded. "I figured you'd want to follow up. Thought you should hear it from me. Thought we could give Cross a visit together."

I studied him, the tension in his shoulders, the way his fingers flexed like he was trying to keep his emotions in check. He cared, even if he wouldn't admit it.

"Thanks, Reyes," I said, softer than I meant to.

He glanced at me, something flickering behind his eyes. "You going to be okay?"

I shook the bag of M&M's. "You worried about me?"

"Always."

The wind whipped between us, carrying the weight of words unsaid.

He sighed, running a hand through his dark hair. "Come on. Let's get back. We've got a case to solve."

CHAPTER FIVE

I watched the road narrow as we left town limits, its edges crumbling into the overgrown ditch that ran alongside like a jagged scar. Jordan drove, his fingers drumming on the steering wheel. He turned off the asphalt onto a gravel driveway.

Dylan Cross's house was a wound on the landscape—a sagging, two-story structure with peeling paint, warped siding, and windows clouded with grime. Jordan parked behind a beat-up Chevy Nova sitting crooked in the driveway, one tail light missing. Rust devoured the metal inch by inch.

Jordan killed the engine.

"Ready?" he asked, though he knew the answer.

I stepped out, my boots crunching on gravel mixed with broken glass. The air smelled of stale beer, motor oil, and rotting trash. We climbed the rickety porch steps, and I rapped on the door with the edge of my knuckle.

A beat. Then another. Then the door creaked open to reveal a shirt-less Dylan Cross, his skinny frame covered with tattoos. His face was all sharp angles and hollowed-out cheeks, eyes bloodshot and rimmed with the kind of darkness that didn't come from lack of sleep alone. A fresh bruise bloomed along his jawline, like he'd picked a fight with someone who hit harder.

"Detective Whitlock," I said, flashing my badge. "This is Officer Reyes. We need to ask you some questions about Leah Emerson."

His eyes flicked from my face to Jordan's, then back again. He didn't move to let us in.

"I already told the cops everything when she went missing," he muttered.

"That was before she turned up dead," I replied.

His face went slack, his cigarette slipping from his mouth and falling onto the porch. Jordan put it out with the toe of his boot.

Dylan just stared at us. Then his knees buckled slightly, and he wobbled over and sank onto the threadbare couch, burying his face in his hands. Jordan and I went inside and stood over him.

"Dead?" he whispered. "No... No, she can't be."

I gave him a moment, watching the rawness ripple across his face. Then I pulled out my notebook. "When was the last time you saw Leah?"

He let out a shaky breath, wiping his face with the back of his hand. His fingers trembled as he lit another cigarette. "Two weeks ago. She left. Said she needed space."

"Space from what?"

He shrugged, avoiding my gaze. "We argued. Stupid shit. Money, mostly."

"Did it get physical?" Jordan asked.

Dylan's jaw tightened. "No! I mean, we yelled. But I never laid a hand on her."

"Where would she go when she needed space?" I pressed.

"I don't know. Sometimes she crashed with friends. Cassie, maybe. Or that dude she worked with at Harlan's."

"What dude?"

"Brent something. He always had a thing for her."

I jotted the name down. "You didn't think to mention Brent when you reported her missing?"

Dylan glared at me. "Didn't think it mattered. Figured she'd come back. She always did."

"Why file a missing persons report this time?"

"Cuz, I… uh, I don't know. It just felt different this time."

"Different how?"

He shifted in his seat. "I called around—Cassie, Harlan's. No one had seen her. Usually somebody's got eyes on her, y'know?"

"But this time, nothing?" I asked.

Dylan just shook his head.

"What does this Brent look like?" I asked.

"I don't know… I only saw him once when I picked Leah up from work."

"Well, what do you remember about him?"

"Just some guy, all nervous. Skinny. He's a cook, I think."

I let the silence stretch, watching him squirm under its weight.

"Where were you the night she died?"

"I don't know when she died."

"Where were you two nights ago?"

Another drag of his cigarette, this one longer, as if he could pull the lie right out of the smoke.

"I was here. Alone."

Jordan shot me a glance, reading my mind. We were getting nowhere fast.

I lowered my voice just enough to make him lean in. "Dylan, if you're lying to me, I will find out. And when I do, I won't be asking questions anymore."

His bravado flickered.

"I didn't kill her," he whispered.

"Then prove it."

Before he could respond, a loud crash echoed from the back of the house. Jordan's hand went to his holster instantly. I drew my weapon, moving fast, my heart a metronome of adrenaline.

We cleared the hallway, the floor creaking beneath our steps. Another sound—a car door slamming shut behind the house.

Jordan kicked the bedroom door open, and we burst into the room.

Empty.

But the window was wide open, the curtain fluttering like a ghost as

I heard the growl of an engine speeding away.

I turned to Dylan, who had followed us. "Who was in this room, Dylan?"

His face had gone pale, eyes darting between us and the open window, lips parted like he couldn't find the words fast enough.

"And why the hell did they take off without introducing themselves?" Jordan asked.

Dylan swallowed hard, his Adam's apple bobbing, but said nothing. The silence felt like it could snap at any moment.

"You better start talking, Dylan. Because whoever just climbed out that window is running from something. And if you're covering for them, that makes you part of this mess."

Jordan stepped beside me. "Tick tock, Cross. We're not in the mood for games."

INTERVIEW WITH DETECTIVE HARLIE WHITLOCK

INTERVIEWER: What did you find out from Dylan Cross?

WHITLOCK: Not much. He gave me exactly what I expected — half-truths, fear, and a whole lot of silence where the important shit should be.

INTERVIEWER: But you think he knows something.

WHITLOCK: Of course he does. Someone was in that house with him when we got there. Someone who didn't want to be seen. You tell me — does that sound like a guy with nothing to hide?

INTERVIEWER: And yet, you don't think he killed Leah?

WHITLOCK: No. He's a mess, but not the right kind of mess. He looked wrecked when I told him she was dead. You can fake a lot of things, but that kind of gut-punch reaction? That was real. He's scared, but not of us.

INTERVIEWER: Then who?

WHITLOCK: That's the question keeping me up at night. Leah was scared before she died. Dylan mentioned she thought she was being watched. And now we've got some unknown runner bolting the second we show up? Doesn't take a genius to put those pieces together.

INTERVIEWER: Sounds like someone didn't want Leah talking.

WHITLOCK: Exactly. And that's what worries me. If she knew something, something worth killing her over, then we're not just dealing with some jealous ex or a crime of passion. This is bigger. And if that's the case, we're already behind.

INTERVIEWER: You think this goes beyond Leah?

WHITLOCK: I don't know. But Sinister Falls has a way of burying things. And I have a bad feeling we're about to start digging up something a hell of a lot uglier than we expected.

INTERVIEWER: Chief Nolan seemed eager to wrap this case up. How much do you think he knows?

WHITLOCK: Nolan doesn't ask questions unless they come with easy answers. He wants this done yesterday, tied up with a neat little bow. But that's not how this is going to go.

INTERVIEWER: So what's next?

WHITLOCK: We find out who Leah was afraid of. We track down who ran from Dylan's house. And we figure out what the hell is going on in this town before another body shows up.

INTERVIEWER: And if Nolan tells you to back off?

WHITLOCK: Then he's going to be very disappointed.

Chief Nolan sat at his desk, rubbing his temples as he stared at the case file in front of him. Leah Emerson's murder case was starting to stink like a rotting wound. A half-empty bottle of whiskey sat in the bottom drawer, but he hadn't touched it—not yet.

The Sinister Falls Police Department was never quiet, but at this hour, the hum of the fluorescent lights was louder than the murmurs of officers wrapping up their reports. His phone rang, cutting through the drone. Nolan let it ring twice before he picked up.

"Nolan."

"This had better be good," Mayor Jenkins sounded like a bear poked awake before spring.

"We've got a problem."

There was a pause on the other end, followed by a long deliberate sigh. "A problem? Define 'problem,' Nolan."

"Leah Emerson. Case is a mess. Whitlock isn't letting it go."

"Christ," Jenkins muttered. "You're telling me this isn't handled yet? You said you'd take care of it."

"I said I'd keep it under control. But Whitlock is digging, and she's not stupid."

"Then remind her why she left Dallas."

Nolan rolled his shoulders. "That leverage only works if she gives a damn about saving herself. Right now, she cares more about solving this case than protecting her own ass."

"Then make her care. She starts sniffing in the wrong direction, we both have a hell of a lot more to lose than a damn detective with a savior complex."

Nolan leaned back in his chair, staring at the ceiling. "It's not just her. Someone ran from Dylan Cross's house when she and Reyes showed up. Someone who didn't want to be seen."

"Do you know who?"

"Not yet. But Whitlock will find out soon if I don't throw her off the trail."

Jenkins was silent for a moment. "I don't want another body showing up, Nolan. Not now. Not with elections coming up. This needs to go away."

"Yeah? Tell that to whoever dumped Leah's body near the old power station. Someone wanted her gone, but they wanted her found, too. That's a message."

"Then find out who the hell is sending it and shut them up. Whitlock can't get to the truth if you get there first."

"And if she's already too close?"

"Then you do what needs to be done. Just make sure it's clean."

The line went dead. Nolan stared at the phone for a long moment before setting it down. His fingers tightened into a fist. The room suddenly felt smaller. He reached into the bottom drawer, pulled out the bottle of whiskey, and poured himself a stiff one.

INTERVIEW WITH CHIEF NOLAN

INTERVIEWER: Rough day, Chief?

NOLAN: Every day's rough in this town.

INTERVIEWER: Is it the Emerson murder?

NOLAN: That's part of it. Add an election year on top, and it's a whole new pile of pressure.

INTERVIEWER: That's got to be frustrating.

NOLAN: Frustrating? No, frustrating is when your car won't start. This? This is a goddamn mess.

INTERVIEWER: Is the Mayor upset?

NOLAN: Milton Jenkins likes things neat. Likes things quiet. Dead girls don't fit into his perfect picture of Sinister Falls.

INTERVIEWER: And yet, this one won't go away.

NOLAN: Because Whitlock won't let it.

INTERVIEWER: You don't seem too fond of her.

NOLAN: She's a pain in my ass. Thinks she's the only one who gives a damn about the truth. Truth doesn't fix things. Truth doesn't keep the peace.

INTERVIEWER: What does?

NOLAN: Knowing when to look the other way.

INTERVIEWER: Tell me about the first time you realized this town wasn't what you thought it was.

NOLAN: I was a rookie. Got called to a domestic dispute out by the lake. Guy beat his wife so bad she could barely breathe. I was ready to haul his ass in. My sergeant — good man, I thought — pulled me aside, told me to let it go. Said, 'Some people in this town, you don't arrest.'

INTERVIEWER: And did you? Let it go?

NOLAN: Yeah. I let it go. And that woman was dead two months later.

INTERVIEWER: And the bodies keep piling up. Doesn't that bother you?

NOLAN: You think I sleep easy? You think I don't hear them? Leah Emerson, that woman by the lake, the ones who came before them. They don't go away. But justice doesn't mean a damn thing if it gets you killed.

INTERVIEWER: So what's the endgame here? Keep looking the other way until there's nothing left?

NOLAN: There is no endgame. There's just keeping your head above water long enough to see the next sunrise.

INTERVIEWER: And Whitlock? What happens when she finds something she can't let go?

NOLAN: Then she's got two choices: learn how to survive, or end up another name on a case file. And I sure as hell don't have room for another open case.

Chapter Seven

I pushed open the front door of my mother's house, the scent of brewed coffee and old wood washing over me like a worn-out memory. It was late, but the glow from the kitchen spilled into the hallway. Mom looked up from the kitchen table as I walked in, studying me the way only a mother could.

"You're late," she murmured, flipping another page of the photo album in front of her.

"Yeah," I said, heading straight for the coffee pot. I poured myself a cup, black, and opened the fridge with my free hand, scanning for leftovers. "What are you looking at?"

She pulled a few photos from the album and laid them on the table. The edges were curled with age, the black-and-white images faded but still clear enough to make out the figures.

I stepped closer, my eyes drawn to one photo in particular. My father, Frank Whitlock, stood in front of Sinister Falls Town Hall, flanked by two other men in dark suits.

"I've never seen this one before." I pointed at the photo then took a sip of my coffee.

Mom sighed, tracing a finger over Dad's face. "Because I never showed you."

I sat down, setting my mug aside and picking up the photograph.

"Who are they?"

"Land developers. Or at least, that's what they claimed to be."

"What do you mean?"

She glanced at me, something unreadable in her expression. "Your father was trying to keep them out of Sinister Falls. He knew they weren't just developers. They were buying up land, forcing people to sell, making threats. Frank tried to stand in their way."

"And?"

Mom gave a humorless smile. "And you know how this town works, Harlie. He made enemies. Powerful ones."

"Why didn't you ever tell me this?"

She met my eyes. "Because I wanted you to leave this place behind. Not end up like him."

"Jesus, Mom."

She leaned back in her chair. "You're tangled up in something now, aren't you?"

"Leah Emerson."

She frowned. "Who's that?"

I let out a tired sigh. "A waitress at Harlan's. Someone left her in the woods near the old power station."

She shook her head. "I don't know her."

I took a sip of my coffee. "Leah's ex, Dylan Cross, is hiding something, but he's more scared than guilty. Nolan just wants me to shut up and go away, and now I'm staring at photos of Dad with men I've never seen before, wondering how deep this town's rot really goes."

Mom watched me carefully. "You sound like you're expecting to find something you won't like."

I huffed a bitter laugh. "I'm expecting to find something that makes sense. But so far, all I have are more questions."

She reached across the table and gently squeezed my hand. "Sometimes, Harlie, the answers don't make things easier. They make them harder."

"Maybe. But I can't stop now."

She sighed, letting go of my hand. "Then be careful. Your father thought he could fight this town and win. Look where that got him."

INTERVIEW WITH MRS. MABEL WHITLOCK

INTERVIEWER: Mrs. Whitlock, Harlie told me you showed her some old photographs. The ones of your husband with a couple of men outside Town Hall. She said you called them 'developers.' But Harlie didn't think that's what they really were. She said you knew something was off about them. What do you remember about those men?

MRS. WHITLOCK: Developers, huh? They wanted people to believe that. Told everyone they were here to 'revitalize' the town, bring in jobs, make Sinister Falls 'better.' All that nonsense. But Frank... Frank wasn't buying it. Not for a second.

INTERVIEWER: What do you mean? Why didn't Frank trust them?

MRS. WHITLOCK: They weren't here for anything good. Frank knew that the minute they started talking about 'redeveloping' everything. You know, Sinister Falls was always... quiet. People minded their own business, kept their heads down. But these men, they came in, all smooth-talking, dressed up in those fancy suits.

INTERVIEWER: Go on.

MRS. WHITLOCK: Frank could see the numbers. He was the one who kept the town's books. He knew what was worth something, and what was being sold for a song. He started asking questions — about who owned what, about where the money was really going. He got a little too close to things. And that... well, that's when things started to get tricky.

INTERVIEWER: They didn't want Frank asking questions. So, what did they offer him? I imagine he wasn't the type to take bribes.

MRS. WHITLOCK: Oh, they offered him plenty. They wanted him to help them — help them track down the best pieces of land. They said, 'We'll give you a cut,' like Frank was some kind of fool who'd just jump at a payday. But Frank wasn't that kind of man. He didn't care about the money, not like they did. He cared about the truth. And that's the problem with people like them. They don't like being challenged. They wanted him to keep quiet, to help hide what they were doing. But Frank wasn't built to keep quiet. He asked too many questions. Started digging into things they didn't want dug up.

INTERVIEWER: So, they weren't just developers. They were after something else. Something bigger, right?

MRS. WHITLOCK: Exactly. They weren't here to make Sinister Falls 'better.' They were here to take. To grab up land on the cheap, flip it, and walk away with a fortune. Sinister Falls? It was the perfect place for them. Old properties, land with potential, but no one paying attention to what was really going on. Frank saw how things were being sold off for nothing — how families were losing their land, all while a few people were making out like bandits. These men were just the latest in a long line of people trying to cash in on the town's decline.

INTERVIEWER: So, Frank must have gotten pretty close to figuring it all out... He was starting to see the whole picture.

MRS. WHITLOCK: He was close. Too close. He started putting it all together — who was selling what, who was getting kickbacks, who was making these shady deals under the table.

And you know what happens when someone gets too close to the truth in a place like this...

INTERVIEWER: Yeah. But then Frank... He died, right? Heart attack, wasn't it? That's what they said.

MRS. WHITLOCK: That's what they said. That's the official story. He had a heart attack. Just like that. But you know, I've never believed that. Not for a second.

INTERVIEWER: You think it wasn't a heart attack? What do you think happened?

MRS. WHITLOCK: I think Frank knew too much. He was getting closer to something — something that would've exposed the whole damn operation. He wasn't someone who just dropped dead of a heart attack. Frank wasn't in poor health. He wasn't the kind to fall apart like that. He was... sharp. But people who get too close to the truth? They tend to meet with 'accidents.' You know how it goes.

INTERVIEWER: So, you think these men... had something to do with it?

MRS. WHITLOCK: I don't have proof. But I've lived in this town a long time. Frank wasn't the first person to die under suspicious circumstances, and I doubt he'll be the last. Frank didn't go quietly, and neither will Harlie if she keeps digging. That much I know.

INTERVIEWER: And Harlie — do you think she'll go as far as Frank did? Will she uncover what he started?

MRS. WHITLOCK: Harlie's like her father — stubborn, determined, doesn't take no for an answer. If she's anything like him, she'll keep digging, no matter what. But this town? It's a hard place to uncover the truth in. And if she gets too close... she'll be walking the same path Frank did. The one that leads you straight into danger.

INTERVIEWER: You've lived here your whole life. You've seen this town's politics — the way it all works. How does it feel, knowing so much of it may have been built on lies?

MRS. WHITLOCK: It's a small town, you know? People think nothing happens here, but that's how they keep things hidden. You live here, you see the same names, the same families always coming out on top. They buy up what they can, take control of what they want, and everyone else just... goes along with it. Frank tried to stand up against that. And look where it got him. This town doesn't change. It never does. And people like Frank and Harlie? They get caught up in it.

INTERVIEWER: Do you think she'll uncover the truth? Or will it just bury her, too?

MRS. WHITLOCK: Truth doesn't always set you free. Sometimes, it just gets you buried deeper than you ever thought you could fall. And that's the real danger. The deeper you dig, the harder it is to get out.

<h1 style="text-align:center">CHAPTER EIGHT</h1>

I sat at my desk, flipping through the crime scene photos again. I picked one up and traced my fingers over the glossy surface. Leah Emerson, sprawled on the damp earth, her hands frozen mid-struggle. The black ribbon tied neatly around her throat.

"Walsh," I called.

Amy poked her head into my office. "Yeah, Detective?"

I lowered my voice. "I need you to pull all missing persons and death cases from the past twenty years."

She blinked. "That's gonna take a while. A lot of those aren't digital."

I nodded, setting the photo down. "Just work on it. Start with anything that might connect to Leah." She gave a quick nod and disappeared.

Nolan's voice barked from down the hall. "Whitlock! My office, now."

I pushed myself up and headed toward the lion's den.

Nolan was slouched in his chair, boots propped on his desk, looking every bit the man who hadn't been home in days. "You wrapping up the Emerson case?" he asked.

I let out a dry chuckle. "Yeah, sure, Chief. I reviewed the autopsy, stared at the crime scene photos until they're burned into my retinas, interviewed the guy who found her, grilled the ex-boyfriend, dug through her social media, and squinted at the grainy footage from the security camera at the gas station down the hill from the power plant. And guess what? I'm coming up with a big fat zero. So no—I'm not."

Nolan's expression didn't change. "I need this wrapped up. The mayor's breathing down my neck with the election coming up. The last thing he wants is panic over some dead girl."

"*Some* dead girl? She was murdered, Chief. She wasn't just *some* inconvenience."

He waved a dismissive hand. "You're chasing ghosts, Whitlock. You don't have a suspect, you don't have a motive, and you sure as hell don't have time to chase after fairy tales."

"I have a body. That's enough for me."

"Listen to me, Whitlock. Some cases aren't meant to be solved. Some leads go nowhere for a reason."

I crossed my arms. "And what reason would that be?"

"Because the people who don't let them go end up regretting it."

A heavy silence settled between us.

"I hope your mess in Dallas isn't clouding your judgment," he growled.

"That supposed to be a threat, Chief?"

A smirk spread across his face. "Just an observation. Maybe dead bodies are starting to get to you. PTSD's a hell of a thing."

"You think I can't handle a murder case because I saw some bad shit in Dallas?" I took a step closer, planted my hands on his desk, and leaned down, meeting him eye to eye. "I worked homicide in a city where we found bodies stuffed in storm drains and burned in abandoned buildings. You really think I scare that easy?"

Nolan's smirk didn't waver, but he looked away. "I think," he said, "you're letting things get personal. And that's dangerous."

I straightened, rolling my shoulders back. "Personal is how cases get solved, Chief. Maybe that's why so many here go cold."

His jaw tightened, but he said nothing.

I turned for the door, adding over my shoulder, "And for the record? If you ever suggest again that I'm too weak to do my job, you'll regret it."

INTERVIEW WITH DETECTIVE HARLIE WHITLOCK

INTERVIEWER: Rough day?

WHITLOCK: You could say that.

INTERVIEWER: Nolan really got under your skin, huh?

WHITLOCK: He thinks I should back off the Emerson case. Tie it up with a neat little bow before it starts unraveling things.

INTERVIEWER: And you're not going to do that.

WHITLOCK: Hell no. A woman is dead. I don't care whose election it might screw up. Nolan is 'worried' about me having PTSD over Dallas. He thinks I'm letting my past dictate how I do my job.

INTERVIEWER: And are you?

WHITLOCK: Every case is personal when you care about the truth.

Chapter Nine

Jordan and I pulled into the parking lot of Harlan's Diner, the kind of place that smelled like burnt coffee and grease no matter the time of day.

Jordan cut the engine and turned to me. "You ready for this?"

"Yeah. Let's see what we can shake loose."

We stepped inside, the bell above the door giving a halfhearted jingle. A few heads turned our way, mostly older men nursing their coffee, staring at us over the rims of their mugs. I scanned the room, looking for anyone who might fit the description of Brent—young, jittery, with too much to say and not enough sense to keep his mouth shut.

A solo waitress hustled between booths, refilling cups and collecting half-eaten plates—moving with the kind of weary energy that came from too many long nights and not enough good tips. She looked us over. "Table for two?"

Jordan flashed his badge. "Actually, we're looking to talk to someone. Brent Matthews. He working today?"

She poured coffee into a waiting cup. "Depends who's askin'."

"Detective Whitlock. This is Officer Reyes. We're looking into Leah Emerson."

Her shoulders stiffened slightly and, for a second, I thought she might tell us to get lost. Instead, she jerked her head toward the kitchen. "He's in back."

Jordan and I made our way past the counter stacked with syrup-sticky menus and a register that looked like it belonged in a museum. I pushed open the swinging door to the kitchen, where the smell of frying onions and overcooked bacon hit me like a wall.

Brent stood at the grill, spatula in hand, flipping a row of burgers. He looked young, early twenties maybe, with shaggy brown hair that curled at his ears. The second he saw us, his grip on the spatula tightened.

"You Brent Matthews?" I asked.

"Yeah. What's this about?"

Jordan leaned against the stainless-steel counter. "Leah Emerson. We heard you two were close."

Brent's face paled under the fluorescent lights. "I—I wouldn't say close. We worked together, that's all."

I folded my arms. "That's not what Dylan Cross said. He told us you had a thing for her."

"Dylan said that? Yeah, well, Dylan's full of shit."

"Then set the record straight," I said. "When was the last time you saw Leah?"

He glanced toward the back door like he was considering making a run for it. "I don't know. Maybe a few weeks ago? She stopped showing up to work. I figured she quit."

"You didn't think to ask?"

Brent shrugged. "Look, people come and go in places like this. You don't ask questions unless you wanna get stuck with the answers."

Jordan exchanged a glance with me before asking, "Did Leah seem worried before she disappeared? Scared?"

Brent's fingers tightened around the spatula again. "Maybe. I mean, yeah. She was acting weird. Kept looking over her shoulder, jumped every time the door opened."

"Did she say why?"

He shook his head quickly. "No. But… she did ask me something strange."

"What was it?"

Brent shifted his weight from foot to foot. "She asked if I knew anything about that old chapel. The one up on the hill."

"What did you tell her?"

Brent licked his lips. "Told her I didn't know much. Just the stories everyone else hears. That some weird shit happened there before it burned. But she was fixated on it. Kept asking about the people who used to go there."

Jordan frowned. "Did she mention any names?"

Brent hesitated. "Just one."

"Who?" I pressed.

He glanced around the kitchen as if someone might be listening, then lowered his voice. "Nolan."

"Chief Nolan?" I clarified, though my gut already knew the answer.

Brent nodded. "Yeah. I don't know why, but she was sure he had something to do with that place."

Nolan had warned me to drop this case. Had gone out of his way to make sure I knew what was at stake. And now Leah had been digging into something that led right back to him.

I stepped closer to Brent and said in a low voice, "Brent, listen to me. If there's anything else you're not telling us, now's the time."

He shook his head quickly. "That's all I know, I swear. Leah was scared."

Jordan put a hand on my arm, a silent reminder to back off. I took a deep breath and stepped away.

"If you think of anything else, you call me," I said, pulling out a card and sliding it across the metal counter. "No matter how small."

Brent took it. "Yeah. Okay."

Jordan and I turned and made our way back through the diner. As we settled into Jordan's cruiser, I said, "Every time I think we're close, someone hands me a match and points to gasoline."

CHAPTER TEN

The station had that smell—faint traces of ink, paper, and old leather chairs—just like my old station in Dallas. As I walked toward Amy's desk, I wondered if all police stations smelled the same. Amy looked up from flipping through reports. I caught the slight shift in her posture.

I pulled up a chair. "We need to talk."

She frowned. "That bad?"

I glanced around the room, making sure no one was within earshot, then leaned in closer. "Is Nolan in?"

Amy shook her head. "No, he stepped out about thirty minutes ago. Didn't say where he was going, just grabbed his keys and left. Looked like he was in a hurry."

"Good. Because we have a problem."

"We do?"

"Nolan's name came up in the Emerson case. Brent Matthews said Leah was convinced that Nolan had something to do with the old church."

Amy's fingers tensed around her pen. "Shit."

"Yeah. And if he knows we're so much as sniffing around this, he'll shut it down before we get anywhere."

"So what's the plan?"

Before I could answer, she slid a folded note toward me. "Anonymous tip came in. Guy wouldn't give his name, but he said Leah was 'asking the wrong people too many questions.' Said we need to find someone named Evelyn Carter."

I turned the note over in my hands. "You tell Nolan?"

Amy shook her head. "Didn't think it was his business yet. Figured you'd want to handle it first."

I nodded. "Good call. From now on, if Nolan asks, keep it surface-level. Give him the basics, nothing else."

She smirked. "You think I'd hand him a loaded gun?"

"Just making sure we're on the same page."

Amy leaned back in her chair. "So, who the hell is Evelyn Carter?"

I tucked the note into my pocket. "That's what I'm about to find out."

"Where are you going?" Amy asked.

"Just following the breadcrumbs," I said, already heading for the door.

INTERVIEW WITH OFFICER AMY WALSH

INTERVIEWER: You look like you're about to jump out of your skin.

WALSH: Can you blame me? This whole thing is insane.

INTERVIEWER: You mean Nolan?

WALSH: Of course I mean Nolan! He's the Chief. He watches everything we do. If he even suspects I know something I shouldn't... I'm in deep shit.

INTERVIEWER: You're worried about slipping up.

WALSH: Yeah. Look, I trust Harlie. If she tells me to keep quiet, I will. But Nolan? He's not the kind of guy you want to be on the wrong side of.

INTERVIEWER: You think he did it?

WALSH: I don't know. I just know Leah was asking questions, and now she's dead. And I know Nolan likes to make problems disappear.

INTERVIEWER: That's a dangerous assumption.

WALSH: Yeah, no kidding. But it's eating at me. I've only been on the force a short time, but I've seen how he operates. He covers for the right people, keeps the politicians happy. I figured it was just... politics. But murder? That's a whole different level.

INTERVIEWER: So what's your move?

WALSH: Keep my mouth shut. Do what Harlie tells me. And pray to God I don't slip up.

INTERVIEWER: And if Nolan finds out?

WALSH: I know how to run.

Chapter Eleven

The wind cut straight through my jacket, carrying the scent of damp earth and stale smoke. I pulled the fabric tighter around me, eyes fixed on the ruins of the old chapel as I climbed the hill toward the burnt-out shell. The last of the daylight was bleeding out behind the ridge.

Funny how no one had ever cleaned this place up. The town left it to rot, left it to sink into the hillside. Maybe they thought if they ignored it long enough, it would just disappear.

It hadn't.

The fire-scarred door hung crooked, barely clinging to its hinges, and I had to force it across the flagstones so I could slip inside.

I walked down the middle aisle, my boots churning up puffs of ash. The walls were charred rock, the roof half-collapsed, and the pews were splintered piles of wood, scattered like bones. At the far end, the altar was nothing more than a slab of scorched stone buried under debris.

I swept my flashlight across the wreckage. Nothing but shadows and silence.

But Leah had come here for a reason. And whatever she had found, someone had wanted it buried.

A gust of wind pushed through the broken windows, rattling what was left of the roof beams. I heard a faint whisper of sound, like voices just out of reach.

I suddenly wanted to get the hell out of there.

As I stepped outside, my flashlight caught something in the distance. A cluster of stone markers, barely visible between the chapel and the tree line. The cemetery.

The town had abandoned the graveyard just like they'd abandoned the church.

I waded through the creeping fog, moving through the rows of leaning tombstones, my flashlight skimming over the inscriptions. Most were too worn to read, their letters lost to time.

Near the far edge, where the land sloped into the darkness of the forest, one headstone stood apart from the others. Half-buried in the tall grass, the name carved deep into the stone stood stubborn against the years.

EVELYN CARTER

The name from Amy's tip. The name Leah had been looking for.

I crouched down, brushing away the dirt from the base of the marker. A sharp gust of wind sent the grass whispering around me, and I felt like something was watching. Like I wasn't alone.

I stood quickly, scanning the darkness, flashlight jerking from one shadow to the next. The trees swayed, the wind howled, but there was nothing.

Leah hadn't just been curious about this place. She had found something. Something she wasn't supposed to. And now, maybe I had too.

INTERVIEW WITH DETECTIVE HARLIE WHITLOCK

INTERVIEWER: You look like you just saw a ghost.

WHITLOCK: Might as well have.

INTERVIEWER: Chapel get to you?

WHITLOCK: It wasn't the chapel. Not really. It was what I found behind it.

INTERVIEWER: The graveyard.

WHITLOCK: Yeah. And one headstone in particular: Evelyn Carter.

INTERVIEWER: Name mean something to you?

WHITLOCK: It should. Amy got a tip, some anonymous call telling her Leah was asking too many questions. That name — Evelyn Carter — was the tip.

INTERVIEWER: And now you've got a dead woman's name carved into a forgotten grave. And Leah went looking for her.

WHITLOCK: Yeah. And now I need to know why.

INTERVIEWER: You're about to go digging, aren't you?

WHITLOCK: Nolan's gone for the night. It's the best time to look through old police files.

INTERVIEWER: You think there's a record on her?

WHITLOCK: There should be. If she lived here, if she died here — there's gotta be something. A death certificate, a missing persons report, hell, even an old speeding ticket.

INTERVIEWER: What if there's nothing?

WHITLOCK: Then that means someone wanted it erased.

INTERVIEWER: You sure you want to do this?

WHITLOCK: Leah went looking for answers, and now she's dead. If I don't figure out what she found — who she was looking for — she won't be the last.

INTERVIEWER: You scared?

WHITLOCK: Not like that.

INTERVIEWER: Then like what?

WHITLOCK: I'm not worried about someone coming after me. I can handle that. What gets me is not knowing what I'm about to dig up.

INTERVIEWER: And if what you find changes everything?

WHITLOCK: Then I deal with it. Whatever it is.

INTERVIEWER: And if you're next?

WHITLOCK: Then at least someone will know what questions to ask. But I don't plan on making it easy for them.

Chapter Twelve

I sat at my desk, overly aware how eerily quiet the station was this late at night. No ringing phones, no voices, just the faint hum of the vending machine down the hall and the occasional creak of the old building settling. I typed **Evelyn Carter** into the department's records database. A progress bar flickered, then the screen refreshed.

```
No Results Found
```

Maybe I had the wrong last name? Maybe Carter was a married name? I tried again, this time broadening the search for anything that might connect to her.

```
No Results Found
```

If the digital records weren't giving me anything, I needed to go to the source: the records room. I pushed back from my desk and made my way to the far end of the station.

After twisting my key in the lock, I pushed the heavy door open and was greeted with the scent of old paper and stale air. I stepped inside and flicked the light switch. Fluorescent bulbs buzzed overhead, flickering once before settling into a steady glow.

The records room wasn't much more than a glorified storage closet. Most of our files had been digitized over the years, but the older ones—

the ones no one cared enough about to scan—still sat in wall-to-wall metal filing cabinets, collecting dust.

I moved to the section labeled 2000–2005, running my fingers along the metal drawers until I reached the year etched into Evelyn Carter's tombstone: 2001.

I pulled the drawer open, wincing at the metallic screech, and started flipping through files packed so tightly they barely moved.

Caldwell… Campbell… Carter.

There it was. A slim manila folder, far thinner than it should have been. I pulled it free and stepped over to a small desk. I laid the folder down and flipped it open. A single sheet of paper, yellowed with age, was clipped to the inside.

Evelyn Carter. Female. Age: 22. Deceased. Cause of Death: Fractured Skull, Car Accident.

That was it. No autopsy report, no witness statements, no next of kin. Just one flimsy piece of paper declaring her dead.

I ran my finger over the ink. This wasn't right. Even the most basic cases had more documentation than this. A death should have had more. Toxicology reports, coroner's notes, something.

Someone had gutted this file.

I turned the page over, looking for any clue as to why. That's when I saw it. Faint, barely legible, scribbled in pencil at the bottom corner of the page:

See File #396B – Restricted

Restricted. Meaning whatever had happened to Evelyn Carter, someone had decided the details didn't belong in the general archive. Someone had locked them away.

There was only one place restricted files were kept: Nolan's office.

I had a choice to make.

I took a steadying breath, my pulse a drumbeat in my ears. This was risky. Hell, it was probably career suicide if I got caught. But I wasn't about to walk away now. Leah had been digging into this for a reason, and now she was dead. Whatever she'd found—whatever she wasn't supposed to find—it had to be in that restricted file.

I shut the manila folder and tucked it under my arm. Time to see just how deep this went.

The hallway felt longer now, every step sending a whisper of doubt creeping up my spine. Nolan's office was at the end of the hall, his door looming like a locked vault. I tried the handle first—locked, of course.

I glanced around, making sure I was alone, then pulled out my pocketknife. I wedged the tip between the frame and the latch, jiggling it just enough to—

A voice, deep and slurred, cut through the silence.

"Well, ain't this a surprise."

I froze, my breath catching in my throat. Then I slowly turned, using my body to shield the pocketknife, hoping he hadn't seen it.

Chief Nolan stood in the hallway, his broad frame blocking my only exit. His tie was loose, his shirt wrinkled, and the unmistakable scent of whiskey clung to him like a second skin.

He took a slow step forward, closing the distance between us. "You wanna tell me why the hell you're breaking into my office, Detective?"

Hopes dashed, I casually slipped the pocketknife back into my jacket. "Door was stuck. Thought I'd give it a try."

Nolan let out a dry chuckle. "Stuck, huh?"

I nodded, keeping my expression even. "Yeah. Needed to grab a case file. Thought I'd save myself a trip in the morning."

He took another step closer, and I resisted the urge to step back. "You always this eager to work after hours?"

"You know me. Overachiever."

He tilted his head, studying me like a predator sizing up prey. "Funny. I don't remember leaving any files out for you."

His voice dropped into a whisper. "You got something you wanna tell me, Harlie?"

I held his stare. "Nope."

His lips curled into something between a smirk and a snarl. "Didn't think so."

I moved to pass him, but he didn't step aside. Instead, his arms shot out, hands planting firmly on either side of the door, caging me in. The stench of whiskey hit me full force, his breath warm and sickeningly close.

My service weapon was sitting on my desk, and I was trapped between a drunk man and a locked door.

Nolan leaned in. "You know, Harlie, you've got this real bad habit of sticking your nose where it doesn't belong. Always digging, always prying. Makes me wonder what else you're good at."

I clenched my jaw, forcing my body to stay rigid, controlled. "Back off, Chief."

He chuckled. "Come on, don't be like that. I've seen the way you look at me. You like a little danger, don't you?" His breath was hot against my cheek. "You and me, we could... come to an understanding."

I didn't flinch. I wouldn't give him that satisfaction. Instead, I tilted my chin up, meeting his gaze with a glare sharp enough to cut. "Move. Now."

He stared at me for a long moment, the drunken haze flickering into something sharper, meaner. Then, slowly, he dropped his hands and stepped back, though the smirk on his face told me he wasn't done playing his game.

"You should be careful, Harlie," he murmured, voice almost sing-song. "Wouldn't want you to get yourself in trouble."

We stood there, locked in a silent battle. Then, just as suddenly as he'd appeared, he stepped aside—just enough to let me pass, but not enough for comfort.

As I moved past, I could feel his breath against my ear, his voice dropping to a near whisper. "You don't want to keep pushing this, Harlie. Some doors, once opened, don't close so easy."

I didn't respond. I didn't trust myself to. Every instinct screamed at me to get as far away from him as possible, but I forced myself to walk, not run. I could feel his eyes tracking my every move, his presence like a dark cloud pressing against my back.

I turned the corner and picked up my pace to collect my things and escape the station. Nolan had been toying with me, letting me know he could stop me anytime he wanted. And maybe next time, he wouldn't just talk.

Chapter Thirteen

The ringtone shattered the thin veil of sleep, vibrating against my nightstand—an alarm I wasn't ready for. I groaned, blindly reaching for my phone and squinting at the screen.

Reyes

I swiped to answer. "This better be good."

"Harlie, you're gonna want to come out here." Jordan's voice sounded tense. "Main Street. Right outside the old post office."

I sat up. "What's going on?"

"Just get here. It's… interesting."

That was enough to shake off the last remnants of sleep. Jordan wasn't one for theatrics, and if he was calling me out of bed, it meant something was off. I swung my legs over the edge of the bed, grabbed my jeans off the chair, and yanked them on. Five minutes later, I was in my truck, speeding toward town.

Main Street was still mostly asleep, but I saw the streetlights flicker as dawn crept in. Jordan's cruiser sat at an angle near the curb, emergency lights flashing. Another unit had just pulled up—Amy Walsh stepped out, adjusted her belt, and scanned the scene.

I parked behind Jordan's car, stepping out into the crisp morning air.

Jordan glanced up as I approached, taking in my disheveled appearance with a smirk.

"You look like hell."

"I'll fill you in later. What do we have?"

My eyes locked onto the beat-up Chevy Nova in front of his cruiser. Inside, gripping the steering wheel like it was the only thing keeping him tethered to reality, was Dylan Cross. In the passenger seat, Seth Jenkins, the mayor's son, was trying too hard to look relaxed.

"Tell me this isn't what it looks like."

"Wish I could. Ran a red light, right in front of me. But they're nervous as hell. Something's not right."

Dylan's knuckles were white, his jaw clenched. Seth's fingers drummed anxiously against his knee, eyes darting to every exit point like he was calculating an escape route.

Amy joined us. "Leah's ex-boyfriend and the mayor's kid? Hell of a pairing."

"Yeah," I muttered. "And they look like they just saw a ghost."

Jordan crossed his arms. "Dylan said they were coming from the lake, but he's tweaking. Seth hasn't said a word."

I rested a hand on the car. "Morning, boys."

Dylan wouldn't look at me. Seth offered a slow smirk. "Detective Harlie. Didn't know a traffic stop warranted such a welcome party."

"That depends. You two always this nervous when you run a red light?"

Dylan finally turned. "We're not nervous."

"Right. And I'm the damn Queen of England." I leaned in. "Why don't you go ahead and tell me what's really going on?"

Seth snorted. "We already told your buddy. We were at the lake. Hanging out."

"At dawn? Just the two of you?"

Dylan shifted. "We didn't do anything wrong."

Amy cleared her throat. "Mind if we take a look in the car?"

Dylan stiffened. "You don't have probable cause."

Seth nudged him. "Shut up."

Jordan rubbed his jaw. "We could call in a K-9. See if they hit on anything."

Dylan's hands unclenched then tightened around the steering wheel again. "This is bullshit."

I leaned in. "You know, Dylan, I was just thinking about Leah this morning. Funny how you pop up."

His head snapped toward me, eyes burning. "Don't."

"Don't what? Say her name? Act like she didn't exist? I bet she's been on your mind a lot lately."

Seth tensed. Dylan looked like he was about to bolt.

Jordan's radio crackled. "Dispatch to Officer Reyes, status check."

Jordan pressed the button. "We're good. Still on scene."

I straightened. "So, here's the deal. You two sit tight while we figure out our next move. You're not under arrest. Yet. But if there's something in this car you don't want us to find, now's your chance to come clean."

Silence.

Then Dylan's voice, barely audible. "We didn't kill her."

"No one said you did."

Dylan's fingers flexed against the wheel. Seth's gaze locked on the dashboard, avoiding eye contact.

"Then why the hell are we still sitting here?" Dylan snapped.

Amy tilted her head. "Because you're acting suspicious as hell."

Jordan ran a hand through his hair. "Look, Dylan, Seth—whatever this is, you're not helping yourselves. The way you're both acting? It makes us think you know more than you're letting on."

Seth's eyes flicked up. "What exactly are you accusing us of?"

"Nothing. Yet," I repeated. "But Leah's murder is still open. And you two are making it real tempting to start asking uncomfortable questions."

Dylan let out a bitter laugh. "This is a joke."

"Maybe," I said. "But if I were you, I'd think real hard about what story you want to tell. Because right now? You look guilty as hell."

Seth's hand darted toward the center console, and I was the first to draw my gun. "Hands where I can see them! Now!"

Jordan yanked Dylan out of the car, shoving him against the hood. "Don't move!"

"Out. Now." I grabbed Seth, spinning him toward the car. "Spread your legs. Hands flat. You so much as twitch—"

"Jesus, we didn't do anything!" Dylan hissed.

"Then this'll be over quick, won't it?" Jordan shot back, patting him down.

Amy worked on Seth, pulling out a small bag of white powder from his jacket pocket. "Well, well."

Seth stiffened. "That's not—"

"Not yours?" Amy held it up. "Yeah, I bet."

"Possession, Seth. Not a good look," Jordan chimed in.

Dylan turned his head. "It's his, not mine."

I rolled my eyes. "That's real loyal of you, Dylan."

"You have no idea who you're messing with," Seth spat. "My dad will have me out of here before you even finish your damn paperwork. And when he does? He'll make sure every single one of you regrets this."

Jordan and Amy led them to the cruisers.

As the doors shut behind them, Jordan let out a slow breath, turning toward me. "Alright, spill it. What the hell happened to you last night?"

"Nolan."

Jordan's expression darkened. "What about him?"

I hesitated, then shook my head. "Caught me outside his office. Drunk. Cornered me. Said some shit I won't repeat. He knows I'm digging, Jordan. He was letting me know he can stop me whenever he wants."

"He touch you?"

"No. But he wanted to make sure I knew he could."

Jordan cursed under his breath and glanced toward the station. "That son of a bitch. You should've called me."

"Didn't have time. I needed to get out of there in one piece."

He looked away for a second before turning back. "Alright. We'll deal with it. But for now, let's figure out what the hell Dylan and Seth are hiding."

I nodded, feeling the weight of the night settle over me. "Yeah. Because whatever it is, it's got them scared shitless and I'd venture it's not the drugs."

CHAPTER FOURTEEN

I stood in the observation room, sipping from a lukewarm cup of coffee that tasted more like burnt dirt, watching through the one-way glass as Seth Jenkins leaned back in the interrogation room chair, arms crossed, his expression carefully indifferent. Amy sat in the chair across the steel table.

Jordan stepped up beside me. "You want Seth, or you want Dylan?"

I tapped my fingers against the side of my cup. "Dylan."

Jordan nodded. "Figured. Amy's got Seth for now."

"Good. She's got a way of getting under his skin."

Jordan smirked. "Yeah, and she actually enjoys it."

I took one last sip of coffee and set the cup down on a file cabinet before pushing open the door to Dylan Cross's interrogation room.

He glanced up as I walked in but didn't say anything. His knee bounced under the table, his hands clenched into fists in his lap. He looked like a guy barely holding it together.

I pulled out the chair across from him and sat down, folding my hands on the table. "Long morning?"

Dylan let out a sharp breath, shaking his head. "What the hell is this?"

I leaned back slightly, watching him. "That's what I'd like to know."

"I ran a red light. Now I'm in an interrogation room. You want to tell me how that makes sense?"

"An anonymous tip came in about Evelyn Carter. I think you know something about that."

Dylan froze for half a second before shaking his head. "I don't know what you're talking about."

I nodded slowly. "Alright. Then let's talk about Leah."

His jaw clenched. "What about her?"

I studied him carefully. "No next of kin has come forward for her, Dylan. We haven't found any family. And if you actually cared about her, which I think you did, you'd help me with that."

He didn't answer.

I leaned in. "Who was Leah's family?"

"She was adopted."

I hadn't expected that. "She ever talk about them?"

He shook his head. "Not much. Her adoptive parents died when she was a teenager. After that, she bounced around. Lived with an aunt for a while, but they weren't close."

"Did she ever try to find her biological parents?"

Dylan hesitated, then shrugged. "Yeah, kind of. It was recent. But you know Leah—she could go on and on sometimes. Half the time, I wasn't paying attention."

I let the silence stretch. "But she found something, didn't she?"

Dylan looked away. "She mentioned stuff. Things she was looking into. But I ignored a lot of it." He gave a hollow chuckle. "Half the time, I was too strung out to care."

I kept my voice steady. "Like what?"

He exhaled hard, staring at the table. "She was obsessed with finding out where she came from. Said she didn't feel like she belonged to anyone. That she wasn't supposed to be here."

A lump formed in my throat, but I swallowed it down. "Did she ever mention names?"

"Not at first. But after a while, yeah. She found a name."

"Whose?"

Dylan looked up, eyes tired and resigned. "Her mother's."

"And?"

"Evelyn Carter."

"Did she find anything else? What about her father?"

Dylan shook his head. "She didn't know. I don't think she ever found out."

I studied him, reading the tension in his body. "Do you have anything of hers? Something she left with you?"

He hesitated, then shook his head. "No."

I let the silence sit. Dylan fidgeted.

"You sure about that?" I pressed.

Dylan swallowed hard, then sighed. "She gave me some stuff to hold onto before she left. Just a notebook, some papers. I didn't look at it."

"Where is it?"

His gaze flickered to the door. "My place. It's in my room."

I didn't let up. "Why were you and Seth out so late?"

"I told you. We were at the lake."

I just stared at him. "Seth said you were meeting someone."

"Seth talks too much."

"We found drugs on him," I said. "I don't care about that—for now. But if you don't start talking, I'll make it your problem."

Dylan's throat worked as he swallowed. "Come on, Harlie. You know I don't—"

"Then tell me the truth."

"We were supposed to meet someone," he admitted finally. "But we never did."

"Who?"

Dylan shook his head. "I don't know. Some guy Seth knew. He set it up."

"What kind of meeting?"

"Seth was trying to get information."

"About what?"

"Leah," Dylan muttered.

"Why?"

"She wouldn't shut up about it. About who she was. Where she came from. She got obsessed."

"And that got her killed?"

Dylan flinched, but he didn't deny it. "She wasn't just looking into her mom," he finally muttered. "She was trying to find her father."

"Did she find out who he was?"

Dylan shook his head. "She thought someone knew."

I held his gaze, reading the fear there. "What did she find?"

"I don't know!"

Seth Jenkins slouched in the metal chair, arms folded over his chest, his expression one of lazy defiance. The smirk tugging at the corner of his mouth was meant to be cocky, but Amy Walsh saw it for what it was— false bravado.

She dropped into the chair across from him, setting a case file on the table between them with a loud thud. "Let's cut the crap, Seth."

He arched a brow, shifting in his seat. "Straight to business? No pleasantries? I'm hurt, Officer."

Amy leaned forward, elbows on the table. "Why were you and Dylan out so late?"

Seth shrugged. "Felt like a drive. Is that illegal now?"

"We both know you weren't just out for a joyride."

He tapped his fingers idly against his arm. "Maybe we just wanted to get some fresh air. Ever think of that?"

Amy wasn't in the mood for his games. "We found drugs on you."

Seth didn't blink. "So?"

Amy tilted her head, watching him. "Where'd you get them?"

His smirk widened. "You tell me. You seem to know everything."

"Cut the act, Seth. You're looking at possession charges. That's not going away just because you think you're untouchable."

His mouth twitched, but he kept up the act. "I don't know what you're talking about."

"Dylan says he didn't know about the drugs. That they weren't his."

Seth let out a low chuckle. "That sounds like Dylan."

"Yeah? Well, Dylan's actually trying to help himself. Maybe you should take notes."

He leaned back, stretching his legs out under the table. "See, here's the thing, Offiiiiicer. You can push all you want, but we both know none of this is going to stick."

"Because your daddy's the mayor?"

Seth's grin turned sharp. "Exactly."

Amy shook her head. "That's cute. But your dad isn't in this room, and he won't be the one prosecuting you when this goes to court."

"You think I'm scared of that?"

"I think you should be. You think your daddy's going to save you, but what happens when he decides you're too much of a liability?"

Something flickered in Seth's eyes, but it was gone just as quickly. He pushed off the table, stood up, stretching his arms above his head. "This has been fun, really. But I think we're done here."

Amy smirked. "Not even close. Sit down!"

"Don't I get a phone call?" Seth asked.

"That's after you get to jail."

Amy shut the door to the observation room with a more force than necessary, exhaling sharply as she turned to face Jordan and me.

"Well?" Jordan asked.

She shook her head. "Seth's full of it, as usual. He thinks he's untouchable because of his dad, but he slipped up."

I frowned. "How?"

Amy leaned back against the table. "He knew too much about Leah's search for her parents. More than he should have."

Jordan raised a brow. "You think he was involved?"

Amy scoffed. "Please. Seth doesn't do anything unless there's something in it for him. If he was looking into Leah's past, it wasn't because he cared about her." She met my gaze. "It's because he wanted to know if it would come back to bite him."

My mind was running through everything I'd just gotten out of Dylan. "Dylan said Leah gave him a notebook and some papers. Stuff she was looking into."

Jordan let out a low whistle.

Amy shook her head and frowned. "She found something, Harlie. Something that got her killed."

I nodded. "And now someone's trying to erase it."

The three of us stood in silence.

Jordan broke it. "So what's the move?"

I glanced at the observation window, where Seth sat alone, still looking smug as hell. "We book him."

Amy nodded, catching on immediately. "Simple possession charge. Nothing major, nothing that'll get his dad breathing down our necks too fast."

Jordan scratched at his jaw. "That buys us what? A few hours?"

"Maybe more, if we're lucky." I met Amy's eyes. "You and Reyes handle the booking. I'll take Dylan home."

"To get Leah's stuff?" Jordan asked.

I nodded. "Whatever's in that notebook, it's important. Leah thought so."

Amy pushed off the table. "Alright. Let's move."

Jordan hesitated. "You sure taking Dylan alone is a good idea?"

I was already heading for the door. "I don't have a choice."

Amy said, "Try not to get yourself killed, Harlie."

I threw her a look over my shoulder. "No promises."

Chapter Fifteen

The doors to the station slammed open so hard they nearly bounced off the hinges. Jordan didn't need to look up to know who had just walked in.

Chief Nolan's steps were full of the kind of restrained fury that meant someone had been chewing him out. And Jordan had a damn good guess who.

"Where the hell is she?" Nolan barked.

Jordan pushed off the wall, arms crossed, and faced him. "Good morning, Chief."

Nolan ignored the dig. His face was set, his mouth a tight line of barely contained rage. "I just got off the phone with an irate Mayor Jenkins demanding to know why his son was booked on a flimsy possession charge." His glare sharpened. "You want to explain that to me?"

Jordan kept his stance relaxed. "Seth had drugs on him. We booked him. It's not complicated."

"Bullshit. That was a petty charge, and you know it."

Jordan shrugged. "Last I checked, possession is still illegal. Unless you've changed the law overnight."

"You don't book the mayor's kid on a nothing charge unless you're looking for trouble." Nolan jabbed a finger in Jordan's face. "And you sure as hell don't do it without clearing it with me first."

Jordan didn't flinch. "Funny, I don't remember needing permission to do my job."

"The mayor says the drugs belonged to Dylan Cross."

Jordan tilted his head. "Oh? Was the mayor in the car with them?"

"Seth says—"

"Seth says a lot of things," Jordan cut in. "Most of them bullshit."

Nolan looked like he was barely holding on to his patience. "Jesus Christ, Jordan. You think this is going to stick?"

"It doesn't have to. It just needs to slow him down."

Nolan's eyes narrowed. "Slow him down from what?"

Jordan didn't answer.

The chief looked around the station. "Where's Whitlock?"

"Following up on a lead."

"What lead?"

"She didn't say."

"Don't lie to me."

Jordan stayed perfectly still, his expression carefully neutral. "I'm not."

They stood there, locked in a silent standoff.

Jordan could see the muscles in Nolan's jaw twitch, the way his fingers curled at his sides like he wanted to lash out.

Jordan saw exactly what Harlie had been talking about.

She'd told him what happened between her and Nolan—her voice calm, her eyes anything but. She hadn't gone into details, hadn't wanted to, but Jordan had read between the lines.

It took everything in him not to hit the son of a bitch right then and there.

Instead, he forced his hands into his pockets. "Anything else, Chief?"

Nolan glared. "Tell Whitlock I want her in my office the second she gets back."

Jordan nodded once. "I'll pass that along."

Nolan turned and stalked toward his office, slamming the door hard enough that the glass rattled.

Jordan didn't move. His fists stayed tight in his pockets.

This whole thing was a goddamn powder keg. And Nolan, whether he knew it or not, was standing way too close to the match.

Jordan let out a slow breath, rolled his shoulders, and grabbed his abandoned cup of coffee sitting on the edge of the nearest desk.

Harlie had her job to do.

And so did he.

Chapter Sixteen

I trailed Dylan to his front door and stepped in behind him as the creaky screen door groaned shut.

Inside, the familiar smell hit me—cigarettes and rotting trash. He moved ahead without a word, and I followed.

The hallway felt narrower than I remembered. A single overhead light bulb buzzed and flickered, sending shadows along the peeling wallpaper.

He stopped at a door, glancing over his shoulder. "You're not gonna like it."

"I already don't like it."

He sighed and pushed the door open.

Dylan's bedroom looked like it hadn't seen a cleaning day in years. Clothes were tossed haphazardly over a rickety desk, and the sheets on the twin mattress were tangled and stained with God-knows-what. An old TV sat on a milk crate in the corner, and the only light came from a half-dead lamp on the nightstand. The air smelled of sweat, weed, and something metallic I didn't want to think too hard about.

"Cozy," I muttered, stepping inside.

Dylan ran a hand through his hair, glancing around like he was seeing the place for the first time. "Yeah, well. It ain't the Hilton."

"Where's the box?"

Dylan rubbed his hands together before clearing his throat. "Look, I need you to turn around for a sec."

"Not a chance in hell."

"Come on, Harlie, it's—"

"Not. A. Chance." I rested my hand on my gun, making sure he saw it. "You want to get the damn box, get the damn box. But I'm not taking my eyes off you."

His shoulders sagged. "Fine."

I watched as he crossed the room, stopping at the far wall where a tattered poster of some half-naked model curled at the edges, barely clinging to the peeling paint. Without a word, he braced himself and shoved the battered dresser beneath it aside.

His breath hitched. His fingers curled and uncurled at his sides. Then, moving stiffly, he knelt down and gripped the frayed edge of the carpet and peeled it back to reveal a section where the wood floor didn't quite sit flush. His hands shook as he wedged his fingers into the gap and pried up a loose floorboard, the nails groaning in protest. The space beneath was dark, the kind of void that swallowed secrets whole.

He hesitated again. Then, with a shallow breath, he reached in.

My fingers flexed over my gun. If he was about to do something stupid, I wasn't in the mood for it.

Dylan pulled out a small metal lockbox, the kind you'd get at a hardware store, dented and scratched from years of use. He held it for a second, staring at it like it might burn him. Then he stood and shoved it into my hands.

I took it, feeling the weight of it. "When did Leah give you this?"

"A few weeks before she was murdered."

"She say what was in it?"

He shook his head. "Just told me to hold onto it. Said if anything happened to her, I'd know what to do."

My grip on the box tightened. "And did you?"

His laugh was hollow. "No. I didn't even look at the damn thing."

I studied him, searching for any sign he was lying, but all I saw was a guy on the edge, one wrong move away from breaking completely.

"What was Seth looking for?"

Dylan hesitated, his fingers twitching at his sides.

"Don't bullshit me," I pressed. "Seth wanted something. Was it this?" I shook the box slightly.

"I don't know," Dylan muttered, but his voice lacked conviction.

I narrowed my eyes. "You do know. And if you're smart, you won't help him."

"You think I want to?"

"I think you're scared of him."

Dylan didn't answer.

I leaned in slightly. "Listen to me, Dylan. Seth is dangerous, and not in the way you think. He's not just some spoiled rich kid playing tough. He's looking for something, and he doesn't give a damn who gets hurt in the process."

"Yeah? And what the hell do you expect me to do about it?"

I met his gaze. "Stay the hell away from him. Whatever he's after, whatever he thinks you know—it's not worth your life."

Dylan's eyes flickered toward the box in my hands. "What if it's already too late?"

"Then you better start making better choices."

Silence stretched between us.

"Just take it and go, Harlie."

I nodded once and slipped the box under my arm. "Stay put. And if Seth comes knocking, you never saw me."

Dylan let out a bitter chuckle. "Yeah. Sure."

I didn't believe him. But I also didn't have time to waste.

Without another word, I turned and walked out the door, gripping the box tight.

I stepped off the porch like I had all the time in the world, like I wasn't carrying the one thing that might explain why Leah Emerson was dead.

I slid into my truck and locked the doors. Only then did I let out a slow breath, glancing at the lockbox on my passenger seat. The thing looked like it had been through hell—scuffed edges, rust biting at the corners.

I had no idea what Leah put in there, but whatever it was, she'd trusted Dylan with it. And now, it was mine to figure out.

Chapter Seventeen

My phone buzzed in the cup holder. I glanced at the screen.

REYES: Nolan's in the office. Wants to talk to you. Now.

I stared at the message for a second before responding.

ME: How bad?

Three dots flickered on the screen, then—

REYES: Pacing.

I gripped the steering wheel. Nolan didn't pace unless he was ready to explode.

I glanced at the lockbox again. I couldn't take it to the station—not with Nolan sniffing around. I needed somewhere to stash it, somewhere no one would think to look. I put the truck in drive and headed toward my mother's house.

Parking in front of the porch steps, I grabbed the box and stepped out, scanning the woods like something might crawl out of the shadows.

Paranoia? Maybe. But in Sinister Falls, paranoia kept you breathing.

I let myself in, the familiar creak of the front door greeting me. The house smelled like coffee and fresh banana bread.

I moved fast, crossing the living room and heading for the hall closet. Inside, I reached up and shoved the box onto the top shelf behind a stack of old blankets.

"Midday house calls now?"

I turned.

Mom stood in the hallway, arms crossed.

"Had to check on you," I lied smoothly. "Everything okay?"

She arched a brow. "Since when do you check on me in the middle of the day?"

I forced a smile. "Since always."

She didn't buy it, but she didn't push either.

"Coffee's fresh and I just took banana bread out of the oven," she said, nodding toward the kitchen.

"Tempting, but I gotta go. Work."

Her gaze flicked toward the closet, then back to me. "Be careful, Harlie."

I nodded and walked out before she could ask anything else.

INTERVIEW WITH DETECTIVE HARLIE WHITLOCK

INTERVIEWER: Can we talk about Nolan?

WHITLOCK: Do we have to?

INTERVIEWER: He's your boss, Harlie. What if he fires you?

WHITLOCK: He won't fire me. I'm the only detective he's got, and he thinks controlling me is a challenge. Keeps him entertained.

INTERVIEWER: That's a weird dynamic.

WHITLOCK: You're telling me.

INTERVIEWER: Alright, so Nolan's not firing you. But he sure as hell doesn't like you going rogue.

WHITLOCK: Oh, he hates it. But he also knows that if he fires me, I'll just keep doing this on my own — except then he won't be able to reel me in when he wants to. Right now, he still thinks he's got a leash on me.

INTERVIEWER: Does he?

WHITLOCK: Not even close.

INTERVIEWER: Alright. What about Seth? How long is he going to be locked up?

WHITLOCK: Hell, he's probably out already or will be soon.

INTERVIEWER: You serious?

WHITLOCK: Dead serious. That kind of money? That kind of family? You really think he's sitting in some holding cell waiting for justice to be served?

INTERVIEWER: Then why arrest him at all?

WHITLOCK: Optics. Makes the department look like they're doing something. Gives Nolan a chance to say, 'Look, we got him!' before quietly letting him walk.

INTERVIEWER: And when he does?

WHITLOCK: Then things get worse. Because now he's pissed.

INTERVIEWER: And dangerous.

WHITLOCK: More than before.

INTERVIEWER: So what's the play?

WHITLOCK: Figure out who's really pulling the strings. Seth's a problem, but he's not the problem. If I just focus on him, I'm missing the bigger picture.

INTERVIEWER: You thinking it ties back to the box?

WHITLOCK: Everything keeps circling back to it. Leah had it. She died for it. Seth — or whoever's pulling his strings — wants it. And now it's sitting in my mom's damn closet like a time bomb.

INTERVIEWER: Then why not open it?

WHITLOCK: Because once I do, there's no going back.

INTERVIEWER: You scared?

WHITLOCK: I'd be an idiot if I wasn't.

INTERVIEWER: So when?

WHITLOCK: Soon. But first, I need to know what I'm walking into.

INTERVIEWER: And if you don't like what you find?

WHITLOCK: Then I deal with it. Like always.

INTERVIEWER: You ready?

WHITLOCK: Not even a little.

Chapter Eighteen

The station looked quiet—too quiet for how tense everything felt. No officers outside, no movement behind the glass doors, just the building holding its breath. I wasn't in a hurry to walk in. Not until I figured out exactly what I was going to say.

But there's only so long you can sit in a parked car before the silence starts pressing in.

I walked straight to Nolan's office, knocked once, then stepped inside, not waiting for an invitation. He was standing behind his desk, arms crossed, face twisted in something between rage and amusement. Jordan stood off to the side, leaning against the wall, arms crossed like he was bracing for impact.

"Whitlock," Nolan said.

"Chief," I replied, shutting the door. "You wanted to see me?"

I felt the weight of what happened the other night. The way he'd cornered me in this very building, drunk and too close, his breath hot with whiskey and arrogance.

He was acting like it never happened. Like it had been just another night at the office.

But I remembered. And judging by the way Jordan was watching Nolan, so did he.

"You want to tell me where the hell you were?" Nolan asked.

"Was there a curfew I didn't hear about?"

"Don't play with me, Whitlock."

I let the silence stretch between us before I answered. "I took Dylan Cross home."

His lip curled. "That what you're calling it?"

"He was tweaking. He wasn't going to make it home on his own."

Nolan leaned forward, both hands braced on his desk. "That's not your job."

I took a slow step closer. "Neither is covering for the mayor's son, but you seem fine with that."

His eyes darkened, and for a split second, I wondered if he'd do something violent.

Jordan shifted to stand beside me. A warning.

Nolan exhaled and sat in his chair. "And after you played babysitter, where'd you go?"

"I checked on my mother."

"How touching."

"Sorry if family responsibilities don't fit your schedule, Chief."

Nolan's gaze bore into me.

"You listen to me, Whitlock," he said finally, voice low and controlled. "I don't care what little games you think you're playing, or what bullshit you're sniffing around. You don't run this department. I do."

"Funny. I thought the mayor did."

Jordan coughed to hide a laugh.

Nolan's eyes snapped to him.

I leaned my hands on Nolan's desk to draw his attention back to me. "You don't scare me, Nolan."

His nostrils flared. "You'd do well to remember—people who dig too deep don't always like what they find."

I held his gaze. "That's what makes it worth digging."

"Get out of my office."

I turned without another word, shoving the door open and stepping into the hall. Jordan followed, his steps easy, like this was just another day.

"You really gotta stop pissing him off," he muttered.

"Keeps me awake."

Jordan shook his head. "One of these days, he's gonna push back."

I looked at him. "Yeah. But not today."

Jordan didn't argue. "Come on. Let's grab a bite to eat before you do something else reckless."

INTERVIEW WITH OFFICER JORDAN REYES

INTERVIEWER: Waiting on Harlie?

REYES: Yeah. She needs to eat, and she sure as hell won't do it unless someone reminds her.

INTERVIEWER: How did it go with Nolan?

REYES: Harlie knows exactly how to push his buttons, and she's got no problem doing it.

INTERVIEWER: Do you think he's scared?

REYES: I know he is.

INTERVIEWER: That's interesting. Because Nolan doesn't strike me as the type to scare easy.

REYES: He's not scared of Harlie. Not in the way she might think. He's scared of what she might find.

INTERVIEWER: So you think she's right? That there's something bigger?

REYES: Look, Nolan's an asshole — always has been. But today? Today he was something else. He wasn't just pissed. He was cornered. And when men like him start feeling trapped, they do desperate things.

INTERVIEWER You think he's going to come after her?

REYES: Not yet. But if she keeps pressing, if she finds something she's not supposed to? Yeah.

INTERVIEWER: You worried about her?

REYES: Worried about her? I've been worried about her since the day she showed up in this town thinking she could fix things.

INTERVIEWER: And now?

REYES: Now I'm wondering how much time she's got before she hits something that can't be undone.

INTERVIEWER: So what's your role in all this?

REYES: Depends on the day. Some days, I'm just the guy trying to keep her from getting herself killed. Other days? I'm keeping a record.

INTERVIEWER: A record?

REYES: You think I don't know how this town works? How Nolan works? If something happens to Harlie — if she disappears, if she turns up dead — I want the truth out there. No cover-ups. No accidents. Just the truth.

INTERVIEWER: That's... unexpected.

REYES: What, you thought I was just here for the ride?

INTERVIEWER: Honestly? A little.

REYES: Nah. I play the long game.

INTERVIEWER: You gonna tell her any of this?

REYES: Not yet.

INTERVIEWER: Why not?

REYES: Because she already knows.

WHITLOCK: Alright, what the hell are you two whispering about?

REYES: Nothing. Just admiring your excellent people skills.

WHITLOCK: Yeah, I'm real good at making friends.

REYES: And pissing off your boss.

WHITLOCK: Gotta have a hobby.

INTERVIEWER: You do realize one of these days Nolan's gonna hit his breaking point, right?

WHITLOCK: Yeah. But not today.

REYES: I'm telling you — she's got bigger balls than any man I know.

The walls of his office, lined with commendations and old case files, seemed to press in as Chief Nolan paced behind his desk. His shirt clung to his back with sweat and his head was pounding.

His phone sat on the desk, vibrating furiously against the wood, demanding his attention. He already knew who it was. He grabbed it and pressed it to his ear.

"Mr. Mayor—"

"Are you out of your goddamn mind?" Mayor Jenkins's voice roared through the receiver with the kind of fury that meant someone was about to get buried six feet under. "Tell me, Nolan. Tell me how the hell my son got arrested this morning while you sat on your ass doing nothing?"

Nolan clenched his teeth. His fat fingers curled tighter around the phone.

"I didn't authorize that," he said.

"No shit you didn't authorize it," Jenkins snapped. "So explain to me how a bunch of your damn officers—including that reckless little bitch detective of yours—thought they had the authority to drag my son in!"

Nolan's free hand slammed onto his desk. "I don't know what the hell Whitlock was thinking, but she sure as hell didn't run it through me."

"Then maybe you're losing your grip, Chief," Jenkins spat. "Because this? This is a problem."

Nolan squeezed his eyes shut. "I'll fix it."

"No, Nolan, you should've fixed it before it happened!"

The mayor's breathing was heavy on the other end, his rage vibrating through the line like a loaded gun with the safety off.

"Do you have any idea what you've done?" Jenkins hissed. "The press is already sniffing around. My son—my only son—was paraded into the damn station like some lowlife junkie! Do you know what that looks like?"

Nolan swallowed hard. He knew exactly what it looked like. Weakness.

And men like Mayor Jenkins didn't tolerate weakness.

"I can control the department," Nolan said quickly. "I'll handle my people."

Jenkins laughed. "Oh, you better handle them. Because if you can't, I will."

Jenkins's voice dropped. "I don't think I need to remind you," he said, "that you wouldn't be wearing that badge if it weren't for me."

Nolan's grip on the phone was so tight his knuckles ached.

"No, sir," he said.

"You remember, don't you?" Jenkins voice was smooth now. "That little problem you had back then? The kind that could've ruined your life?"

"I remember."

"Damn right you do. You were spiraling, Nolan. You had blood on your hands, and not just figuratively. You were sloppy, desperate. But I took care of it for you."

Nolan's throat felt tight.

"I cleaned up your mess," Jenkins continued, "and in return, you got to keep your badge. You got to keep your life."

A cold sweat broke out along Nolan's neck. The weight of old sins settled deep in his chest.

"I made you," Jenkins said, voice like steel. "And I can unmake you just as fast."

Silence.

"Now," Jenkins said, all business again. "I don't care what you have to do—pull strings, plant evidence, hell, set a damn fire if you have to. But I want this shit buried. No more cops sniffing around Seth. No more arrests. No more Whitlock."

Nolan grunted his assent.

"She's a problem," Jenkins continued. "Always has been. You should've taken care of her a long time ago."

"She's useful."

"She's a liability," Jenkins corrected. "And if you don't handle her, I will."

Nolan grunted again.

"Nolan," Jenkins said, "do we understand each other?"

"Yes, sir."

"Good."

The line went dead.

Nolan stared at the phone. His fingers twitched, and before he could stop himself, he slammed the phone back down on the desk.

The damn nerve of Whitlock. Arresting Seth Jenkins without his approval. She was already a thorn in his side, but this? This was going to get them all killed.

He turned toward the window. Somewhere out there, Harlie Whitlock was probably strutting around like she had just done the department a favor.

She had no clue what she had just set in motion.

INTERVIEW WITH CHIEF NOLAN

INTERVIEWER: Rough day, Chief?

NOLAN: You got a talent for understatement.

INTERVIEWER: Must be a real headache, your officers arresting the mayor's son without running it by you first.

NOLAN: You think? I've got the mayor breathing down my neck, my department acting like a damn free-for-all, and Whitlock making a career out of pissing off the wrong people.

INTERVIEWER: Sounds like she's got a habit of that.

NOLAN: You have no idea.

INTERVIEWER: So, what's next? You going to rein her in?

NOLAN: You ever try leashing a wolf?

INTERVIEWER: Nope. Can't say I have.

NOLAN: Yeah, well, it doesn't end well for the one holding the leash.

INTERVIEWER: The mayor really put the pressure on you, huh?

NOLAN: You don't get it. This isn't just political bullshit. He's not just pissed because his kid spent a night in a cell.

INTERVIEWER: Then what is it?

NOLAN: Let's just say Mayor Jenkins and I... have history.

INTERVIEWER: History?

NOLAN: He did me a favor once. A big one. And big favors? They come with even bigger strings attached.

INTERVIEWER: How big we talkin'?

NOLAN: The kind you don't walk away from.

INTERVIEWER: So, he owns you.

NOLAN: He thinks he does.

INTERVIEWER: Does he?

NOLAN: We'll see.

The scent of peppermint tea clung to the air as I pushed open the front door of my mother's house. The television hummed softly from the living room, playing an old crime drama at low volume. My mother sat in her recliner, bundled in one of her favorite knitted blankets, her thin fingers curled around a mug.

"Well, look what the cat dragged in," she said, setting her tea on the side table. "Jordan Reyes, you got some nerve, boy."

Jordan's brows shot up. "Me?"

She nodded, her voice laced with playful accusation. "Bringing my daughter around without so much as asking permission. Where are your manners?"

I groaned, dropping my keys on the counter. "Mom."

Jordan smirked, playing along. "You're right, Mrs. Whitlock. That was rude of me. But in my defense, I was more worried about her dragging me into trouble."

Mom let out a raspy chuckle, shaking her head. "That, I believe." She turned to me, eyes sharp with mischief. "I raised you to have better taste in men, sweetheart. At least find someone who asks before stealing you away for the night."

Jordan laughed, holding up his hands in surrender. "Don't worry, Mrs. Whitlock. Your daughter is entirely too scary for me."

"Shame. You're handsome enough."

I rolled my eyes. "Alright, before you start planning a wedding, we've got work to do."

She waved a hand dismissively. "Go on, then. I'll be right here, pretending I'm not incredibly nosy."

Jordan followed me to the hall closet. I reached up and pulled down the metal lockbox.

Jordan eyed the rusted latch. "This thing's seen better days."

I carried it to the kitchen and set it on the table. "You got that fancy tool of yours?"

Jordan grinned. "You mean the one that keeps saving your ass?"

I gestured at the box. "Less talking, more prying."

He pulled the multi tool from his duty belt, wedging the flat end under the latch. With a firm push, the metal groaned and popped open. The hinges creaked as he lifted the lid.

Inside, a small stack of yellowed papers lay neatly folded. Among them were two photographs. I carefully lifted the first one.

It was a portrait of a woman—early twenties, maybe. She had soft features, high cheekbones, and deep-set eyes framed by wavy chestnut-colored hair. There was a quiet sadness in the way she stared at the camera, like she carried more experience than someone her age should.

"No name," Jordan muttered, glancing at the back. "Nothing written on it."

I set it aside and picked up the second photograph. A baby, dressed in an old-fashioned white christening gown, small hands curled into tiny fists. No name, no date.

Then there was a baptismal certificate—faded, nearly unreadable. I squinted at the ink.

Catherine Sylvia Carter
Baptized at St. Thomas Chapel

"That's the chapel that burned down, right?"

"Yeah," I said. "And look who signed it."

At the bottom of the certificate, barely legible through the fading ink and water damage, was a signature.

Reverend Stephen Polanski

Jordan let out a low whistle. "That's the guy who runs the new church on Main Street."

I nodded slowly, my fingers tracing over the old document. "He's been in town long enough to know what happened."

Next, I picked up the adoption papers.

Leah Abigail Emerson, adopted at two months old by Carl and Irma Emerson

Jordan leaned back in his chair. "So Leah was born a Carter."

The sound of shuffling slippers caught our attention. Mom walked into the kitchen, heading toward the sink for a glass of water. She glanced at the table and stopped mid-step. She frowned and reached for the photograph of the woman.

"Well, I'll be damned," she murmured.

"You know her?" I asked.

Mom nodded slowly, studying the image. "She worked at Corbin's Department Store back in the day. Always in the men's section—I used to see her when I went in to buy shirts for your daddy."

"What was her name?"

Mom's lips pressed together in thought. "Evelyn… something. Carter, I think."

Jordan and I exchanged a glance.

"She was real young when I met her," Mom continued. "Pretty thing, but always looked worried, like she was carrying too much on her shoulders."

I nodded toward the table. "Did you know she had a baby?"

"Oh, everybody in town knew. It was all anyone could talk about."

"She wasn't married?"

"No," Mom said, shaking her head. "And back then, that meant people talked." She sighed and set the photo down. "I felt bad for the girl. She was sweet, polite, kept to herself. Never made a fuss about anything."

"What happened to her?" Jordan asked.

Mom's fingers lingered on the edge of the table. "She died."

"How?"

"Car accident," she said. "Up near the mountain road. Paper said she must've fallen asleep at the wheel. Drove right off into the trees."

Mom let out a small sigh. "I never heard what happened to the baby."

I glanced at the documents spread out before us—the birth certificate, the adoption papers, the baptismal certificate. Leah was Evelyn's daughter. Before she was Leah Emerson, she was Catherine Sylvia Carter.

"Mom, did you know Carl and Irma Emerson?"

Mom frowned, thinking for a moment before shaking her head. "Doesn't sound familiar. Were they from around here?"

"I don't know. They adopted Leah when she was a baby."

"If they were local, I would've remembered. People around here don't forget much, especially something like that."

"So maybe they weren't from Sinister Falls?"

Mom pursed her lips. "That'd be my guess. If Evelyn gave the baby up, they probably took her somewhere else. Away from the gossip."

Away from the gossip. Or maybe away from something worse.

I closed my eyes, trying to piece together what I knew. Then I opened them and stood. "If I can't get into Nolan's office," I muttered, grabbing my jacket, "then I'll find another way."

Jordan frowned. "Where are we going?"

I grabbed the baptismal certificate and held it up.

"To see Reverend Polanski."

INTERVIEW WITH MRS. MABEL WHITLOCK

INTERVIEWER: Harlie mentioned that you knew Evelyn
Carter from Corbin's Department Store. What else do you
remember about her?

MRS. WHITLOCK: Oh, honey, that was a long time ago. Let me
think... She was real young, probably barely out of high school
when I first saw her working there. Always in the men's section,
folding shirts and straightening ties like she had something on
her mind.

INTERVIEWER: Did you ever speak to her?

MRS. WHITLOCK: A few times, sure. She was polite, always
smiled, but you could tell there was a weight on her. Like she
was carrying something too heavy for a girl her age.

INTERVIEWER: Do you remember when she got pregnant?

MRS. WHITLOCK: Oh, everybody in town talked about that.
Poor thing, being unmarried and all. Back then, people weren't
as forgiving as they are now. Some folks whispered, some
judged. I just felt bad for her.

INTERVIEWER: And then she passed away.

MRS. WHITLOCK: Tragic accident, they said. Drove off the
mountain road. People barely talked about her after that. Like
she was just a passing headline... Now, is this all you wanted to

ask me, or are you just trying to keep me talking so you don't have to leave my kitchen?

INTERVIEWER: Well, I did have another question. Earlier, you were teasing Jordan Reyes when he stopped by with Harlie. You've known him a long time?

MRS. WHITLOCK: Oh, Lord, yes. I've known that boy since he was a teenager, back when he and Harlie were raising hell together in high school.

INTERVIEWER: Raising hell?

MRS. WHITLOCK: Not the bad kind, just... well, let's say, if there was a party, they knew about it. If there was trouble, they weren't far behind. But Jordan, he was always a good boy. Real respectful.

INTERVIEWER: You seem fond of him.

MRS. WHITLOCK: I am. Always have been. His home life wasn't easy. His daddy — that man was mean. Real mean. The kind of mean that seeps into your bones if you're not careful.

INTERVIEWER: Abusive?

MRS. WHITLOCK: Oh, yeah. More than people liked to admit. But Jordan? He never let it turn him bitter. He took care of his mother, took care of himself. And he turned out real good, despite all that darkness.

INTERVIEWER: And Harlie? Has she ever had a steady boyfriend?

MRS. WHITLOCK: You're asking the wrong person, honey. My daughter doesn't talk about her love life — mostly because she acts like she doesn't have one.

INTERVIEWER: So no serious relationships?

MRS. WHITLOCK: She had one in Dallas, but that didn't last.

I think she's afraid of slowing down, afraid of what getting too close to someone might mean.

INTERVIEWER: And you? What do you think?

MRS. WHITLOCK: I think she's got a good head on her shoulders. But I also think if she ever lets someone in, it'll be when she's good and ready. And heaven help the poor fool who falls for her.

INTERVIEWER: Why's that?

MRS. WHITLOCK: Because my daughter is stubborn as hell.

Chapter Twenty-One

Even though it was late, the lights were still on at the rectory behind St. Thomas Chapel on Main Street. The stained-glass windows of the chapel glowed faintly in the dark, throwing fractured light across the lawn as Jordan and I made our way to the back entrance.

He knocked gently. A minute passed. Then footsteps.

The door opened to reveal Reverend Polanski, older now than I remembered—stooped slightly, his thin white hair combed back neatly. He blinked at us through wire-rimmed glasses.

"Harlie Whitlock?" His voice was soft but surprised. "And… Jordan Reyes?"

"Sorry to come so late," I said. "We wouldn't be here if it wasn't important."

He raised a bushy brow. "Haven't seen either of you at Sunday service in a while."

Jordan cleared his throat. "We've been… busy."

Polanski gave a wry little smile. "Aren't we all. But the doors are still open, you know. Even for lapsed believers."

"I'll try to stop by," I said, though we both knew I wouldn't.

He studied us for a moment, then stepped aside. "Come in."

The inside of the rectory was modest—warm light, old wood, the faint scent of candle wax. A bookshelf sagged under the weight of old theological texts, and a kettle hissed softly from somewhere in the back.

We followed him to a small sitting room where he gestured for us to sit.

"What can I help you with?" he asked, settling into the armchair across from us.

I pulled the faded baptismal certificate from my coat pocket and handed it over. "Do you remember this name? Catherine Sylvia Carter. She was baptized at St. Thomas Chapel. You signed it."

Polanski squinted down at the paper, then nodded slowly. "Yes... yes, I remember that. Evelyn Carter. Young girl. Very quiet."

"She wasn't married," I said.

"No. She came to me with her mother, I think. Or maybe an older aunt. Asked if I would baptize the baby. I didn't ask questions—I never do. Just did what was asked." He ran a thumb along the edge of the certificate. "She seemed... scared. But determined."

"What happened to her after?" Jordan asked.

"I never saw them again. Not until the accident." He looked up at me. "She died. Car accident, just outside town. She's buried near the old chapel."

I leaned forward. "Did you ever hear what happened to the baby?"

"No," he said, frowning. "There were rumors, of course. Some said she gave her up. But no one ever really knew. Evelyn wasn't from here originally. She kept to herself."

"You didn't see her again after the baptism?" Jordan asked.

"Not once," he said.

I glanced down at the certificate, then back at him. "Do you remember anyone else being involved? Anyone pushing her to give up the baby?"

His eyes narrowed in thought, then he slowly shook his head. "If someone was, she didn't say. And I didn't pry."

There was a long pause. The kettle in the next room clicked off.

"I wish I could tell you more," he said. "But that's all I know."

I stood, slipping the certificate back into my coat. "Thank you, Reverend. This helps more than you know."

He walked us to the door, hands folded in front of him. He opened it, then paused.

"Catherine," he said, almost to himself. "It was a beautiful name." He softly closed the door behind us.

Jordan looked over at me. "You believe him?"

"Yeah," I said. "I do."

Chapter Twenty-Two

The road up to Devil's Backbone was all sharp turns and uneven pavement, the kind of place you only drove to if you were looking to disappear for a while. Jordan handled the curves like a pro, but I could see the tension in his grip on the wheel.

Amy had sent the message an hour ago: Meet me near Devil's Backbone. Can't talk at the station. Got something you need to hear.

I wasn't thrilled about the secrecy, but I understood. If Nolan was around, we couldn't risk him catching wind of anything before we had a chance to act on it.

Jordan pulled off at the designated turnout, the cracked pavement giving way to dirt. Amy's car was already there, parked nose-out like she was ready for a quick getaway.

She stepped out as soon as we did, arms crossed over her chest, her face tight with something between urgency and irritation.

"Took you long enough," she said.

"Well, excuse us for not wanting to fly off the side of a mountain," Jordan muttered, slamming the door shut.

Amy rolled her eyes, then turned to me. "I found something. And you're gonna want to hear it before Nolan starts sniffing around."

I gestured for her to continue.

She pulled out her phone, tapped the screen, then turned it toward me. A mugshot filled the screen—a man in his mid-thirties, rough-looking, with shaggy brown hair and a scar running down the side of his face. His eyes were the kind that had seen too much and trusted too little.

"Travis Hale," Amy said. "Served three years on an assault charge. Got out a couple of years ago. Lives off the grid now, out in a trailer in the woods near Rosedale."

I frowned. "And why do I care?"

Amy smirked. "Because he used to date Leah Emerson. Back when she was in high school."

"Wait. What?"

"Yeah," Amy said, shifting her weight. "He was a lot older. Shouldn't have been with her, but he was. They were together her senior year. And I think he might know something about what got her killed."

Jordan let out a low sarcastic whistle. "An ex-boyfriend with a record? That's a hell of a lead."

I nodded, already making a plan. "Where's this trailer?"

"That's the problem. He's not exactly listed in the phone book. I had to do some digging, but I got a rough idea of where he's staying." Amy pulled out a folded map and handed it to me. "It's deep in the trees, off an old hunting road. No neighbors, no address. Just a trailer and a whole lot of nothing."

"Sounds charming," Jordan muttered.

"Does he know we're coming?"

Amy gave me a pointed look. "Would you want to give a guy like him a heads-up?"

"Fair point."

We found Travis Hale's trailer exactly where Amy said it would be—a rusting heap of aluminum shoved so deep into the trees it was practically part of the landscape. A dirty blue tarp flapped from the roof, barely holding up against the wind.

Jordan cut the engine. We sat in silence for a few minutes.

"Place gives me the creeps," he muttered.

"Let's just get this over with," I said, opening my door.

We approached the trailer cautiously. I wasn't expecting a warm welcome, but I also wasn't in the mood to take a bullet through the door. My hand hovered near my holster as Jordan knocked—two sharp raps.

A long pause. Then movement inside.

The door cracked open, and Travis peered out. He looked exactly like his mugshot—grimy flannel, grease-streaked hands, and the kind of permanent scowl that made it clear he had no patience for strangers.

"What the hell do you want?" he muttered, his gaze flicking between us.

I pulled my badge. "Detective Whitlock. This is Officer Reyes. We need to ask you a few questions."

Travis rolled a cigarette between his fingers. "Yeah? Well, I already gave that other cop all the info I know."

I exchanged a look with Jordan before turning back to Travis. "What other cop?"

Travis shrugged and moved to close the door.

I wedged my boot in before he could. "I'll ask again. What cop?"

"I don't make it a habit to ask for names, but—" He scratched the back of his neck. "Big guy. Balding. Hadn't shaved in a while. Beer gut. Total asshole."

Chief Nolan.

I kept my voice even. "What did he want to know?"

"Wanted to know if Leah ever left anything here. And when the last time I talked to her was."

I kept my face neutral. "And what did you tell him?"

"Same thing I'm telling you. I ain't got nothin' of Leah's."

I studied him, watching the nervous twitch in his fingers, the way his eyes darted away like he wanted this conversation over.

Jordan took a step forward. "When's the last time you talked to Leah, Travis?"

His lip curled. "Why the hell does it matter?"

"Because she's dead," I said flatly. "Murdered."

Travis swallowed hard, his Adam's apple bobbing. His gaze flickered with something—not just guilt. Fear.

"She called me," he muttered. "About two weeks ago."

"What did she say?" I asked.

Travis hesitated, glancing past us like someone might be listening.

"Travis. Tell me."

He let out a breath. "She was freakin' out, man. Said she found somethin'—somethin' big. Somethin' about her real parents."

"What do you mean, her real parents?" I asked.

Travis shrugged. "She was always talkin' about not knowin' where she came from. But this time, she said she had proof. Names. Dates. Said she was onto somethin'."

"Who else knew about this?" Jordan asked.

Travis hesitated again. "She was gonna meet someone. Said they had answers. But she wouldn't tell me who."

"Damn it, Travis." I was losing patience. "I'm not in the mood to play twenty questions."

Travis ran a hand over his unshaven jaw. His discomfort was clear in the way he shifted his weight from one foot to the other.

"Look, I hadn't talked to Leah in months before she called me," he muttered. "She was a nice girl, but I don't want no trouble."

His fingers tapped against the door frame. "I don't get why everyone's comin' to me."

I narrowed my eyes. "Everyone?"

Travis let out a bitter laugh. "Yeah, some skinny meth head came knockin' a week ago."

Jordan stiffened beside me.

Travis scoffed, shaking his head. "Guy was tweakin' bad. Thought at first he was lookin' for drugs, but then he started rambling on about some chick. Took me a minute, but I figured out he meant Leah. Said she owed him somethin'."

"Did he say what?"

Travis shook his head. "Didn't ask. Didn't care. I slammed the door and told him to get the hell off my property."

"You sure that's all he said?" Jordan pressed.

Travis scowled. "I'm sure I wanted him off my damn porch."

I studied him, weighing whether or not to push further. There was something else in his expression—something that told me this wasn't just about avoiding trouble.

He was afraid.

"Travis," I said, "if you know anything else, now's the time to say it."

For a second, I thought he was about to slam the door. But instead, he muttered, "All I know is, that guy? He wasn't just some junkie looking to score. He was desperate. Desperate and scared."

Desperate. Scared. And looking for something Leah had.

Travis straightened. "That's all I got. And I mean it—I don't want no part of this. Leah's dead. That ain't got nothin' to do with me."

I stared at him for a long moment, reading the tension in his shoulders, the way he kept glancing past us toward the tree line.

He was lying. Not about everything. But about something.

But I also knew we weren't getting anything else out of him. Not right now.

Jordan took the cue and nodded once. "Alright. If you think of anything else—"

"I won't," Travis cut in. "And I'd appreciate it if you two never came back."

I held my ground for a second longer, then gave a slow nod. "Stay safe, Travis."

He didn't answer. Just shut the door and locked it.

Jordan and I turned back toward the car, neither of us speaking until we were halfway down the dirt path leading to the road.

"Seth," Jordan finally said.

I nodded. "Seth."

Jordan drummed his fingers against the steering wheel, staring at the road like he was trying to fit the pieces together. "If Seth was looking for something Leah had, and now Nolan's out here poking around too..." He glanced at me. "What the hell did she find, Harlie?"

INTERVIEW WITH DETECTIVE HARLIE WHITLOCK

INTERVIEWER: Jordan didn't seem like he was in a rush to leave when he dropped you off here.

WHITLOCK: He wasn't. Just gave me the usual don't do anything stupid speech before he left.

INTERVIEWER: And?

WHITLOCK: And I promised him I'd go straight home.

INTERVIEWER: But you're still here.

WHITLOCK: Guess I lied.

INTERVIEWER: You planning on going back in the station?

WHITLOCK: That depends. You gonna report me?

INTERVIEWER: Not my job. I just ask the questions.

WHITLOCK: Lucky me.

INTERVIEWER: So, what's your plan?

WHITLOCK: Same as it was this morning. Figure out what Leah found, who she pissed off, and why the hell Seth and Nolan were both sniffing around Travis Hale. And if there's one thing I know about Seth, it's that he doesn't go looking for things unless he's desperate.

INTERVIEWER: What would make him desperate?

WHITLOCK: Money. Drugs. Leverage. But Leah? She wasn't mixed up in his usual bullshit. Whatever she had, it wasn't about getting high.

INTERVIEWER: And Nolan?

WHITLOCK: That one's trickier. He's got no reason to be involved in this case — unless he does, and he just doesn't want anyone knowing why.

INTERVIEWER: You think he knows who Leah's father is?

WHITLOCK: I think he knows a hell of a lot more than he's letting on.

INTERVIEWER: And that's why you want back in his office.

WHITLOCK: You catch on quick.

INTERVIEWER: And if you get caught?

WHITLOCK: Then I'll have to start lying to more than just Jordan.

INTERVIEWER: He won't like that.

WHITLOCK: No, he won't.

INTERVIEWER: But you're going to do it anyway.

WHITLOCK: I don't really have a choice, do I? Leah's dead. Nolan's hiding something. And I'm supposed to just go home and pretend I don't know any of this?

INTERVIEWER: And if you find what you're looking for?

WHITLOCK: Then I figure out my next move.

INTERVIEWER: And if you don't?

WHITLOCK: Then I keep looking.

INTERVIEWER: And if Nolan catches you?

WHITLOCK: Then I hope Jordan bails me out before I do something stupid.

INTERVIEWER: This is personal for you, isn't it?

WHITLOCK: You ever see someone's face the moment they realize they're about to die? Leah knew. She was looking for answers, and she ran out of time to find them.

INTERVIEWER: Do you think you'll find answers before you run out of time?

WHITLOCK: I guess we'll find out.

CHAPTER TWENTY-THREE

I stood just inside the doors, listening. The station was empty.

No witnesses.

I moved toward Nolan's office. The place felt unnatural when it was quiet like this—like it was holding its breath, waiting for something to go wrong.

When I reached Nolan's door, I pulled a thin piece of plastic from my pocket—an old hotel key card I'd been keeping for situations exactly like this. Sliding it between the frame and the latch, I jimmied it carefully, applying just enough pressure to pop the lock without making a sound. The knob turned easily in my hand.

I slipped inside and shut the door behind me.

Nolan's office had the scent of a man who spent too much time in here and not enough time giving a damn about the people who worked for him. Much less the town he was supposed to be protecting.

His desk was cluttered but not careless. Papers stacked in piles that looked haphazard but were too evenly spaced to be accidental. The man was arrogant, but he wasn't sloppy.

Which meant whatever I was looking for wouldn't be out in the open.

I moved to the file cabinet against the far wall. Locked, of course. Pulling my pocketknife from my boot, I wedged the tip into the seam just above the lock and twisted until I heard a quiet pop as the deadbolt released.

I pulled the drawer open and scanned the folders. Names, case numbers, dates. Some recent, some old.

```
Carter, E.
```

I grabbed the folder and flipped it open just enough to catch the first few lines of the accident report. Death certificate. Accident photos. *Bingo.*

I tucked the folder inside my shirt, pressing it flat against my stomach, and took one last look at the drawer, making sure nothing looked disturbed. Then I slid it shut and pushed the deadbolt to relock it.

As I moved back to the door, I scanned Nolan's desk. Something about it made my skin crawl—maybe it was the thought of him sitting here, drinking himself stupid, covering up whatever the hell he was trying to bury.

I turned the knob slowly, cracked the door, and listened. Still empty.

I relocked the door, slipped out, and pulled the door shut behind me, then walked back through the station as if everything was normal.

As if I hadn't just stolen a file from my chief's office.

I stepped outside into the cool night air and walked across the parking lot, letting my breathing return to normal. After sliding into my truck, I locked the doors, then reached under my shirt to pull out the folder.

I stared at the neatly printed name on the label, then I set the file on the seat beside me, gripped the steering wheel, and turned the key in the ignition.

I parked the truck in my mother's driveway, shutting off the engine and sitting in the quiet for a moment.

I grabbed the file from the passenger seat, tucking it under my arm as I climbed out and walked toward the house. The porch light was on, but the house was quiet. Mom was probably already asleep.

Fine by me. I didn't want to explain why I looked like I'd just dug up a ghost.

I let myself in, locked the door behind me, and went straight to my bedroom. The walls were still the same pale blue they'd been since high school, but most of my old things were long gone—except for a corkboard on the far wall, filled with newspaper clippings, crime scene notes, and photos from past cases. It was my personal war room.

I tossed the folder onto my desk and flipped on the lamp. I pulled out my notepad and pen, then opened the folder.

The first thing I saw was the handwritten accident report from Officer Ray Bridges.

I knew the name. Couldn't put a face to it, but I'd heard it before. He used to work here in Sinister Falls before moving to Portland. Someone had mentioned he'd joined the Portland Police Department—probably retired by now.

I made a note:

Find Ray Bridges. Portland PD? Retired?

I glanced at the death certificate, nothing special.

```
Cause of Death: Fractured Skull
Manner of Death: Car Accident
```

There were a few grainy photos of the scene, showing the crumpled wreckage of a car at the bottom of the rocky ravine and a woman's body lying near the wreckage. I suspected there had been more photos, but they had long since been lost—or more likely destroyed. No autopsy report.

I turned back to the report.

```
Accident Report
```

Pinnacle Road, 2.3 miles past mile marker 18
Clear, dry pavement
Reporting Officer: R. Bridges

Summary:
Vehicle, a 1986 Ford Taurus, red, registered to
Evelyn Carter, left the roadway and plunged down
a 50-foot embankment.
Vehicle was found upside down at the bottom of
the ravine.
Driver, Evelyn Carter (age 22), was ejected from
the vehicle.
Body was located 25 feet from the wreck, face
down.
Visible injuries: severe head trauma, lacerations,
abrasions, bruising.
Pronounced deceased at the scene.
Body transported to county morgue for autopsy.

I scribbled notes beside each detail and circled *ejected from the vehicle.*

Witness Report – Siam Barok:
Driving east on Pinnacle Road.
Saw fresh skid marks.
Stopped to investigate.
Observed vehicle at the bottom of the embankment.
Saw a female lying motionless near the wreckage.
Left scene, drove to Pinnacle Inn, and called
911.
Additional Note:
Shortly before the accident, Barok observed a
dark blue sedan traveling at a high rate of speed
in the opposite direction.

I stopped reading, my pen frozen above my notepad.
I underlined *a dark blue sedan.* Twice.

I flipped to the next page. The rest of the report was routine, just documentation of the recovery of the vehicle, towing logs, coroner's intake records. But at the bottom, there was something scratched out. I grabbed my phone, switched on the flashlight, and tilted the page, trying to read the faded imprint left behind.

No blood inside vehicle. No sign of

INTERVIEW WITH DETECTIVE HARLIE WHITLOCK

INTERVIEWER: Did you find the file on Evelyn Carter?

WHITLOCK: Yeah, I did.

INTERVIEWER: Anything helpful?

WHITLOCK: Maybe. I need to track down a former officer — Ray Bridges. He's the one who took the original accident report. There was a little tidbit in there that caught my eye... looks like it says No blood in vehicle — but the rest of the sentence cuts off.

INTERVIEWER: So, what's next?

WHITLOCK: A hell of a lot. First, I need to make sure Nolan hasn't noticed his office was accessed.

INTERVIEWER: You think he will?

WHITLOCK: He's not stupid. He'll notice eventually, but if I did my job right, he won't know when. Hopefully, that buys me some time.

INTERVIEWER: And Bridges? How are you going to track him down without Nolan catching on?

WHITLOCK: You ever heard of a little thing called subtlety?

INTERVIEWER: Not exactly your strong suit.

WHITLOCK: Yeah, well, I'll manage. Bridges is probably retired by now, which means no department email, no easy access. But I know a few people in Portland who owe me favors. I'll start there.

INTERVIEWER: And if you find him?

WHITLOCK: Then I see if he's got a story worth telling.

INTERVIEWER: You've already got one story worth telling. The autopsy report — or lack of one.

WHITLOCK: Yeah, and that's why I'm stopping by the morgue before heading to the station.

INTERVIEWER: Dr. March?

WHITLOCK: He wasn't the coroner back when Evelyn died, but he's thorough. If there's anything left of that report, anything that wasn't conveniently misplaced, he'll find it.

INTERVIEWER: If he's willing to help.

WHITLOCK: He likes me more than he likes Nolan. That's a good start.

INTERVIEWER: And if there's nothing to find?

WHITLOCK: Then I keep looking. Time to see what the dead have to say.

Stepping into the morgue, I saw Dr. March standing over a table holding whatever poor soul had landed in his care this morning. His back was to me, but I could see his hands moving over the body.

"You know," I said, "most people find this place creepy as hell, but I bet you sleep like a baby."

March didn't even look up. "That's because the dead don't talk back. Unlike you."

"I'll take that as a compliment."

He sighed, finally turning toward me. "I assume you didn't come here to admire my work."

"Not unless your latest guest has something to say about Evelyn Carter."

March frowned. "That name doesn't sound familiar."

I held up the folder. "Because someone went through a hell of a lot of trouble to make sure no one ever talked about her again."

March pulled off his gloves, tossing them into a biohazard bin before nodding toward his office. "Alright, let's see what the system has to say."

I followed him past the exam tables, trying not to breathe too deeply—the morgue always smelled too clean, like the cleaning chemicals were trying to scrub away death. March's office was packed with shelves stacked with medical textbooks and old case files that hadn't made it into the digital era.

"Carter, Evelyn," he muttered as he typed. The computer screen showed a list of records. He frowned.

"What?" I asked, leaning forward.

"Her file is sealed."

"By who?"

March clicked a few more times, then let out a low whistle. "Sealed by court order."

"What judge signed off on it?"

March adjusted his glasses. "Milton Jenkins. Back when he was Judge Jenkins."

Seth's father. The same man who gave Nolan his orders.

"That son of a bitch."

March gave me a knowing look. "Starting to wonder if you should have stayed home today?"

"Oh, I knew today was gonna suck. Just didn't expect to be right this fast."

March smirked. "Well, congratulations. You win absolutely nothing."

"Ha ha. Any way to unseal it?"

"Not without a court order."

"And that's not happening."

"Not unless you know a judge who doesn't mind pissing off the mayor."

Even if I did, that paper trail would lead straight back to me.

"What about a hard copy?" I asked. "Would the original autopsy report still exist somewhere?"

March leaned back in his chair. "Possibly. The coroner before me wasn't exactly organized, but he didn't believe in throwing things away. A lot of those old cases are still in the basement archives."

"Can you check?"

"It'll take a while. I have an autopsy to do first."

"Of course you do," I muttered. "Dead people come first."

March smirked but then turned serious, watching me for a long beat before speaking again. "Be careful with this, Whitlock."

"You worried about me, Doc?"

"Yeah, actually. I'd rather not see you end up on one of my tables."

I grinned. "That's sweet. But I'd rather you not see me naked."

March let out a rough chuckle, shaking his head. "You're a pain in my ass."

"And yet, you still take my calls."

"Yeah, yeah." He waved a hand. "I'll let you know if I find anything in the archives. Until then, try not to do anything that gets you killed."

"No promises," I said, grabbing my folder and heading for the door.

INTERVIEW WITH DR. LIONEL MARCH

INTERVIEWER: So, how bad is it?

MARCH: You mean how much of a mess is Whitlock about to step in? Because if you're asking me that, I'd say she's already knee-deep.

INTERVIEWER: She ever ask for anything simple?

MARCH: Nope. She doesn't bring me easy cases. If she's knocking on my door, it means something's been rotting for a while, and now it's starting to stink.

INTERVIEWER: And this one?

MARCH: This one smells worse than most.

INTERVIEWER: She ask you to talk her out of it?

MARCH: Hah. No, Whitlock doesn't come looking for permission. She comes looking for confirmation. And, unfortunately, I think she found it.

INTERVIEWER: And you're gonna help her?

MARCH: Against my better judgment? Yeah.

INTERVIEWER: Why?

MARCH: Because I like the kid. And because if I don't, she's gonna get herself in trouble anyway — only this time without backup.

INTERVIEWER: You ever see a file sealed by a court order before?

MARCH: Can't say I have. And I've been here a long time. Even the messiest cases, the high-profile ones — hell, even the botched ones — they stay in the system. You don't just erase a death like that unless there's something worth hiding.

INTERVIEWER: So what are the odds you can find an archived file?

MARCH: Not sure. Never had to go digging around in the basement archives. But I'm gonna give it one hell of a try.

INTERVIEWER: What happens if you find something?

MARCH: Then Whitlock gets another reason to keep pushing. And I start wondering how long before someone tells me to back off.

INTERVIEWER: You worried about that?

MARCH: Look, I'm not looking to make enemies. But I also don't like being told what I can and can't know. Especially when it smells like bullshit.

INTERVIEWER: So, if the file exists, you'll find it.

MARCH: Damn right I will.

INTERVIEWER: And if it doesn't?

MARCH: Then that means someone wanted it gone badly enough to make sure it disappeared. And that? That tells me more than any piece of paper ever could.

<h1 style="text-align:center">Chapter Twenty-Five</h1>

The moment I stepped through the front doors of the station, I could feel the tension. The place had a charge to it, like everyone was waiting for something to explode.

I ignored it.

I ignored the way a couple of officers glanced up at me, then quickly looked away. I ignored the whispers coming from the bullpen. And most of all, I ignored the dozen frantic, all-caps text messages Jordan had sent me while I was at the morgue.

```
REYES: Where the hell are you?
REYES: Nolan is LOSING HIS SHIT.
REYES: Seriously, Harlie, did you do something??
REYES: He's throwing things.
REYES: THROWING. THINGS.
REYES: Call me before he murders someone.
```

I smirked, sliding my phone back into my pocket and making a bee-line for my office. I shrugged off my jacket, tossed it over the chair, and sank down into my seat like I didn't have a care in the world.

That lasted about ten seconds.

Jordan appeared in my doorway, a half-eaten breakfast burrito in one hand, a paper napkin in the other. He looked at me, chewed, then swallowed.

"Where the hell have you been?"

"Good morning to you too."

Jordan stepped inside and shut the door just enough to keep prying ears out. "Nolan is acting crazy. Like, crazier than usual. He came in, went into his office, and not even five minutes later, he started cussing worse than a sailor. Slammed his chair down. Threw something against the wall."

Jordan took another bite of his burrito, watching me carefully as he chewed, then wiped his mouth with a napkin. "You have any idea what's gotten into him?"

I leaned back, my hands steepled in front of my chest. "I have no idea."

"Bullshit."

I grinned. "Hey, you asked if I knew what got into him. I don't. I can take a guess, though."

"And what's your guess?" Jordan bit off a huge chunk of his burrito.

I shrugged. "Maybe he lost something important."

Jordan inhaled sharply, and when he finished coughing up the fragment of burrito lodged in the wrong pipe, he deadpanned, "You broke into his office, didn't you."

"Break-in is a strong word."

Jordan groaned. "Harlie—"

"I borrowed something."

"Jesus Christ."

I shrugged again. "It's fine. I put everything back exactly the way it was. He doesn't know for sure it was me."

Jordan pointed at me with the burrito. "No. But he sure as hell suspects. And guess who he's been taking it out on?"

I smirked.

"Me," Jordan grumbled. "Me, Harlie. I have spent my entire morning dodging questions I don't have answers to and pretending I have no idea why he's losing his damn mind. You owe me for this."

"I do appreciate your sacrifice," I said, nodding solemnly.

Jordan glared at me, then shoved the last of his burrito into his mouth.

"So," he said, still chewing, "are you gonna tell me what you found, or do I get to die of curiosity?"

I propped my elbows on my desk. "Long story short? Evelyn Carter's autopsy report was sealed by Judge Milton Jenkins. As in, Seth's dad. Before he was mayor."

Jordan stopped mid-chew. "You're joking."

"Wish I was."

He swallowed, shaking his head. "A judge sealing an autopsy report? That's—"

"Not normal?"

"No. Not unless someone had a damn good reason to bury it."

I nodded. "And something tells me it wasn't done out of the kindness of his heart."

Jordan began pacing the small space of my office. "Alright. What's next? Because Nolan's gonna be breathing down your neck after this morning."

"Let him breathe. He doesn't have proof."

"That won't stop him from trying to get it."

"I'm not worried about Nolan right now. I've got something more important to focus on."

"Like what?"

I tapped the desk. "Dr. March is looking for a hard copy of the autopsy report in the morgue's archives."

Jordan blinked. "You got him digging through the archives?"

I grinned. "Hey, he offered."

Jordan shook his head. "You are a menace."

"And yet, you stick around."

"Yeah, because if I don't, you're gonna end up dead or fired, and I'm not sure which would be worse."

"Probably dead. I make a damn good cop."

Jordan sighed and rubbed his temples. "Alright, Whitlock. Just...

watch your back. Nolan might not have proof yet, but we both know that's never stopped him before from screwing people over."

"I know. I'll be careful."

Jordan studied me for a moment. "I gotta get back before someone realizes I've been hiding in here. Try not to set anything else on fire before lunch, alright?"

"No promises."

Jordan rolled his eyes and disappeared down the hall, leaving me alone with my thoughts. Nolan was pissed. Milton Jenkins had buried something. And March was digging.

INTERVIEW WITH OFFICER JORDAN REYES

INTERVIEWER: Didn't Harlie promise you she wouldn't try to get into Nolan's office when you dropped her off in the parking lot last night?

REYES: Yeah, she did.

INTERVIEWER: And you believed her?

REYES: Oh, hell no. I just wanted to see how long it'd take before she broke that promise.

INTERVIEWER: And?

REYES: Judging by the way Nolan came in this morning foaming at the mouth? I'd say under eight hours.

INTERVIEWER: You think she actually found something?

REYES: Oh, I know she did. You don't break into Nolan's office and walk away empty-handed. Not if you're Harlie.

INTERVIEWER: You confronted her about it?

REYES: If you call asking her point-blank and getting a smug little smirk in response a confrontation? Then yeah.

INTERVIEWER: What'd she say?

REYES: 'I have no idea why Nolan's in a mood, Jordan.'

INTERVIEWER: And you just let it go?

REYES: What was I supposed to do? Yell at her? She'd just lie better next time.

INTERVIEWER: You ever get tired of this game?

REYES: It's not a game. It's just... Harlie. She's gonna do what she does, whether I like it or not. So, I figure I might as well keep her from getting herself killed in the process.

INTERVIEWER: You sound more like a babysitter.

REYES: Yeah, well, tell me something I don't know.

INTERVIEWER: Nolan's losing it. Do you think he'll come after her?

REYES: Nolan? No. Not directly. He's too much of a coward for that. But he'll make her life hell in other ways. Try to box her in. Wear her down.

INTERVIEWER: And what about you?

REYES: Oh, he's already taken a couple swings at me. Nothing new there.

INTERVIEWER: You ever think about stepping back?

REYES: Every damn day.

INTERVIEWER: And?

REYES: And then I remember if I'm not around, she's got nobody watching her back. And let's be real — you think Harlie Whitlock's gonna stop just because someone tells her to?

INTERVIEWER: No.

REYES: Exactly. So, I stay. And I keep my eyes open.

INTERVIEWER: You ever worry she's gonna take it too far?

REYES: I know she will. Question is, who's gonna be there to pull her back when she does?

INTERVIEWER: So what now?

REYES: Now? Now I finish my soda, pretend I don't know a damn thing, and wait for the next mess she drags me into.

REYES: Shouldn't take long.

Chapter Twenty-Six

Nolan's voice cut through the station.

"Whitlock! My office. Now."

Jordan glanced up from his desk, the crumpled burrito wrapper and empty soda can pushed to the side. I met his gaze briefly, offered a dismissive shrug, then turned and made my way toward the chief's office. I stepped inside, pulling the door shut behind me with a deliberate click.

"Sit down," he snapped.

I felt the weight of the unspoken challenge between us. Moving with measured ease, I adjusted my jacket, smoothed a nonexistent wrinkle on my sleeve, and finally lowered myself into the chair opposite his desk.

The muscle in Nolan's jaw ticked—a tell I knew well. He was trying to rein himself in.

"You remember the last time I caught you somewhere you weren't supposed to be?"

I let a smirk pull at the corner of my mouth. "Couple days ago, if I recall."

He knew exactly what I had done. But if he admitted it, he'd have to acknowledge there was something in that file worth stealing. And he wasn't about to do that.

I tilted my head, studying him like a puzzle with a missing piece. "You look kinda tired, Chief. Wake up on the wrong side of the bed?"

Nolan leaned back in his chair, the leather groaning. He clasped his hands over his stomach, fingers tightening for just a second before relaxing. "How's the Leah Emerson case coming along?"

"It's coming along."

"That right? You got any leads?"

"A few," I said lightly. "But I know how much you want this case wrapped up, so I wouldn't want to bore you with the details."

His lips pressed into a thin line. "Anything you think I should know?"

I leaned back, mirroring his posture. "Yeah. I need a couple days off. Taking my mom to Portland. Specialist appointment for her rheumatoid arthritis."

Something flickered behind his eyes—not sympathy, not quite suspicion. Calculation.

"That so?"

I nodded. "She needs real care. Portland's got the best options. Figured I'd actually do something decent for once."

A moment of silence stretched between us. Nolan watched me like he was reading between the lines of a book that hadn't been written yet.

"When are you leaving?"

"Tomorrow morning. Should be back in a couple days."

"And while you're gone?"

"Reyes and Walsh can handle anything that comes up. You should be happy to get me out of your hair for a while."

He let out a short huff of breath. "Oh, don't flatter yourself."

"Come on, Chief. You know you'll miss me."

"Just don't take too long, Whitlock. We wouldn't want things getting too quiet around here."

"Oh, I don't know. Has the mayor recovered yet from the arrest of his young prodigy of a son?"

"Watch yourself, Whitlock."

I pushed up from my chair, adjusting my jacket with a casual flick of my wrist. "Always do." I turned and walked out, feeling his eyes on my back.

Jordan looked up when I stopped at his desk. "Figured you'd be leaving on a stretcher."

"Disappointed?"

"A little," he admitted, setting his pen down.

I leaned in slightly and lowered my voice. "Meet me for lunch in twenty minutes at Marcelle's Cafe. We need to talk."

"That serious?"

I nodded once. "Yeah."

INTERVIEW WITH DETECTIVE HARLIE WHITLOCK

INTERVIEWER: Alright, I gotta ask — what happened in there?

WHITLOCK: What do you think? Nolan yelled a little, glared a lot. Standard procedure.

INTERVIEWER: Did he know you stole the file?

WHITLOCK: Borrowed. I borrowed the file.

INTERVIEWER: Right. Borrowed. And did you, uh, 'return' it yet?

WHITLOCK: Not exactly. Let's just say I'm holding onto it for safekeeping.

INTERVIEWER: You really like walking that line, don't you?

WHITLOCK: It keeps life interesting.

INTERVIEWER: So, what's next?

WHITLOCK: Meeting Jordan for lunch. There's something I need to run by him.

INTERVIEWER: Work-related? Or... other?

WHITLOCK: It's complicated.

Chapter Twenty-Seven

Portland crept up on us in waves—first the thickening traffic, then the city skyline breaking through the gray haze, its jagged silhouette softened by the ever-present drizzle. The wet roads reflected the streetlights and neon signs as I drove into the city. Its energy was a stark contrast to Sinister Falls, where time seemed to crawl.

"I still don't understand why you're doing this," Mom murmured. She sat with her hands folded over her purse, her gray braid resting against her shoulder. "You didn't have to drive me all this way."

"What, you think I'm that heartless?"

She huffed. "You've just never been the sentimental type, that's all. You've always been…" She waved a hand, searching for the word.

"Practical?" I supplied. "Efficient? A little cold?"

"Independent. Stubborn as a mule, but you get that from your father."

"Yeah, well, don't get used to it. This is a one-time deal."

She chuckled, but I caught the way her fingers curled against the fabric of her coat. The truth was, I knew what this trip meant to her. It had been twenty years since she'd last seen Ernestine Popovich, her best friend from childhood.

I'd grown up hearing stories about Ernestine—her wicked sense of humor, the way she and my mother had been inseparable once upon a time. Then life happened. Ernestine moved to Portland, my mother stayed behind in Sinister Falls, and the distance between them stretched thin by time, by life, by the quiet guilt of not making the effort.

I turned onto a tree-lined street, the houses small but well-loved, and pulled up in front of Ernestine's place—an old craftsman-style bungalow, its porch lined with mismatched flower pots, some thriving, some long dead. A wind chime, crafted from seashells and bits of glass, dangled above a fat orange cat lounging on the front step, eyeing us with lazy suspicion.

The front door flew open, and Ernestine Popovich, all five feet of her, wrapped in a thick knit sweater, her silver hair in a messy bun atop her head, practically barreled down the steps toward us.

"Mabel Whitlock, you old woman!" she bellowed, arms outstretched.

Mom barely had time to unbuckle before she was being crushed in a fierce embrace. I watched as my mother—normally composed—melted into the hug, her face buried in Ernestine's shoulder. When they finally pulled apart, both their eyes were suspiciously damp.

"Forty years, and you still don't call?" Ernestine scolded, swatting my mother's arm. "I should break my own rule and start drinking just to deal with this betrayal."

Mom laughed. "I could say the same about you."

"Come, come," Ernestine waved a hand, already ushering Mom toward the house. "Inside. I have tea and cookies—not those store-bought things, real cookies, made with love."

I grabbed Mom's bag from the backseat and followed them inside. The house was warm, filled with the scent of cinnamon and something savory, like beef stew simmering on the stove. The walls were lined with bookshelves overflowing with old novels, knickknacks from various travels, and framed photographs.

The orange tabby who'd been sunning himself on the porch slipped past my legs and trotted inside like he owned the place. I bent down to scratch behind his ears.

"That's Tubs," Ernestine said with a smile. "He's harmless—unless you're a mouse."

I stood and she nodded toward the hallway. "Guest room's down there, second door on your right. You can just set her bag on the bench by the window, dear."

The guest room was a cheerful space with a patchwork quilt, a pair of mismatched lamps casting a golden glow against the lace curtains, and a faint trace of garden roses in the air. It was unmistakably Ernestine: warm, vibrant, a little chaotic in the best way—and it reassured me that bringing Mom here had been the right call.

As I wandered back into the living room, my gaze drifted over the bookshelves. A tarnished silver frame caught my eye. I picked it up, staring at the two dark-haired girls in frilly dresses, their Cheshire grins wide as their arms draped over each other's shoulders. At their feet, a black Labrador lay chewing on a bone, oblivious to the moment being captured.

"That was summer of '63," Ernestine said from behind me. "Your mother and I—best troublemakers in the whole damn county. That dog, Duke, followed us everywhere. Mabel tried dressing him up once, put a bonnet on his head—he just sat there looking miserable."

I smirked, glancing toward my mother. "You never told me you used to torture animals."

Mom chuckled, shaking her head. "Ernestine exaggerates. Duke loved the attention."

"Uh-huh, keep telling yourself that," Ernestine teased, plopping into her armchair. "Harlie, sit. You're making me nervous hovering like that."

I took a seat on the couch. Ernestine poured tea into mismatched cups, handing one to Mom then holding out a plate of cookies to me. "So, what's really going on? You didn't drive all this way just to drop off your mother."

I took a bite of cookie. "Just needed a change of scenery for a couple of days."

"Bull. You have that same look your mother used to get when she was hiding something. You gonna tell me, or do I have to drag it out of you?"

I shook my head. "Not much to tell. Work's been... complicated."

Mom's eyes flicked to me, but she didn't press. Instead, she reached for another cookie, her fingers trembling slightly. Ernestine covered Mom's hand with her own. "You doing alright, Mabel?"

Mom sighed. "I've had better years. But I'm managing."

"You're allowed to lean on people, you know."

"I know," Mom murmured, but I wasn't sure she believed it.

I glanced at the clock. "I'll be back in a couple of days."

Mom's gaze turned to me. "Harlie—"

"Just relax, okay? Catch up, reminisce, drive Ernestine crazy."

Ernestine waved a hand. "She'll have to try harder than that."

I kissed Mom's cheek and gave Ernestine a nod. "Thanks for this."

"Don't thank me yet. I might keep her," Ernestine joked.

As I stepped out onto the porch, the evening air cool against my skin, I pulled out my phone and hovered over one name in my contacts.

Mark Callaway

It had been six years since he left Dallas, and nearly that long since I'd had anything more than a casual text exchange with him. My thumb trembled over the call button.

I didn't even know why I was hesitating. Mark had always been solid—good, honest, dependable. The kind of man you didn't just walk away from unless you were me.

It rang. Once. Twice.

Then, "Callaway."

His voice. Familiar in a way that sent something warm curling through my chest.

"Hello?"

"Mark, it's Harlie." My voice came out steadier than I felt.

Chapter Twenty-Eight

"Well, I'll be damned. Harlie Whitlock."

Six years, and his voice still had the same effect. A bittersweet feeling settled in my stomach. But I hadn't called for nostalgia.

"Hey," I said.

A pause. Not long, but enough to make me think he was trying to figure out why, after all this time, I was suddenly on the other end of the line.

"Didn't think I'd hear your voice again," he said. "What's going on, Harlie?"

I gripped the railing of the porch. "Yeah, I know. Sorry for the ambush."

"Harlie." He cleared his throat. "You don't call unless something's wrong. So, tell me. What's wrong?"

Of course he could see through me, even over the phone. Mark had always been able to read me better than anyone. That was half the reason I'd ran back then, why I couldn't bring myself to move to Portland when he'd asked. Being with Mark meant being seen, truly seen, and that had always scared the hell out of me.

"I'm in Portland, and I was wondering if you could meet me for dinner?" The words tumbled out, and I cringed, realizing that had sounded like I was asking him on a date.

What the hell was I thinking? Calling Mark out of the blue and expecting him to drop whatever life he'd built here just because I suddenly decided to waltz back in? For all I knew, he was married now, settled and happy with someone who hadn't left him standing there with an unspoken promise shattered at his feet.

I almost backtracked, almost told him to forget it, but before I could, Mark spoke.

"Dinner?" His voice was slower now, like he was testing the word, trying to read between the lines. "Yeah, alright. There's a café on Hawthorne. Cherie's. It's quiet. We can talk."

A small café. Not a busy steakhouse where the noise could swallow up the tension, but somewhere quiet. Intimate. Where there'd be nothing but the two of us, and the past sitting between us.

"Okay," I said, trying to sound unaffected. "Seven?"

"Seven," he agreed, but then added, "Harlie… you sure you're okay?"

That damn concern.

"I just… need to talk. In person."

Mark was silent for a beat. "Okay, Harl, I'll be there."

"Thanks, Mark."

"See you soon."

I lowered the phone slowly, fingers aching from how hard I'd been gripping it. My chest felt too tight, my thoughts scrambled. It had been years, but somehow, Mark still saw the parts of me I tried to bury.

Like that night in Dallas, after we found a missing teen—barely sixteen—curled up in an alley behind a laundromat, a needle still jammed in her arm. Too late to save her. I sat in my car, hands shaking, pretending I was fine until Mark knocked on the window. He didn't say a word. Just handed me a cup of coffee and waited.

I needed to pull myself together before I walked into that café. Because if I wasn't careful, Mark Callaway would see right through me. And there'd be no hiding just how much trouble I was really in.

I arrived at Cherie's fifteen minutes early, stepping inside the dimly lit café with its assorted mix of chairs and walls adorned with eclectic art-work—bold abstract paintings, moody black-and-white photography, and the occasional splash of neon street art. Each piece felt like a story waiting to be told, mismatched yet strangely cohesive, much like the city itself. The scent of fresh coffee and baked bread lingered in the air, wrapping around me like a familiar comfort. I found a booth near the window, settling in with a view of the street outside.

I watched as people passed by—tattooed artists, a woman in a bright pink tutu with combat boots, a man walking a dog in a stroller. Portland Weird, they called it. The city thrived in its own eccentricity, a stark contrast to the rigid predictability of Dallas. It was the kind of place where people reinvented themselves, where pasts could be left behind, and yet here I was, dragging mine back into the light.

The door opened and Mark walked in, and the sight of him stole my breath.

Dressed in uniform, his badge gleaming, the lieutenant bars on his shoulders confirmed he had done well for himself. The years had sharp-ened him, giving him an air of authority that hadn't been there before. But beyond the uniform, beyond the polished strength, his face was the same. Familiar. Unshakable.

Our eyes met, locking for a long charged moment. I pushed my-self up, hesitating only a second before stepping toward him. His arms wrapped around me, warm and unyielding. The scent of worn leather and faint cologne clung to him, stirring something deep inside me. I let myself relax into it, into him, into the security he'd always carried so effortlessly.

When we pulled apart, he studied me, those piercing blue eyes searching, assessing. "You look good, Harlie."

"Not too shabby yourself." I nodded toward his uniform. "Lieu-tenant, huh?"

Mark smirked as he slid into the booth across from me. "Got pro-moted last year."

I took in his easy confidence. "Look at you. Moving up in the world."

"More like stuck with more paperwork." He chuckled, shaking his head. "And you? How's Dallas?"

My fingers absently traced patterns against the smooth ceramic of my coffee mug. The question wasn't unexpected, but it still made me uncomfortable.

"I left Dallas last year," I admitted. "Moved back to Sinister Falls to take care of Mom."

"How is she?"

He wasn't asking out of politeness. He knew her. Mom had adored him from the start, always giving me that knowing look whenever his name came up, as if she'd already planned our whole future before we had. A future I hadn't been brave enough to step into.

I sighed, wrapping my hands around the warmth of my coffee cup. "You know her. Tough as ever. Pretends the arthritis isn't slowing her down. Still insists she can do everything on her own, even when she can't."

"She's an amazing woman." Mark's mouth quirked into a half-smile. "Like her daughter."

I broke eye contact by taking a sip of coffee. "You always were a smooth talker."

He let out a low chuckle. "So," he said, tilting his head, "what are you doing in that crazy little town of yours? Thought you swore off Sinister Falls for good."

"Yeah, well. Turns out life's full of bad decisions."

He huffed. "Tell me about it."

I took another sip before finally saying it. "I'm working for the PD."

"Sinister Falls PD? You?"

"What? Thought I'd end up running an underground poker ring instead?"

"Just… never thought you'd go back. You always swore that town was the last place you'd ever be."

I rolled the mug between my palms, keeping my voice casual. "Yeah. Well. Things change."

Mark studied me for a long moment, his fingers tapping absently against his coffee cup. I could see him piecing things together, the way he always had. He didn't ask why I'd really left Dallas. Didn't press about what had really pulled me back home. But I could tell he was thinking it.

I wasn't ready to have that conversation. Not yet.

"You still overworking yourself?" I asked.

His lips quirked, his shoulders easing just a little. "You know me."

"Yeah," I murmured, watching him. "I do."

The waitress set our plates down with a practiced ease, barely sparing us a glance before moving on. Mark picked up his fork, spearing a bite of his steak like he hadn't eaten in days.

"Still eating like a man who forgets to cook for himself?"

He chewed, then grinned. "Guilty as charged."

The easiness of being in Mark's company again was a relief—like slipping into a well-worn jacket you'd forgotten you owned. The years hadn't erased our rhythm, hadn't made the silences uncomfortable. It was just us, the way it had always been.

We fell into idle conversation, the kind that made the years melt away.

He told me about life in Portland—the cases, the long hours, the city's particular brand of crime. Nothing too deep, just enough to paint a picture. He'd just come back from a weeklong fishing trip with some guys from the department. "Didn't catch much," he admitted, shaking his head. "But it was nice to be off grid for a while."

I let the conversation flow, let myself sink into the comfort of it. For a little while, it was just two old friends catching up, not a detective with a murder on her hands and a favor to ask.

But eventually, dinner was over. The plates were cleared, the coffee refilled.

Mark leaned back in the booth, arms folded, studying me with a familiarity that made it hard to breathe. He wasn't just making conversation anymore—he was waiting.

I stared into my coffee, fingers curled around the mug. "I need your help, Mark."

I saw the subtle shift in his posture, the way his fingers drummed lightly against his bicep. "Knew this wasn't just a social call," he said.

"What, I can't just want to see you?"

He wasn't buying it.

I sighed, leaning forward, elbows on the table. "I've got a big problem on my hands."

Mark set his coffee down. "Go on."

It wasn't easy asking for help—especially not from him. But if there was anyone I could trust outside of Sinister Falls, it was Mark Callaway.

"I'm working a murder back home. Young woman, Leah Emerson. Strangled. Staged." I let the words sink in. "There's something not right about it, Mark. Something bigger than just a one-time killing."

His brows knitted. "And your boss? He giving you trouble?"

"Nolan wants me to tie it up in a neat little bow and walk away."

Mark shook his head. "Figures."

"I can't walk away from this."

"Yeah. I didn't think you could."

"So where do I come in?"

I glanced around the café. "I need to find someone. Ray Bridges."

Mark's brows shot up. "Ray Bridges?"

"You know him?"

"Knew of him," Mark corrected. "Former Sinister Falls PD, right? Moved to Portland ages ago. I heard his name a couple of times when I started with the department, but nothing in years."

I nodded. "He left Sinister Falls nearly twenty years ago. I don't know why exactly, but I do know he didn't leave on good terms. And now… I think he might have answers about my case."

Mark studied me for a moment. "And you think he's still in Portland?"

"I don't know," I admitted. "But if he is, I need to find him. And fast."

He rubbed the back of his neck. "Harlie, if this guy's been off the radar for two decades, he's not gonna be easy to track down."

"I know."

"You think he's involved?"

"I think," I said carefully, "that he knows something. And no one back home is exactly eager to talk."

Mark ran a hand over his chin. Then, "You're really in the thick of it, huh?"

I felt bone tired. "Welcome to Sinister Falls."

Mark let out a quiet chuckle, shaking his head. "Alright. I'll see what I can dig up."

Relief flooded through me, but I kept my face neutral. "I owe you one."

He smirked. "Damn right you do."

I grinned. Same old Mark.

The waitress passed by, dropping off the check. He reached for it, but I slid it out from under his hand before he could grab it.

"Harlie—"

"What? A girl can't buy a guy dinner?"

"This is starting to feel like a date."

I rolled my eyes. "You wish, Callaway."

For the first time in a long time, I didn't feel completely alone.

"I'll see what I can find. Where are you staying?"

I opened my mouth, then realization hit me and I let out an embarrassed chuckle. "Well, I actually hadn't thought that far ahead."

Mark's brows lifted in exaggerated disbelief. "Hold on." He leaned forward, resting his forearms on the table, eyes dancing with amusement. "The great Detective Harlie Whitlock made it all the way to the big city without a plan?"

I smirked, shaking my head. "I know. Try to contain your shock."

"Honestly, I feel like I should take a picture of this moment. Frame it. Proof that you're actually human."

"Don't push it, Callaway."

He held up his hands in mock surrender. "You know, you're welcome to stay with me."

"What?"

"I've got an extra room. Nothing fancy, but it's got a bed, a door, and," he smirked, "indoor plumbing."

I scoffed. "Wow. Luxury accommodations."

"Hey, I try to keep things classy."

The idea of being under the same roof as Mark—of having that much proximity to him again after all these years—sent a wave of unease through me. Not because I didn't trust him. Because I did.

Mark must've sensed my apprehension because he quickly added, "Look, no pressure. I just figured it's better than wandering around at midnight looking for a motel that doesn't double as a crime scene."

"Okay, fair point."

He smiled. "My shift starts at eleven, but I can take you to my place first, drop off your stuff. It's just a few blocks from here."

This was Mark. The same Mark who had once been my best friend, who had once been the person I trusted most in the world. But things were different now. Years had passed. There were things we'd left unsaid, things neither of us had been willing to face back then.

Could I really stay under his roof without those ghosts creeping in? Without old memories clawing their way back to the surface?

"Harlie, it's just a place to crash. No expectations, no strings." His lips twitched. "I promise not to talk your ear off about fishing."

"Okay. Fine. But if you start snoring like you used to, I'm moving out immediately."

His laugh settled something inside me.

"No guarantees," he said, standing up. "Come on. Let's get you settled before I have to clock in."

As I followed him out into the cool night air, I hoped Mark could settle something in my case, too.

CHAPTER TWENTY-NINE

I settled into the guest room at Mark's house easily enough, exhaustion dragging me under the moment my head hit the pillow. Portland's nighttime hum drifted through the window, the occasional car passing, but otherwise, it was quiet. Safe.

The vibration of my phone yanked me out of sleep.

It took a moment to register the noise, for my limbs to move. My hand fumbled across the nightstand, fingers grazing the cool surface of my phone before I grabbed it and held it up to my face.

2:04
Reyes

I swiped to answer. "Reyes?"

"Harlie. Someone broke into your mother's house."

"Talk to me!"

I swung my legs over the edge of the bed, my bare feet hitting the cool hardwood. I was still in my T-shirt and shorts, the bed's warmth lingering, but adrenaline was starting to kick in, waking me up fast.

"Talk to me," I said, gripping the phone tighter.

"No forced entry. Whoever it was either had a key or knew how to pick a lock without leaving a trace. Nothing stolen, but the place was searched.”

“How bad?”

“Not ransacked. Just… specific. Desk drawers opened, papers shifted. Almost like they knew exactly what they were looking for.”

“Then they took the bait.”

Jordan was quiet for a second. “Looks that way. Good thing you set up that silent alarm.”

Jordan and I had planned for something like this. We knew someone would come sniffing around while I was out of town, looking for the Evelyn Carter file. A file that, to the outside world, didn’t exist anymore.

“They must have thought I left it there.”

“Yeah. Question is, who?”

A soft knock at the door. I turned my head toward it as Mark’s voice, low and groggy, came through.

“Harlie?”

“Come in,” I muttered.

The door creaked open. Mark stepped in, hair tousled, eyes heavy with sleep. He wasn’t supposed to be off until 6:00.

“What are you doing home?”

“Got off early.”

He crossed the room and sat next to me on the bed without a word, his knee brushing against mine.

Jordan’s faint voice broke through the silence.

“Harlie… who the hell is that?”

I put him on speaker, knowing I was going to regret this. “It’s—”

“Mark Callaway,” Mark answered for me. “And you are?”

“No way.” Jordan sounded thoroughly unimpressed. “Tell me you are not sitting in a bedroom with your ex-boyfriend in the middle of the damn night.”

I groaned. “Jordan—”

“Oh, this is rich,” he continued. “I call to tell you someone broke into your mother’s house and you’re off screwing around?”

Mark smirked, clearly entertained. “Co-worker of yours?”

“Her favorite one,” Jordan deadpanned. “You know, I was wondering why she didn't answer my first couple of calls. Guess I got my answer."

I glared at the phone. "Both of you need to shut up."

Mark huffed a small chuckle but asked in a serious tone, "What's going on?"

I hesitated then said, "Alright, Reyes. Start from the top."

"Someone broke into Harlie's mom's house. Didn't take anything, just searched. No forced entry."

"What were they after?"

"The Evelyn Carter file," I said. "We figured someone would come looking for it while I was gone. Guess we were right."

Mark rubbed his jaw. "And I'm guessing you didn't actually leave the file there."

"Nope," Jordan confirmed. "She's not that dumb."

"Gee, thanks, Reyes," I muttered.

Mark shook his head, his mind already working. "So whoever it was came up empty. Which means they're going to keep looking."

"Exactly," Jordan said. "And if they were willing to risk a break-in for it, they're not going to stop now."

Mark glanced at me. "You've got bigger problems, Whitlock."

"Yeah. I know."

Jordan asked, "What's the plan, Harlie?"

I glanced at Mark. "We don't flinch," I said. "Whoever's looking for that file… we let them think they're getting close."

Mark nodded. "And then?"

"We make them show their hand."

Chapter Thirty

Mark's Jeep rumbled as we left the last stretch of city behind, rolling into the sprawling wilderness outside of Portland. It felt like old times—long drives with nowhere in particular, just the open road and the occasional argument over who had the worse taste in music.

"So, just to make sure I got this straight," Mark said, "Chief Nolan had the Evelyn Carter file locked in his office."

"Yep."

"You broke in and took it."

"I retrieved it."

"You stole it."

I didn't respond.

"And," he continued, "someone thought you left it at home, so they broke into your mom's house looking for it."

"Correct."

"And now we are driving two hours into the mountains, in search of a retired cop who might be able to tell us more about a fatal accident that happened twenty years ago."

"That's the plan," I said, taking a sip of my lukewarm coffee.

He chuckled. "Just making sure I got it all straight."

"Starting to regret coming along?"

"Hell no. I haven't had this much excitement since my last fishing trip."

I rolled my eyes. "Did you catch anything, or did you just sit around drinking beer with a fishing pole in your hand?"

"Excuse you," he said. "I caught a very respectable trout."

"Uh-huh."

Mark smiled as he downshifted, taking us onto a narrow road that wound higher into the mountains.

"What did your sources tell you about Bridges?" I asked, breaking the steady hum of the Jeep's engine.

"Pretty much the same thing across the board. Everyone says he was a good cop—never had any issues, never made waves. He did his job, didn't step on toes, and then one day, he retired. No fanfare, no drama. Just walked away."

"No rumors? No whispers about why he left?"

Mark shook his head. "Nothing concrete. If there was bad blood, he never let it show." Mark glanced at me, then back at the road. "What exactly are you hoping to get out of him?"

I sighed, shifting in my seat. "For starters, I want his take on Evelyn Carter's accident. He was the investigating officer—he's the one who wrote the original report before everything got scrubbed."

"You think he remembers something?"

"If he does, he might be the only one left who can tell me what really happened that night." I hesitated, then added, "But I also want to know what else was going on in Sinister Falls at the time. Who was pulling the strings? What cases might've been connected?"

"So, best case scenario, he gives you something solid."

"Worst case," I said dryly, "he tells us to get the hell off his porch."

"Well, good thing I'm the charming one."

I scoffed. "Right. Because that's worked out so well for you."

He chuckled but didn't argue. Instead, he pressed down on the gas, the Jeep roaring as we climbed higher into the mountains. Civilization had officially faded behind us. The only signs of life now were the occasional weathered road signs and the distant calls of birds echoing through the pines.

"I think if there's any version of the truth left, he's the one who has it," I concluded.

Mark adjusted his grip on the wheel. "Man really wanted to disappear, huh?"

"Or he just likes his privacy," I said.

"Same thing, when you live this far off the grid."

The Jeep bumped over a patch of uneven dirt, and I reached for the dashboard to steady myself. "This is the kind of place horror movies start," I muttered.

"Good thing I brought you along, then."

I shot him a glare. "If this turns into a slasher flick, I'm tripping you first."

Mark laughed. "Cold, Whitlock. Real cold."

We kept driving, the road twisting deeper into the woods until it revealed a small cabin, the wood dark with age and wear. Mark cut the engine, and the Jeep rumbled to a stop. The sudden silence was eerie.

I stared at the cabin, watching a thin wisp of smoke curl from the chimney. "You ready for this?"

Mark's hand lingered on the gear shift. "Are you?"

My fingers tightened around the door handle. "Guess we're about to find out."

Mark nodded, then pushed open his door. I did the same and stepped out, my boots sinking into the soft ground. The air was thick with the scent of pine and damp earth, untouched by city smog or the figurative smog of Sinister Falls.

As we started toward the porch, I caught the flicker of movement behind the window. Mark knocked on the door. I waited to meet the man who may know the truth.

Chapter Thirty-One

The door creaked open. Ray Bridges looked older than I expected but in a way that suggested experience rather than frailty. His silver-streaked hair was cropped short, his lean frame still sturdy, his blue-gray eyes scanning us with quiet scrutiny. He was dressed in jeans and a plain red flannel shirt, the sleeves rolled up to reveal strong forearms.

"You're either lost," he said, "or you're looking for trouble."

Mark, ever the diplomat, offered an easy smile. "Neither, I hope. My name's Mark Callaway—Portland PD." He gestured toward me. "This is Harlie Whitlock, Sinister Falls PD. We're looking for Ray Bridges."

The moment Ray heard the word "PD" his entire posture shifted. Not in a defensive way, but in a way that read understanding. He pulled the door open wider.

"Well, hell," he said, stepping aside. "Come on in."

I shot Mark a glance before stepping across the threshold. The inside of the cabin was exactly what you'd expect from a retired cop who had traded city streets for solitude. The place was rustic but clean, the kind of neatness that wasn't obsessive, just practical. The floors were polished wood, a stone fireplace dominated the main living space, a stack of firewood arranged neatly beside it. Shelves lined one wall, filled with books—real books, old and well-read, not just there for decoration.

"Have a seat," Ray said, motioning to the sturdy wooden chairs at the kitchen table. "You want something to drink?"

"Coffee if you've got it," Mark said.

Ray smirked. "I *always* got coffee. You?" He turned to me.

"Water, if you've got it," I said, not quite in the mood for more coffee.

He nodded, moving to the fridge. He pulled out a glass pitcher filled with water and poured me a generous glass before setting it down with a quiet thunk. Mark got a fresh mug of hot black coffee.

Ray grabbed a pipe from the kitchen counter and sat down across from us, lighting it and taking a few puffs of the aromatic tobacco. "So, what brings Sinister Falls PD and Portland PD knocking on my door?"

Mark cradled his coffee. "I actually reached out to some of my old colleagues in Portland. They all had good things to say about you."

Ray's mouth quirked up in amusement. "Yeah? That so?"

Mark nodded. "Nothing but respect. Said you did your job, did it well, and didn't get caught up in the department politics."

Ray chuckled. "That's a nice way of saying I kept my head down and my mouth shut."

"A survival tactic I think we both understand," Mark said.

"Who do you know over there?"

Mark rattled off a couple of names—officers, detectives, people who had been around long enough to cross paths with Ray at some point.

Ray nodded as he listened. "Good guys. Not all of them, but most." He took another puff from his pipe. "You still dealing with Captain Murray's messes?"

Mark laughed. "Every damn day."

"Yeah. That figures."

It was classic cop shop talk—two guys who had worked the same streets at different times, exchanging war stories, testing the waters. I let them talk, sipping my water, watching the way Ray measured every response.

Finally, he turned his attention to me. "You came a long way to find me. What does Sinister Falls want after all these years?"

I set my glass down carefully. "I need to ask you about Evelyn Carter."

The easy amusement in his expression faded.

Ray leaned back in his chair, and for a moment, the only sound was the faint creak of the wooden beams settling.

"That name hasn't crossed my lips in a long time," he said finally.

"But you remember her."

"Yeah. I remember."

"You were the responding officer to her accident. You took the original report."

He nodded slowly. "That's right."

I reached into my bag, my fingers brushing against the edges of my copy of the Evelyn Carter file—the real one was hidden somewhere safe. I pulled the accident report free and slid it across the table.

Ray's gaze flickered to it, his teeth clamping down on the pipe. He didn't move to pick it up, didn't even reach for it. Just stared at the pages as if they carried more weight than paper should.

"I don't need to read it," he said. "I remember what I wrote."

"I have some questions I was hoping you could answer," I said.

Ray's expression remained unreadable. "What do you want with a twenty-year-old accident?"

I braced my elbows on the table. "A few weeks ago, there was a homicide. Young woman. Leah Emerson. She was found strangled, her body laid out near the old power station. Staged. Like someone wanted to send a message."

Ray didn't react.

"During the investigation, I found out Leah was adopted. In the weeks before she died, she'd been searching for her birth parents."

Ray didn't look surprised.

"And you know where this is going, don't you?"

Ray said nothing.

"Leah Emerson's birth mother was Evelyn Carter."

Ray nodded. Once.

Mark said, "Harlie thinks Evelyn Carter's accident is somehow related to Leah's murder."

Before I could answer, Ray spoke up. "That's because they are."

"So you do remember," I said.

"I'll never forgot."

Ray stared at the table, his fingers tapping absently against his pipe. "The night Evelyn Carter died… was the night I stopped believing that justice existed in Sinister Falls."

Mark and I exchanged a look before I turned back to Ray.

"Tell me everything."

"Evelyn Carter's accident," he shook his head, "wasn't just an accident."

"What do you mean?"

Ray paused, as if pulling himself back in time twenty years.

"I mean," he tapped the accident report, "the accident scene didn't add up, not the way they wanted it to. The official story was simple: single-vehicle crash, driver loses control, car goes over the edge. But when I got there, things didn't look right."

He ran his finger against the edges of the report. "This is what I wrote. The truth." He let out a slow breath. "But, key details were omitted, reworded. And one thing in particular?" His eyes flicked up to meet mine. "Was erased altogether."

"What was erased?" I asked.

Ray pointed at the line I had circled.

"Ejected from the vehicle," he said. "That was a lie."

"What?"

Ray nodded grimly. "Evelyn Carter was not ejected from that car. She was placed outside of it."

Mark sat forward. "Placed?"

Ray nodded again. "Her injuries didn't match an ejection. Not even close."

"Then how did she get twenty-five feet from the car?"

Ray shook his head. "She was never in the damn car when it went over the edge."

I could hear the faint ticking of the clock on the wall, the sound of wind moving through the trees outside. I looked down at the report. "Her body… if she wasn't thrown, then someone—"

Chapter Thirty-One

Ray nodded. "Someone put her there. After the crash."

Mark's fingers curled around his coffee mug. "Christ."

I flipped a page to the witness report. "Siam Barok saw the wreck, saw Evelyn lying near it. But he only stopped after seeing the skid marks—which means those marks were fresh."

Ray leaned back and relit his pipe. "Exactly. And that blue sedan he mentioned? You think it's a coincidence that a car was seen speeding away from the crash site?"

"No," I murmured. "Someone staged Evelyn's death too."

"They wanted it to look like an accident. A clean story, no questions asked." Ray added, "And someone in Sinister Falls PD made sure it stayed that way."

I stared down at the last part of the report—the faded imprint of the words that had been scratched out.

I read, "No blood inside vehicle. No sign of—" I looked up at Ray.

"Not a drop of blood inside." He nodded. "Which means Evelyn was never driving that car when it went over."

Mark cursed under his breath. "Then where the hell was she before the crash?"

"That's the part I never got the chance to find out," Ray answered.

I asked, "Who was the chief back then?"

"Forrest Sellinger."

Sellinger had been chief when I was a kid, long before I ever put on a badge in Sinister Falls. I didn't know much about him—only that he had retired early and left town without a word.

I frowned. "Sellinger was in charge, but he wasn't really the one pulling the strings, was he?"

"Not even close." Ray scoffed. "Beutrand Hoffermeir ran the show."

"The mayor back then." I knew this—not from any case files, not from department records—but because my father had worked for him.

Ray nodded. "Hoffermeir was as dirty as they come. He had his people in place—inside the department, inside the courts. He didn't just run Sinister Falls. He owned it."

"Who did he have inside the PD?"

"William Nolan."

I stared at Ray, my fingers curling into a fist against my thigh. "Nolan was the mayor's stooge back then, too?"

Ray nodded. "Back then, he was just Detective Nolan. But he wasn't just another guy on the force—he was Hoffermeir's guy. He made problems disappear, made sure some cases never saw the light of day." Ray exhaled. "And when Sellinger stepped down? Nolan was the one who climbed the ladder."

"You're telling me that the current Sinister Falls's police chief was covering up crimes for the mayor twenty years ago?"

Ray nodded. "And he wasn't the only one. Hoffermeir had a judge in his pocket, too."

"Who?"

"Milton Jenkins."

Mark stiffened beside me, glancing between us. "Wait—are you telling me the current mayor of Sinister Falls used to be its corrupt judge?"

Ray nodded. "That's exactly what I'm telling you."

"Jesus."

My dad had been a city accountant back then, handling budgets, payroll, financial reports. I remembered his clipped tones, the way his jaw would tighten, when the name Hoffermeir came up. "A man like that doesn't build an empire without stepping on bodies," he'd muttered once. I had been too young to understand what he meant at the time.

Hoffermeir, Nolan, and Jenkins had formed the foundation of Sinister Falls on corruption, rigged cases, silenced victims, and buried truths. And two decades later, Nolan and Jenkins were still in power.

Mark broke the silence. "And if Nolan was cleaning up messes back then, what are the chances he's still doing it now?"

I pressed Ray. "I just don't understand why someone would go through all the trouble of staging a car accident to cover up the death of Evelyn Carter. I mean, she was only twenty years old—what kind of threat was she?"

"Evelyn Carter had a reputation, if you know what I mean."

I frowned. "What kind of reputation?"

Ray sighed. "She liked the men. And well… you know." He gave me a look, letting the words settle. "It's all fun times and parties until she got greedy. Thought she could play people off each other."

"Are you telling me Evelyn was sleeping with all the powerful men in town? And she decided to blackmail them?"

Ray spread his hands. "That was her reputation." He glanced at Mark before turning back to me. "I never could prove it, but do you want my honest opinion?"

"Yes. Yes, I do."

"I think you find out who Leah's biological father was… and you'll have your killer."

Chapter Thirty-Two

During the drive back down the mountain, Mark and I were silent—and not the comfortable kind we'd settled into on the way up. I gripped the Jeep's door handle, staring out the window at the endless trees rushing past.

William Nolan.

Milton Jenkins.

One of them could be Leah's father.

One of them had killed her.

"So," Mark said, adjusting his grip on the wheel. "Hell of a story, huh?"

I huffed. "Story? More like a damn Greek tragedy."

He glanced at me. "You believe him?"

I turned my head toward him. "Every word."

Mark nodded, like that was the answer he expected.

"Leah's father has to be someone powerful enough to have staged then erased Evelyn Carter's death." I shook my head. "That's not just anyone. That's someone with real power."

"And right now, you're thinking about Nolan and Jenkins."

"Who the hell else could it be?"

Mark didn't argue.

"You ever hear anything about Evelyn Carter before this? Anyone ever mention her name growing up?"

"No. Nothing. She was erased. Like she never existed."

I leaned my head back against the seat, staring at the roof of the Jeep. "I just keep thinking… what if Leah had no idea what she was walking into? She was looking for her birth father, Mark. What if she came face to face with him and didn't even know it?"

"And when she got too close, she ended up dead."

He shot me a look. "I mean, you're talking about high-profile men— powerful men. If one of them is Leah's father, and he killed her mother then her to keep it quiet? That means you're chasing a guy who's willing to kill to keep his secrets buried."

"Then I better find him before he kills again."

Chapter Thirty-Three

The tires crunched over loose gravel as Mark eased the Jeep into a small turnout. I saw a weathered wooden sign swinging in the breeze: Evergreen Café. A tiny roadside diner nestled between towering pines, with an old-fashioned porch wrapped around the front and a handful of metal chairs scattered beneath the eaves.

"What are you doing?"

He shifted into park and cut the engine. "Taking a break."

"A break? Mark, we don't have time for a break. I need to get back to Portland."

He reached across the console and grasped my hand, his fingers warm against mine. "Can we please forget the world for an hour?"

I had spent the last few weeks running full speed toward answers, toward the truth, barely stopping long enough to catch my breath. And I'd pulled Mark into all of it. I had crashed back into his life like a storm, and now here we were, sitting on the edge of something neither of us had planned for.

He squeezed my hand lightly. "Come on, Whitlock. Just one hour."

"You're impossible."

Mark smirked. "And yet, you're still here."

I rolled my eyes, but I didn't pull my hand away.

With a resigned sigh, I pushed open the door. The café looked like something out of another time—the kind of place that had probably been sitting in this spot for decades, untouched by modern chains or flashy renovations. The wooden porch creaked under our boots as we stepped up to the entrance.

Inside, the place felt warm and familiar, the scent of bacon and buttered toast lingering in the air. A long counter stretched across the back, behind which an older woman with silver-streaked hair moved effortlessly between the coffee pots and griddle, flipping pancakes and refilling cups with practiced ease. A few locals were scattered at the booths, wrapped in easy conversation, their voices a low hum beneath the classic rock playing from the old jukebox in the corner.

Mark led us to a booth by the window, the worn vinyl seats cracking as we slid in. The view outside was breathtaking—a stretch of green pines tumbling down into the valley below, mist curling through the trees.

The waitress approached, a notepad in hand. She had a smile that made you feel like you belonged even if you'd never set foot in the place before.

"What can I get you two?"

Mark glanced at me. "Coffee?"

"Sure. Why not?"

The waitress nodded. "Two coffees. You want food?"

Mark grinned. "What's the pie of the day?"

"Blackberry. Fresh baked this morning."

Mark nudged my foot under the table. "We need pie, right?"

"If we must."

The waitress chuckled. "I like you two already. Be right back."

I leaned back against the booth, studying Mark. "So," I said. "What is this, Callaway? A nostalgia trip? A hostage situation? What's your angle?"

He smiled. "You never could take a break, could you?"

I shrugged. "Never saw the point."

"I never expected you to come waltzing back into my life like this, Harlie."

"Yeah. I didn't exactly plan it, either."

"And now that you're here? I'm not sure I want to let you go."

The waitress returned, setting down two steaming mugs of coffee and two thick slices of blackberry pie, the crust golden and flaking.

Mark picked up his fork and stabbed into the pie. "So what do we do now, Whitlock?"

He wasn't just talking about the case. And we both knew it.

I took a sip of my coffee, the bitterness settling against my throat. "I don't know."

"You don't know?"

I pushed my fork through the pie. "I didn't expect this, okay? Any of it. Not the case. Not coming back here. Not… you."

Mark smiled. "I have that effect on people."

"Don't push your luck."

He chuckled, taking a sip of his coffee before setting the cup down to take another bite of pie. "You ever think about staying?"

"In Portland?"

He shrugged. "Or Sinister Falls. You always talked about leaving Dallas, but… I don't know. Maybe it's not about where you are. Maybe it's about what you're running from."

"That's deep, Callaway. You been reading self-help books on your off days?"

"Nah, I just know you."

I savored a bite of pie then chased it with a sip of coffee.

"I don't know, Mark. I don't even know what next week looks like. My whole life right now is wrapped up in figuring out who killed Leah. And after that?" I shrugged. "I don't know what happens after that."

"Fair enough." He leaned forward and tapped his fork against my plate. "But, for what it's worth, if you ever decide to stop running—I wouldn't mind sticking around to see where you land."

I wanted to say something back. Wanted to tell him that I hadn't stopped thinking about him since the moment I saw him again. That maybe, just maybe, this thing between us wasn't as dead as I had convinced myself it was.

But I couldn't. I wasn't ready to say it out loud.

So instead, I picked up my fork, took a bite of the pie, and smiled just enough to keep things steady. "You're right about one thing."

"Oh?"

"This is some damn good pie."

"Classic Whitlock. Always avoiding the important stuff."

I smiled, but deep down, I knew he was right. Because if I let myself think about what this really was—what it could be—I wasn't sure I'd be able to walk away.

Chapter Thirty-Four

Mark pulled into his driveway and cut the engine. I pulled out my phone and dialed Jordan.

He answered on the second ring. "Tell me you're on your way back."

I sighed, rubbing my forehead. "Nice to hear your voice too, Reyes."

"Yeah, yeah," he muttered. "What do you need?"

I glanced at Mark, sitting silently beside me. "Any more bites?"

Jordan was quiet for a second, then I heard the familiar click of his pen tapping against something. "Not yet. But I've got eyes on the department. If anyone's still looking for that file, they're being a hell of a lot more careful."

That wasn't comforting.

"Nolan?" I asked.

"Still watching everyone. Still acting like he runs the damn world. He's keeping tabs, but he's playing it cool. Too cool."

"You think he's waiting for something?"

"I think he's trying to figure out what you know before he makes a move," Jordan said. "He asked me if you'd checked in."

"What did you say?"

"Told him you were in Portland like you said you'd be. Didn't give him anything else."

Mark shifted beside me. I knew what he was thinking: Nolan was testing the waters.

"He buy it?" I asked.

"He didn't press me for details, but let's be real, Whitlock. You and I both know Nolan never asks a question unless he already knows the answer."

"Keep me posted." I hung up the phone.

Mark didn't say anything as we got out of the Jeep and made our way to the house. He unlocked the door, pushing it open, and we stepped inside. The warmth of the house wrapped around us, a stark contrast to the chill outside. I could still smell the faint trace of his cologne, a clean woodsy scent that was distinctly him.

I sighed. "I'm gonna turn in. It's been a long—"

Mark's hand closed around my wrist. I stopped, my breath catching as he gently turned me around to face him.

My eyes snapped up to his, my heart hammering against my ribs. "What are you doing?"

Mark didn't answer right away. He just looked at me, really looked at me, like he was memorizing every damn freckle, every sharp edge that had softened in the last twenty-four hours. His blue eyes were filled with a heat that made my stomach flip.

"What I've wanted to do since I saw you in the café last night."

He kissed me.

It was fierce, demanding, like he'd been holding it back for years.

His hands slid to my waist, pulling me flush against him, and as my body molded against his, a shiver ran down my spine.

I should've pulled away. I should've said something, anything.

But I didn't.

Instead, my fingers curled into the fabric of his shirt, gripping it like it was the only thing keeping me upright. I felt the taut muscles beneath it, the solid warmth of his chest pressing into mine.

His lips were hot, insistent, relentless, moving against mine like he was trying to remind me of something we both had tried too damn hard to forget.

I kissed him back.

Hard.

It was a battle neither of us wanted to win. A collision of past and present, of frustration and longing, of something too powerful to ignore.

His hands skimmed up my back, fingers sliding into my hair, tilting my head slightly, deepening the kiss.

Mark groaned, like he was barely holding himself together.

I wasn't doing much better.

I felt the heat, the hunger, the years of everything unspoken spilling out between us. Every unsaid word, every lost moment, every damn thing we should have talked about but never did—it was all there.

The only thing in my head was Mark. The way he felt, the way he tasted, the way he was kissing me like I was the only thing in the world that mattered.

Then suddenly, he broke away.

Breathing hard, his forehead resting against mine, his hands still firm on my waist.

I was afraid to open my eyes, afraid to see whatever was written across his face.

"Tell me to stop."

I didn't say a damn thing.

Because stopping was the last thing I wanted.

I stood there, trapped in the gravity of him, my breath still uneven, my body still humming from our kiss.

Mark exhaled sharply, his grip on my waist loosening, but he didn't move away. His forehead was still resting against mine, his breath warm against my lips.

"Harlie…"

I forced myself to take a small step back, though it felt like ripping myself away from something I wasn't ready to let go of. His hands didn't leave my waist.

I looked up at him. "What are we doing, Mark?"

"That depends." His eyes were locked onto mine. "Are you gonna pretend that didn't just happen?"

I opened my mouth. Then shut it.

I let out a slow breath, crossing my arms over my chest like it might somehow keep me steady. "This is complicated."

Mark gave a quiet laugh, shaking his head. "It's always been complicated with us."

He wasn't wrong.

"Mark, I didn't come here for this."

Mark studied me for a long moment, his expression unreadable. A smile pulled at his lips.

"I know."

But he wasn't backing away.

His hands were still warm where they rested against my waist, like he was waiting to see if I'd pull away first. I should've. I needed to.

But I didn't.

He lifted a hand and brushed his thumb softly over my cheek.

"I know you didn't come here for this, Harlie. But that doesn't change the fact that it's here."

I shouldn't do this. I couldn't.

Not just because of the case, or because of Nolan and everything waiting for me back in Sinister Falls. But because I had spent years convincing myself this was over. That whatever had existed between Mark and me was buried in the past.

And now, in the span of a single day, because of a single kiss, all of that was unraveling.

I shook my head, stepping back. "This isn't the time."

Mark let his hands drop. "Then when, Whitlock?"

"I don't know."

And that was the truth. I had no damn clue what this was, or where it was going, or what it even meant.

Mark studied me for another long moment, then finally nodded. "Alright. I won't push."

"Thank you."

"Just don't expect me to pretend like it didn't happen."

I bit the inside of my cheek. "I wouldn't ask you to."

"Go get some sleep, Whitlock." Mark nodded toward the hallway.

I hesitated, then turned toward my room and slipped into the bedroom, shutting the door behind me. I leaned against it, closing my eyes and trying to catch my breath.

For the first time since this whole damn case started, I wasn't just worried about finding the truth.

I was worried about what it was going to cost me.

Chapter Thirty-Five

I was losing the battle with sleep. Every time I closed my eyes, my mind wouldn't shut off. The pieces of Evelyn Carter's case, Leah Emerson's murder, Nolan's maneuvering—it all spun through my head like a broken reel, images overlapping, colliding, unraveling.

And then there was Mark.

The warmth of his hands, the press of his lips, the way he looked at me like I was something he wasn't ready to lose again.

I groaned, rolling onto my back and staring at the ceiling.

At some point, I must've drifted off because the next thing I knew, sunlight was sneaking through the blinds, casting pale streaks of morning across the room.

I dragged myself out of bed, my limbs heavy with exhaustion, my head still clouded with the weight of everything waiting for me in Sinister Falls.

The house was quiet when I stepped out into the hall.

No sign of Mark.

I wasn't surprised—he had to work today, and after last night, I had no idea where we stood.

I shuffled into the kitchen. The scent of coffee lingered in the air, and I found myself silently thanking Mark for at least leaving the machine set up.

I poured a cup, inhaling the warmth, then carried it to the table.

There was a note on the table.

I set my coffee down and picked up the handwritten note, my heart doing something strange in my chest.

Harlie,

Have a safe trip back to The Falls. If you need anything, you know how to find me.

Mark

I stared at the note longer than I should have, my fingers absently running along the rough edges of the paper.

No talk about last night.

No mention of the kiss.

Just a simple, careful message, like he knew I'd be overthinking everything already.

I pressed my thumb against the ink.

This was probably for the best. Mark had a life here in Portland. A normal one. A safe one. And I was heading back to a town built on lies, corruption, and secrets that got people killed.

I set the note back down and took a sip of coffee while I stared out the kitchen window. The morning was peaceful, untouched by the chaos waiting for me.

It wouldn't last.

I stepped onto the porch of Ernestine's house, lifted my hand and froze, my finger poised just above the doorbell button.

Music.

The velvety notes of an old jazz record floated through the open window, the sound of a saxophone weaving through the air.

Laughing.

Not just a chuckle, not just polite conversation—but full, unfiltered laughter.

I hadn't heard my mother laugh like that in years. Not since before Dad died.

I took a step closer to the window and looked through the sheer curtains.

Dancing.

Not just swaying, not just tapping her foot—my mother was dancing.

Mabel Whitlock, the woman who constantly reminded me of how stiff her joints were, how tired she was, how she didn't have the energy for nonsense, was twirling in the middle of the living room, her arms loose, her face glowing with joy.

And opposite her, grinning like the devil herself, was Ernestine. The two of them were laughing, twirling in circles to the crooning jazz, moving like they weren't two women in their seventies, but two reckless girls caught up in a summer night.

I couldn't remember the last time I'd seen my mother look that free.

Ernestine clapped her hands as Mom spun, calling out, "See? You still got it, Mabel! You always did!"

My mother giggled. "Oh, hush. I'm rusty."

Ernestine waved her off. "Rusty, my ass. You were always the best dancer in town. You just forgot how to have fun."

I swallowed past the sudden tightness in my throat.

This was not the mother I had come to rescue in Sinister Falls. I wondered if maybe she didn't need me as much as I thought.

I tried the front doorknob and let myself in, calling out "Hello" as I entered the living room. I looked between them, still trying to piece together what the hell was happening. "So... what exactly have you two been up to?"

Ernestine clasped her hands together. "Oh, honey, we've been having the best time. We went down to that little bakery on Maple Street and got fresh cinnamon rolls. Then we walked along the river, fed the ducks, and spent half the afternoon reminiscing about the trouble we got into when we were kids."

I looked at my mother. "You? Trouble?"

"I had my moments."

I shook my head, still reeling from the shift in her demeanor. I'd spent so long worrying about her, watching her withdraw into herself, that seeing her like this felt almost… unnatural.

But in a good way.

Ernestine patted my shoulder. "I was just telling your mother she ought to stay here a while. A few weeks, at least. No sense in rushing back to that big empty house when she can stay here with me."

My mom watched me, waiting for my reaction.

The lightness in her expression, the way she moved without wincing, the genuine joy I saw in her—this was the best she had looked in a long time.

I nodded. "If that's what you want, Mom, it's fine by me."

"Are you sure?"

I nodded again. "Yeah."

Mom deserved to be happy, deserved to be out of Sinister Falls. And I needed to go back to Sinister Falls to find a killer.

Chapter Thirty-Six

Sinister Falls looked the same. It felt like I'd never left.

I tossed my bag inside the house before heading straight to the county coroner's office. If Dr. March had anything for me, I needed to hear it now.

I parked outside the squat, windowless building that had probably been built sometime in the 1950s and never updated. I pushed open the door and walked inside, the scent of antiseptic smacking me in the face.

The front desk was empty, but faint sounds of jazz music—a preference Dr. March and Ernestine weirdly shared—drifted from the back.

I followed the sound and found March hunched over a file at his cluttered desk, his lab coat half-buttoned over a wrinkled shirt, reading glasses perched at the tip of his nose.

Without looking up, he muttered, "Unless you're bringing me lunch, you better have a good reason for interrupting my very important work."

"And here I thought you'd be happy to see me."

"Whitlock. What an absolute delight." His gaze swept over me, then he leaned back in his chair. "I take it you're here to pester me about a twenty-year-old corpse?"

I plopped down into the chair across from him, tossing my badge on his desk for dramatic effect. "Evelyn Carter. Tell me you found something."

March picked up my badge, inspected it like he'd never seen one before, then tossed it back like it was worth about fifty cents. "You know, normal people ask me about fresh corpses. New mysteries. But not you, Whitlock."

I grinned. "That's why I'm your favorite."

"Favorite pain in my ass."

I gestured toward the file on his desk. "Come on, Doc. Tell me you've got something."

March pulled a thin worn-out folder from the pile beside him. "I don't know what you did to piss off the gods of record-keeping, but this file?" He held it up. "It shouldn't exist."

"What do you mean?"

He opened it, flipping through the few yellowing pages inside. "This is what's left of Evelyn Carter's autopsy report. It's incomplete. Half of it is missing."

I leaned forward. "What's there?"

March took off his glasses and rubbed his eyes. "Cause of death is listed as blunt force trauma. Severe head injury, multiple fractures consistent with a high-velocity impact."

I nodded. That lined up with the official accident report.

"But here's where it gets interesting." He pulled out a separate, faded sheet of paper. "There's a reference to a toxicology screening."

"And?"

"And it's not here."

"You mean it was never run?"

"No, it was run. There's a line in the notes indicating that toxicology was ordered. But the results? Poof. Gone."

"Convenient."

"Extremely."

March drummed his fingers on the desk. "Tell me, Detective. Why would someone go through the trouble of making a whole car accident look legit, but then remove only one part of the autopsy report?"

"Because whatever was in her system was proof she was dead before the crash."

March nodded. "That'd be my guess."

"You sure there's no way to find out what was in her system?"

"Toxicology reports aren't just floating around in cyberspace, Harlie. If someone buried it this deep, it's because they had the power to make sure it never saw the light of day."

"What about records from the lab that ran the test? Maybe they have—"

March cut me off. "You think I haven't already tried that? That lab doesn't even exist anymore. Shut down years ago."

INTERVIEW WITH DR. LIONEL MARCH

INTERVIEWER: Dr. March, let's talk about the autopsy file for Evelyn Carter. You told Detective Whitlock that it shouldn't exist. How difficult was it to find?

MARCH: You ever go looking for something you know should be there, but every turn you take, every damn file you pull, it's like someone got there first and wiped the slate clean? That's what this was.

INTERVIEWER: That sounds intentional.

MARCH: Oh, it was. I've worked here long enough to know that sometimes things go missing because of human error — someone files a report in the wrong cabinet, records get mislabeled, hell, even a flood in the basement took out a chunk of old archives years back. But this? This wasn't misplaced. This was removed. Deliberately.

INTERVIEWER: Walk me through how you managed to find it.

MARCH: It wasn't easy. I started where I always start — with the death records. Should've been simple, right? Look up Evelyn Carter, pull the corresponding file, boom — case closed. Except when I did that? Nothing. No file, no official record in the coroner's log. It was like she never even existed in my system.

INTERVIEWER: But you didn't stop there.

MARCH: Of course not. I started digging — cross-referencing paperwork, checking old intake logs from the morgue. Found her name scribbled in a handwritten log from twenty years ago. That told me she was processed, that an autopsy was performed. But when I went looking for the full report? Half of it was gone.

INTERVIEWER: Gone?

MARCH: The first few pages were still in the system, just enough to support the official story — blunt force trauma, consistent with a high-speed crash. But everything after that? Missing. And the toxicology report? Completely wiped out.

INTERVIEWER: Could it have been lost over time? A clerical mistake?

MARCH: Do I look like a man who buys into coincidences? That wasn't lost. That was erased. The kind of thing that only happens when someone with the right access and enough pull decides it needs to disappear.

INTERVIEWER: How long did it take you to track down what little you did find?

MARCH: Let's put it this way — I've spent less time identifying actual murder victims than I did looking for this damn file. I had to comb through old physical logs, search for duplicate paperwork that might've been stored offsite, even go through handwritten reports from twenty years ago. And the only reason I even found the fragment that still existed? Because whoever erased it didn't realize one thing.

INTERVIEWER: What was that?

MARCH: Paper trails have a funny way of surviving. Someone removed the toxicology results, but they didn't erase the fact that a test was ordered. That little detail was buried in an old intake log, a single line written by a morgue assistant confirming that the test had been requested. That's how I knew it was missing.

INTERVIEWER: And missing for a reason.

MARCH: Exactly.

INTERVIEWER: And whoever covered it up all those years ago... do you think they're still around?

MARCH: Oh, they're around. People like that don't just disappear. And whoever tried to cover it up won't hesitate to do it again. And this time, they won't just erase a file.

INTERVIEWER: Meaning?

MARCH: Meaning if Detective Whitlock's not careful, she might be the next name in my morgue.

INTERVIEW WITH DETECTIVE HARLIE WHITLOCK

INTERVIEWER: Harlie, you've been chasing the truth about Evelyn Carter's death and Leah Emerson's murder. But let's talk about the moment things really started shifting — your interview with Ray Bridges. What was that like?

WHITLOCK: That conversation changed everything. Up until then, I knew something was off, but Ray? He confirmed it. He gave me the missing pieces — the ones nobody wanted found.

INTERVIEWER: You didn't go to Ray Bridges alone. You brought Mark Callaway with you. Why?

WHITLOCK: Because I'm not stupid.

INTERVIEWER: Meaning?

WHITLOCK: I knew what I was walking into. If Ray had slammed the door in my face? Fine. If he had decided he didn't want to talk? I could've handled that. But if someone had gotten wind that I was sniffing around and tried to make sure I never walked out of those mountains? Well. Having Mark there made sure that didn't happen.

INTERVIEWER: Why reach out to Mark? I mean, he's your ex-fiancé. That's not a small ask.

WHITLOCK: Because I trust him.

INTERVIEWER: Just like that? After all these years?

WHITLOCK: Just like that.

INTERVIEWER: That says a lot.

WHITLOCK: We spent years having each other's backs. That kind of bond doesn't just disappear, no matter how much time has passed.

INTERVIEWER: But you left him.

WHITLOCK: Yeah. I did.

INTERVIEWER: Why?

WHITLOCK: Because I didn't know how to stay.

INTERVIEWER: Explain that.

WHITLOCK: You want me to lay out all my emotional baggage for you?

INTERVIEWER: If you're willing.

WHITLOCK: Mark and I... we were fire and gasoline. Passion, trust, heat — we had all of it. But we also had expectations. Plans. He wanted forever, and I... I didn't know what the hell I wanted.

INTERVIEWER: Did you love him?

WHITLOCK: I never stopped.

INTERVIEWER: Then why run?

WHITLOCK: Because running is what I do. Commitment? That's another story.

INTERVIEWER: And now that you're back in each other's lives?

WHITLOCK: Now it's messy. Because for the first time in years,

I have to face the fact that I never really let him go.

INTERVIEWER: And neither did he.

WHITLOCK: No. He didn't. And that scares the hell out of me.

INTERVIEWER: Let's talk about Portland again. Bridges told you Evelyn Carter's accident was staged — that she wasn't even in the car when it went over the edge. What was your reaction when you heard that?

WHITLOCK: You ever have a moment where everything you thought you knew just... blows apart in front of you? That was it. That single detail changed everything. Evelyn Carter didn't die in a car accident. Someone killed her, then dumped her body at the scene to make it look like one. And the people who covered it up? They made sure it stuck.

INTERVIEWER: Did you expect Bridges to tell you that?

WHITLOCK: I hoped he'd talk, but I didn't expect him to lay it all out like that. But I think he knew... once I knocked on his door, there was no more running from the past.

INTERVIEWER: You sat across from a man who had been holding onto the truth for twenty years. What was going through your mind?

WHITLOCK: I remember watching him, waiting for him to say something, and in that moment, I could tell — he wasn't just remembering Evelyn Carter's death. He was remembering every decision he made after that. Every time he looked the other way. Every moment he stayed quiet when he knew damn well something wasn't right.

INTERVIEWER: You don't sound angry about that.

WHITLOCK: Ray was a cop in a corrupt system. He knew how things worked, and back then, he had two choices — shut up and survive, or speak up and end up buried right next to Evelyn

Carter. I get it. Doesn't mean I like it, but I get it.

INTERVIEWER: But he spoke up now.

WHITLOCK: Yeah. Because he saw that I wasn't going to stop. And maybe, just maybe, he didn't want to carry it anymore.

INTERVIEWER: Let's talk about the people you suspect — Chief Nolan and Mayor Jenkins. Do you really believe one of them could be Leah Emerson's father?

WHITLOCK: I think someone in power had a reason to keep Evelyn Carter quiet. And when Leah started looking into her birth parents, she got too close. She didn't even know she was walking into a death trap.

INTERVIEWER: That's a bold theory.

WHITLOCK: It's not a theory. It's a pattern. And if you connect the dots, they all lead to the same place.

INTERVIEWER: And what do you think Mark took away from that conversation with Bridges?

WHITLOCK: That Sinister Falls isn't just corrupt. It's rotted. And that whatever we're digging into? It's dangerous.

INTERVIEWER: Did it complicate things between you and Mark?

WHITLOCK: If you think things weren't already complicated between me and Mark, you clearly haven't been paying attention.

INTERVIEWER: So where do you two stand now?

WHITLOCK: Right now? We're in this together. That's all I know.

INTERVIEWER: No regrets about calling him?

WHITLOCK: None.

INTERVIEWER: What about Ray Bridges?

WHITLOCK: Ray spent twenty years trying to outrun this. He finally told the truth. Now, we'll see what it costs him.

INTERVIEWER: And what about you? What's this all going to cost you?

WHITLOCK: I guess we're about to find out.

Chapter Thirty-Seven

I pulled into the station's parking lot. I sat behind the wheel debating whether I had it in me to waltz through the doors like I didn't have a million things weighing on me. Between Evelyn Carter's case, Leah Emerson's murder, and Mark Callaway kissing me like he meant it, my brain was running on fumes.

But I had work to do. And the sooner I got through my backlog of paperwork, the sooner I could refocus on the real reason I'd come back. I made my way inside.

The station had its usual buzz—phones ringing, the hum of conversation, and the low whir of the copy machine. Jordan Reyes was at his desk, as expected, leaning back in his chair and scrolling through something on his phone. His boots were kicked up on the edge of his desk like he had nowhere better to be. The second he spotted me, he dropped his feet and smirked.

"Well, well, well. Look who decided to return."

I rolled my eyes but couldn't fight the smile tugging at my lips. "I wasn't aware I needed your permission."

"You don't. But I know a couple of people who were wondering if you were ever coming back."

I didn't need to ask who he meant.

Across the room, Amy was by the copy machine, stacks of papers in her arms. She turned, noticed me, and gave a short wave. "Welcome back, Whitlock."

I nodded. "Good to be back."

Jordan snorted behind me. "That sounded convincing."

I ignored him, making a beeline for my office. The second I stepped inside, I plopped down into my chair and sighed. The place was exactly how I left it—controlled chaos. Papers stacked on the desk, a few messages left beside my phone, and mail I'd need to sort through. I flipped through the notes absently, my mind only half-focused.

I had a feeling at least one of these messages was from Nolan, and I was not in the mood for whatever game he wanted to play today. I had just started sifting through the paperwork when Jordan walked in, mid-chew, holding another damn breakfast burrito.

He dropped into the chair across from my desk like he owned the place, his knee bouncing as he unwrapped his food. "So… Portland, huh?"

I kept my attention on my papers. "Yup."

"That's all I get? Just yup?"

I set down a report and leveled him with a look. "What do you want, Reyes?"

He leaned forward, grinning around a bite of his burrito. "Come on, Whitlock. Spill. You were in Portland. You met up with Callaway. I'm dying to know—how's Officer Blue Eyes these days?"

"He's fine, Jordan."

"Just fine?" He wiggled his eyebrows. "Because the way he answered my call at two in the morning, I was getting some very interesting ideas about how you two spent your time together."

I rolled my eyes. "Oh my God, stop."

Jordan laughed. "I will not. This is the most entertainment I've had in weeks."

"Should I be concerned that my love life—or lack thereof—is your idea of entertainment?"

He shrugged. "Small town. Gotta take what I can get."

I tossed a pen at him. He dodged it easily, still grinning.

"Alright, alright," he said, holding up a hand in surrender. "I'll be serious." He leaned back in the chair and bit off another chunk of burrito. "So… Bridges?"

I rested my elbows on my desk. "We found him. He talked."

"And?"

"It's worse than we thought."

"That bad?"

"Yeah."

Jordan set his burrito down, his smirk finally gone. "Alright, Whitlock. Tell me everything."

"Bridges confirmed what we suspected—Evelyn Carter's accident wasn't an accident. She was dead before that car went off the road."

"Shit."

"Yeah." I rubbed my thumb over the edge of a file on my desk. "And it gets worse. Bridges wrote the original report, but it was altered. Someone scrubbed key details—the toxicology report, the lack of blood in the car."

Jordan let out a low whistle. "That's some next-level cover-up."

"Which brings us to the why," I said. "Why go through the trouble of staging the whole thing? Bridges had a theory."

Jordan narrowed his eyes. "Let me guess. Evelyn was sleeping with the wrong people?"

"Correct!" I tapped my fingers against the desk. "She had a reputation for getting involved with powerful men. Bridges couldn't prove it, but he thinks someone got nervous. Maybe she got too greedy, thought she could play them against each other. And then…" I spread my hands. "She ended up dead."

Jordan was quiet for a long moment. "And Leah?"

"Bridges believes if we find out who Leah's father is, we'll have our killer."

"You think it's Nolan, don't you?"

I hesitated. "It makes sense. He was Hoffermeir's guy back then, covering things up for the mayor. He had access to the police files, the power to make things disappear. If Evelyn was sleeping with him, and she got pregnant…" I trailed off, watching as the thought settled over Jordan.

"And now Leah pops up out of nowhere, looking for her birth parents."

"Exactly and if Leah went public, Nolan could lose everything. Career, reputation, maybe even his freedom. That kind of fear makes people desperate."

"What about Jenkins?"

"He was in Hoffermeir's pocket too. Bridges said he made sure the right cases got dismissed, kept the wrong people protected."

I stared at my desk. "And if Bridges is right, Leah's murder is just another loose end getting cleaned up."

Jordan shook his head. "Jesus, Whitlock. What the hell did we walk into?"

I met his gaze. "The biggest case this town has ever seen."

"So, what's next?"

"I gotta prove it."

INTERVIEW WITH OFFICER JORDAN REYES

INTERVIEWER: Jordan, let's talk about the moment Harlie came back to the station after Portland. What was your first impression?

REYES: First impression? She looked like hell. Tired, like she'd been running on fumes and caffeine for days. But that's just Whitlock. She doesn't stop. If she's got a case on her mind, she'll drive herself into the ground before she even considers tapping out.

INTERVIEWER: Did she seem different to you?

REYES: Yeah. There was something in her eyes when she walked in — like she was carrying more than just the case on her shoulders. And then there was Callaway. I mean, come on, she spent time with her ex-fiancé for the first time in years, you think I wasn't gonna ask about that?

INTERVIEWER: What was her reaction?

REYES: Oh, she hated it. But that just told me everything I needed to know. If there was nothing there, she would've brushed me off without blinking. Instead, she got defensive, changed the subject — classic Whitlock deflection.

INTERVIEWER: So, be honest, Reyes — are you jealous of Callaway?

REYES: You really went straight for it, huh? Look, I've admitted before that I have a thing for Whitlock. And yeah, there was definitely a twinge of jealousy knowing she was with Callaway in Portland. But deep down? I know where we stand. Harlie and I... we work as partners, as friends. That's what we'll always be.

INTERVIEWER: But it still got to you a little?

REYES: I mean, yeah, a little. Callaway's got history with her, and history like that? It doesn't just disappear. Doesn't matter how much she pretends it does. I saw the way she reacted when I brought him up — there's something still there.

INTERVIEWER: Do you think Callaway is a distraction for her?

REYES: He's definitely something. But distraction? I don't know. He's also the only person I've seen get through that damn wall she keeps around herself. And that? That might be exactly what she needs right now.

INTERVIEWER: Let's shift gears. Ray Bridges. Harlie filled you in on what she learned in Portland. What was your reaction?

REYES: Honestly? It was worse than I expected. I mean, I knew we were dealing with something deep, but a twenty-year-old cover-up, corruption that goes all the way to the top? That's not just a case, that's a damn war waiting to happen.

INTERVIEWER: And you believe Bridges?

REYES: Yeah, I do. That man had nothing to gain by talking to Harlie. He could've told her to get lost. Instead, he laid it all out. And what he said? It makes too much sense.

INTERVIEWER: What about the part where he suggested Leah's biological father could be Nolan?

REYES: Hell, I didn't see that coming. When Harlie told me, I just sat there thinking, holy bleep. Nolan? Leah's father? That's some next-level insanity. But the more I think about it... the pieces fit.

INTERVIEWER: You really think it's possible?

REYES: Yeah. It would explain everything — the cover-up, the way Evelyn Carter's death was staged, and now, Leah turning up dead. If Leah found out Nolan was her father? And she started asking questions? That could be enough motive. Maybe.

INTERVIEWER: And Jenkins?

REYES: You mean our dear, respectable mayor? Please. That man's been greasing palms since before I had a badge. If he was in Hoffermeir's pocket, then he's just as dirty as Nolan. Maybe even worse.

INTERVIEWER: So what's next?

REYES: That's the question, isn't it? We need proof. And if Leah found something before she died? We need to know what it was.

INTERVIEWER: Are you worried?

REYES: Oh, I'm always worried. But that's not what's keeping me up at night.

INTERVIEWER: Then what is?

REYES: Harlie. She's pushing too hard, and if Nolan realizes just how much she knows? He's not the kind of guy to just sit back and let her keep digging.

INTERVIEWER: You think she's in danger?

REYES: I think she already has a target on her back. And if she doesn't start playing this smart, I'm afraid we're gonna find her the same way we found Leah.

Chapter Thirty-Eight

Chief Nolan sat behind his desk, a steaming cup of coffee in one hand, the other flipping through a case file. He didn't look up right away after I knocked. Instead, he finished whatever note he was scrawling in the margin of a document before finally lifting his gaze to me.

"Whitlock." He gestured to the chair across from him. "Sit."

I did, crossing one leg over the other, keeping my posture casual. Not too stiff, not too relaxed. Just enough to make him think nothing had changed.

Nolan leaned back, regarding me for a long moment. "How was Portland?"

I smiled. "Productive."

His dark eyes studied me, looking for cracks. I gave him none.

"Good," he said slowly. "And your mother?"

"She's doing remarkably well," I answered, keeping my voice light. "Best idea I ever had—taking her to Portland."

I saw the flicker of curiosity in his eyes, the slight tightening of his jaw. He was trying to read between the lines, wondering if I meant something more.

"Glad to hear it," he said after a beat, lifting his coffee and taking a slow sip. "Family's important."

I let the words hang.

"Now that you're back, I expect you to get caught up. You've got a backlog of cases sitting on your desk." He set his mug down with a quiet thunk against his desk. "Including Leah Emerson's."

My fingers curled against my knee.

"I assume you're close to wrapping that one up?" he continued, his tone as smooth as glass. "It's been weeks, and the department has more pressing matters to deal with."

Rage threatened to rise inside me, but I swallowed it down.

"Of course," I said, nodding. "I'll make sure everything is handled properly."

Nolan studied me for another minute, searching for something in my face. Doubt. Fear. Resistance. I gave him nothing.

"That's what I like to hear," he said, picking up his pen and tapping it lightly against his desk. "We can't afford to waste time chasing shadows, Whitlock. Some cases just don't have clean endings."

I clenched my jaw but forced my lips into an agreeable smile. "Understood, Chief."

I let my smile fade. "Can I ask you something, Chief?"

"Depends on the question."

"Why didn't you ever get married?"

His reaction was subtle. The briefest flicker of surprise in his eyes, the almost imperceptible pause in his movements.

"Why do you ask?"

I shrugged, feigning nonchalance. "Just curious. You've been in this town a long time. Seems like a guy in your position would have settled down, maybe had a family." I paused, letting my voice take on just the right amount of self-reflection. "I guess I've been thinking a lot about my own future. Whether I want marriage, kids… the whole picture." I smiled. "Figured I'd ask someone who's been around a while."

"I was married to the job," he finally said. "Didn't leave much room for anything else."

I nodded as if that made perfect sense. "No serious relationships, then?"

Nolan's fingers tapped against the arm of his chair. "I had my share."

I waited, keeping my gaze steady.

"But nothing that stuck."

"Because they didn't want to be with a cop? Or because you didn't let them?"

"You ask a lot of questions, Whitlock."

I shrugged. "Like I said, just curious."

"If I had a daughter, I imagine she'd be a lot like you."

The statement caught me off guard, but I didn't let it show.

"All piss and vinegar," he continued, shaking his head. "Headstrong. Stubborn. Can't let anything go, even when it's in her best interest."

I chuckled. "Sounds exhausting."

"Oh, it would've been. No doubt about that." He lifted his coffee mug, watching me over the rim as he took another sip. "But that kind of fire? It gets people far in life."

"Or burned," I said evenly.

"That, too."

Nolan leaned forward. "You should take my advice, Whitlock. Close the Leah Emerson case. Move on."

I held his stare. I wondered if he could see past the mask I was wearing. If he could sense that I knew more than I was letting on.

I smiled. "Noted, Chief."

Nolan studied me for another long second before nodding, dismissing me with a flick of his fingers. I stood, smoothing my hands down my jeans, and turned for the door.

As I reached for the handle, Nolan's voice stopped me.

"And Whitlock?"

I turned my head just slightly. "Yeah?"

His dark eyes locked onto mine. "Some things are better left alone."

I smiled. "Good thing I don't believe in leaving things alone."

INTERVIEW WITH DETECTIVE HARLIE WHITLOCK

INTERVIEWER: Harlie, looks like you just had a rather... interesting conversation with Chief Nolan. How would you describe it?

WHITLOCK: Oh, you know. Just your average, run-of-the-mill power struggle.

INTERVIEWER: Did he ask about your trip to Portland?

WHITLOCK: Yeah, but I didn't give him anything. Nolan doesn't like loose ends, and right now, I'm one of them. He knows I went out of town, suspects I met with people he doesn't control, and that eats at him. The more I keep him in the dark, the more he's going to wonder what I really know.

INTERVIEWER: You seem to enjoy that — keeping him guessing.

WHITLOCK: I'd be lying if I said it wasn't a little fun. He's been playing chess with this town for twenty years, moving pieces exactly where he wants them. The moment someone makes a move he didn't predict? He starts to slip. That's what I'm looking for — a crack in his control.

INTERVIEWER: Did you see a crack?

WHITLOCK: Yep. He called me into his office to remind me who's in charge, to put me in my place. So I flipped the script.

Instead of reacting, I threw him off balance. I asked about his personal life.

INTERVIEWER: He didn't see that question coming, did he?

WHITLOCK: Not at all. Nolan's the kind of man who expects every conversation to go the way he directs it. When I asked why he never got married, you could almost see the wheels grinding to a stop in his head. He had to shift gears, had to rethink his approach. That's rare for him.

INTERVIEWER: Why that question, though?

WHITLOCK: Because he has too many secrets. And sometimes, the best way to get to the truth isn't by asking directly, but by watching how someone reacts to something unexpected. I didn't need him to say anything outright — I just needed to see what he didn't say.

INTERVIEWER: And what did he not say?

WHITLOCK: He didn't deny having relationships. But he was quick to brush them off. Said he was 'married to the job.' That's a nice, clean answer. Safe. But when I pushed a little — asked if it was because women didn't want to be with a cop or because he didn't let them — he shut that door real fast.

INTERVIEWER: You hit a nerve.

WHITLOCK: Oh yeah. That little flicker of irritation? That's gold. That means I was too close to something. It means there is a past there, something he doesn't want me looking into. And now? I definitely want to look into it.

INTERVIEWER: You enjoy pushing his buttons.

WHITLOCK: Damn right I do.

INTERVIEWER: Do you think you'll get more out of him?

WHITLOCK: Maybe. But not directly. Nolan isn't stupid — he's not going to suddenly spill his deepest, darkest secrets just because I ask the right questions. But now? Now he knows I'm watching him. Now, every time I walk into a room, he's going to wonder what I know, how much I've figured out. That's power.

INTERVIEWER: You think he's nervous?

WHITLOCK: Not nervous. Not yet. But he's paying attention. And when people like Nolan start paying attention, they make mistakes.

INTERVIEWER: He told you to close the Leah Emerson case?

WHITLOCK: Of course he did.

INTERVIEWER: What are you going to do?

WHITLOCK: Not that.

INTERVIEWER: What is it about Sinister Falls that won't let you go?

WHITLOCK: It's not about Sinister Falls. It's about what happens when people with power think they can do whatever the hell they want. About what happens when the people who should be protected — the people who don't have the means or the voice to fight back — get left behind.

INTERVIEWER: So, this is personal?

WHITLOCK: Everything's personal, whether you admit it or not.

INTERVIEWER: Tell me.

WHITLOCK: Maybe... maybe it's because I wasn't there when it mattered.

INTERVIEWER: What do you mean?

WHITLOCK: I wasn't there when my best friend Shelby died. I

wasn't there when my dad... when he needed me most.

INTERVIEWER: You blame yourself?

WHITLOCK: I don't know. Maybe. Maybe not. But I do know that there's no changing the past. I can't go back and be the person I should've been back then. But I can make sure no one else gets left behind the way they did.

INTERVIEWER: That's a heavy burden to carry.

WHITLOCK: Guess it's a good thing I have broad shoulders.

Chapter Thirty-Nine

The diner was half-full when I walked in, the usual lunchtime crowd filling up the booths and counter seats. The scent of grilled burgers, coffee, and fresh pie filled the air, mingling with the quiet hum of conversation and the occasional clatter of plates from the kitchen.

Amy was already waiting for me, scanning the menu like she was preparing for battle. She was barely a year on the force, full of energy and a little too much caffeine most of the time. She had her light brown hair pulled back into a ponytail, her uniform shirt unbuttoned at the collar, radio clipped to her belt. She looked up as I approached, a grin spreading across her face.

"Hey, Whitlock. Thought you might ditch me."

I smirked, sliding into the booth across from her. "Tempting, but I figured I'd at least let you buy me lunch first."

"Dream on, Detective. You make more than me."

The waitress came over with two glasses of ice water. "What can I get you ladies?"

"Burger, fries, and a chocolate shake," Amy said without hesitation.

"You still eat like a teenager?"

"Hey, some of us have fast metabolisms." She pointed at me. "Bet you're getting a salad or something boring."

I turned to the waitress. "Patty melt, extra onions, and a black coffee."

Amy grinned as the waitress jotted it down and walked off. "See, that's more like it. I knew you had it in you."

"So, what's up, Walsh? You never invite me to lunch."

She leaned forward, resting her elbows on the table. "Oh, Portland. How was it? Jordan said you were, and I quote, 'tied up with some unfinished business'."

"Reyes talks too much."

Amy's grin widened. "He also said you were with your ex-fiancé."

"Are we seriously doing this?"

She gasped, eyes wide with mock horror. "You were engaged?"

"It was a long time ago."

"Wait—Detective Whitlock was almost a Mrs.? Mind blown."

"You're being dramatic."

"That's because I had no idea! I've never even seen you date!" She leaned back. "So, this guy—what's his deal?"

"He's… an old friend."

"Jordan made it sound like a lot more than that."

"That's because Reyes loves to run his mouth."

"So, what happened?"

I shrugged. "Life."

Amy let out a disappointed groan. "That's all I get? Come on, Whitlock. I need at least one fun fact about this guy."

I set my water glass down. "Fine. He's the only person who's ever beaten me at darts."

Amy blinked. "That's it?"

"That's all you're getting."

"Lame."

"Too bad."

The waitress returned and set down our food. Amy immediately dug into her fries, still grinning like she was sitting on the best gossip of the year.

"Alright, fine. I'll drop it—for now." Amy popped another fry into her mouth.

"Appreciate the mercy."

She shrugged, chewing. "You're a mystery, Whitlock. It's half the reason I like working with you."

I took a sip of my coffee while I studied her. The grin was still there, but beneath it was the Amy who was still trying to figure out how to carry a badge without letting it change her.

"You want some advice?" I asked.

"Are you about to get all mentor-y on me?"

"Just listen."

She nodded.

"You're good at this job," I said. "You've got instincts, and you care. That's rare. But you need to understand something early—this work? It'll take pieces of you. Not all at once, just a little at a time. If you don't know who you are outside the badge, you'll wake up one day and realize you gave too much of yourself away."

Amy was quiet for a minute. "Has that happened to you?"

I looked down at the swirl of black coffee in my cup.

"Yeah," I said finally. "More than once."

She nodded slowly, the smile gone now, replaced with something like respect.

"Thanks," she said. "For being straight with me."

"Don't thank me yet," I said, picking up my patty melt. "You'll hate me the first time I make you chase a suspect through a cow pasture."

INTERVIEW WITH OFFICER AMY WALSH

INTERVIEWER: Officer Walsh, you recently had lunch with Harlie. From what I understand, you had quite an interesting conversation.

WALSH: Oh yeah. Anytime you can get Whitlock to talk about herself, it's a win.

INTERVIEWER: You didn't know she was engaged before, did you?

WALSH: Nope. Not a clue. You have to understand, Harlie's not exactly the type to chat about her personal life. She's all about the job. But when Jordan casually mentioned she was off in Portland with her ex-fiancé, I was floored.

INTERVIEWER: So, you had to press her for details.

WALSH: Of course! I mean, come on — Harlie Whitlock, engaged? It's like finding out your high school principal used to be a rock star. It just doesn't compute.

INTERVIEWER: And what did she tell you?

WALSH: Practically nothing. She dodged every question like she was in an interrogation room. I got one fun fact out of her — he's the only person who's ever beaten her at darts. That's it. I mean, I was expecting something juicy, but nope, just Whitlock being all business as usual.

INTERVIEWER: You really admire her, don't you?

WALSH: Yeah, I do. She's tough as hell, and she doesn't take crap from anyone. She's the kind of cop I want to be.

INTERVIEWER: And now, you're working with her on a case that might be bigger than either of you realized.

WALSH: Exactly.

INTERVIEWER: Aren't you worried? If this goes as deep as you and Harlie think, then digging too much could put both of you in danger or lose your jobs?

WALSH: Look, I didn't become a cop to sit behind a desk and ignore the bad things happening in this town. I became a cop to help people, to get justice for the ones who don't have a voice.

INTERVIEWER: You sound a lot like Harlie.

WALSH: Guess I've been learning from the best.

INTERVIEWER: If Nolan orders Harlie to drop the case, do you think she will?

WALSH: Not a chance in hell.

INTERVIEWER: And you?

WALSH: I made a promise to her — to help. And I don't break promises.

Chapter Forty

Gravel crunched beneath my boots as I stepped toward the guardrail, the clouds above heavy with the promise of rain.

2.3 miles past mile marker 18

This was where Evelyn Carter's car had careened off the road twenty years ago. I braced my hands against the metal, peering over the edge. The slope was almost vertical, disappearing into a mess of trees and rocks far below.

I studied the curve of the road, imagining Evelyn's car speeding along that night, headlights cutting through the dark, the drop-off waiting. There had been no guardrail back then.

If someone had forced her off the road, they would've had to anticipate her exact path—timing it perfectly to make it look accidental.

I braced my hands against the guardrail again, peering down into the ravine. The trees were thick, with jagged rocks protruding between them. If she had truly been ejected from the vehicle during the crash, she should've looked like she'd been through a blender. The sheer force of the car tumbling down the rocky ravine should've shattered her body.

The report had noted blunt force trauma, skull fracture consistent with a high-velocity impact. But not the kind of injuries she should have had if she'd been in the car. Ray Bridges said her body hadn't been ejected.

I closed my eyes, forcing myself to see it differently. Reverse the scene. Not from the perspective of a victim, but from the mind of someone staging it.

Maybe she was killed somewhere else, and her body dumped down the cliff like evidence they didn't know what to do with.

Or maybe it was a panic move. An argument turned deadly, and they staged the crash in a rush, hoping no one would question the wreckage.

What if there were two of them?

I'd been thinking of one killer this entire time—but what if there were two?

One to drive Evelyn's car and send it over the edge. And a second person following behind with Evelyn's body. Two sets of hands to throw Evelyn's body over the edge. And a getaway car. A dark blue sedan.

I glanced back down the ravine. They would've needed to act fast to complete all the steps before someone else drove by. Get to the right spot. Send her car over the edge. Pull her body out of the second vehicle then throw her over the edge.

If there were two of them, why not just push the car over with Evelyn inside?

It began to rain. I rubbed my fingers against the railing in tribute to Evelyn Carter then stepped back to my truck. I climbed in, started the engine, and eased onto the road, letting gravity pull me back down the mountain.

Pinnacle Road wound down in sharp switchbacks, the asphalt already wet. I kept my grip steady, tires hugging the pavement, my headlights slicing through the dimming light. The rain drummed on the truck's roof.

In my rear-view mirror, I caught sight of headlights.

Coming fast.

BAM!

My entire truck jolted forward, my seatbelt locking against my chest. The steering wheel wrenched in my hands as the truck skidded off the road, gravel spraying as I fought to regain the asphalt.

BAM!

My body slammed against the seatbelt as metal crunched, my tires kissing the edge of the road.

Stay calm, Whitlock. Focus.

I flicked my gaze to the rear-view mirror. I couldn't tell what kind of truck it was or see the color. The headlights were blinding, the glare obscuring any view of the driver.

This was intentional.

They weren't just trying to scare me.

They were trying to send me over the edge.

I reached for my radio, fingers grasping for the mic.

BAM!

I snapped my hand back to the wheel just in time to keep my truck from fishtailing into the abyss.

The curve ahead was coming fast.

I gritted my teeth, forcing my breathing to steady. My truck was heavy, stable, but the truck behind me was relentless. If I lost control, if I let them push me just one inch too far—I wasn't walking away from this.

I had one shot.

I took a deep breath and jerked the wheel hard left—into the oncoming lane, onto the gravel, right up against the guardrail.

The truck followed.

At the last second, I ripped the wheel right, tires spinning as I threw my truck back onto solid pavement and braked hard.

The other truck wasn't as lucky.

Its tires skidded on the loose gravel, momentum carrying it through the guardrail.

It teetered—caught between balance and gravity.

Then it was gone.

The sounds filtered through the rain.

A sickening scream, metal crunching, tree branches snapping like bones.

Then—silence.

I sat frozen, my breath ragged, my fingers locked around the wheel so tight they ached.

I stared at the empty space where the truck had been. The darkness had swallowed it whole.

Then, with shaking hands, I grabbed the radio.

Static hissed before I keyed in.

"This is Whitlock." My voice was steadier than I felt. "Vehicle accident off Pinnacle Road, past mile marker 18. Need immediate response."

Jordan's voice crackled through. "Harlie? What the hell happened?"

I swallowed hard, eyes still locked on the darkness below.

"Somebody just tried to run me off the damn mountain."

CHAPTER FORTY-ONE

The wail of sirens echoed through the trees, flashing red and blue lights cutting through the dark as rescue vehicles wound their way up the mountain. Gravel crunched under tires as first responders pulled in behind my truck, radios crackling with clipped voices.

I didn't move from my spot at the edge of the road. The sky had cleared and the full moon spotlit the truck below. My hands gripped the guardrail, my breath steady despite the dull throb radiating from my back and neck. I could feel my body protesting, muscles stiffening, but I shoved it down.

Two paramedics jumped out of their rig, moving toward me with medical bags slung over their shoulders. One of them, a stocky guy in his forties with salt-and-pepper hair, narrowed his eyes at me like he already knew I was going to be difficult.

"Detective, we need to check you out," he said.

I shook my head. "Not a chance." I jabbed a finger toward the wreckage below. "Your priority is down there. Get your team ready. I want to know if the driver's alive."

The paramedic sighed, glancing at his partner, a younger woman who looked equally unimpressed. "Detective Whitlock—"

"I'm fine," I cut in. "Get your ropes, get your gear, and get down there. I'll be fine."

Before they could argue, Jordan Reyes's car slid into a stop, his door open before the engine had even finished shutting off.

"What the hell, Whitlock?" Jordan stormed toward me, his dark eyes scanning me up and down before flicking toward the ruined guardrail. "Are you okay?"

Amy Walsh wasn't far behind, scrambling out of the passenger seat, her face pale in the flashing lights. "Jesus, Harlie—what happened?"

Jordan stepped closer to the edge, his gaze locking onto the wreckage below. "Holy shit."

I exhaled, rolling my sore shoulders. "If you're wondering if it's the truck that tried to run me off the road, then yeah."

Jordan swore under his breath, hands on his hips. "Someone really tried to kill you?"

"You think I just enjoy running people off cliffs for fun?"

Amy's gaze darted between me and Jordan, her hands gripping the straps of her duty belt. "Who was driving?"

"No clue," I admitted. "Didn't get a look. Too busy trying to keep from dying."

Amy's expression twisted. "You're seriously hurt, aren't you?"

I ignored her and turned to Jordan. "Where's Nolan?"

Jordan frowned. "No idea. He left the station earlier this afternoon. Didn't say where he was going or when he'd be back."

"Convenient."

Jordan didn't argue. He looked down at the wreck again, his mind clearly working through the same possibility I was.

The rescue team was moving into position. A fire crew had arrived, led by Captain Bill Mercer, a seasoned firefighter with arms like tree trunks and a no-nonsense expression.

"Whitlock," he greeted, barely looking at me before turning to his team. "We've got a steep descent, loose terrain, and a wreck that might not be stable. We're going in slow and careful."

He turned to one of his men, nodding toward the tangled metal below. "Set up the anchor points. We'll lower two down to assess the scene before we call in heavy rescue."

Firefighters moved with trained efficiency, securing ropes and harnesses while one of the paramedics coordinated with them. I watched as two men clipped in, testing their weight before beginning the rappel.

Amy shifted beside me, arms crossed tightly over her chest. "This is insane."

I didn't answer. My eyes were locked on the scene below, watching every movement.

Jordan, standing behind me, said, "Harlie, you're hurting. Just sit down for a minute."

I didn't move.

"Seriously," he pressed. "You just survived a damn attempted murder. Let the medics do their job."

I shook my head. "Not until I see the bastard that tried to kill me."

"You're impossible."

Amy tried again. "Harlie, let them check you…"

"No," I muttered, my fingers tightening on the guardrail. "Not until I see."

Jordan muttered something under his breath, but he didn't push me further.

Minutes stretched into eternity as the rescue team worked. The men below moved with precision, clearing debris, checking for any sign of movement. The radio crackled to life, Mercer answered.

"Got anything?" he asked.

"We've got a body."

Mercer's grip on his radio tightened. "Status?"

"Deceased."

The tension in my muscles didn't ease—it coiled tighter.

"Can you identify?" Mercer asked.

Static crackled. "Hard to say. Face is—" The voice hesitated. "It's bad."

Mercer's tone remained even. "Male or female?"

"Male."

"Alright, bring him up. Nice and slow."

The rescue team moved the body onto a stretcher basket and attached it to ropes. The pulleys creaked under the weight as the body began its slow ascent from the depths of the ravine, dirt and small rocks dislodging as the basket bounced softly off the cliffside.

I caught myself holding my breath, fighting the dizziness creeping at the edges of my vision. The weight of the moment pressed against my chest, but I forced my feet to stay planted, my eyes locked on the tangled metal below.

Jordan stepped a little closer, but he didn't say a word. He knew better than to tell me to sit down again.

The basket inched higher, emerging from the darkness below. My heartbeat pounded against my ribs. The body inside was strapped down, covered with a heavy tarp.

One of the paramedics moved forward, gripping the edge of the tarp with gloved fingers. The fabric lifted slowly, peeling away from the body. Even with the bruising, the gashes, the twisted, lifeless features— my mind refused to believe what I was seeing.

No.

No, this wasn't possible.

I must have gasped, because suddenly Jordan was at my side, his hand gripping my arm. Amy was saying something, her voice distant, muffled, like I was underwater. One of the EMTs stepped closer, urging me to sit down, his hands hovering near me like he thought I might drop at any second.

I couldn't move.

The body strapped to the stretcher—the person who had just tried to kill me—wasn't Nolan.

But it was someone I knew.

Everything I thought I understood about this case was unraveling right in front of me.

Chapter Forty-Two

The ride back to town was silent except for the hum of the engine and the occasional sigh from Amy. I felt her glance at me more than once, but she didn't say anything. Jordan hadn't stopped gripping the steering wheel since we left the crash site, his knuckles white against the leather.

The tow truck had taken my wrecked police truck away, the rescue team had finished their work, and after letting the EMTs poke and prod at me until they deemed me "okay" outside of some whiplash, I'd climbed into Jordan's cruiser.

And now we were driving through the winding back roads of Sinister Falls, heading toward the last place I wanted to be.

"You sure you want to do this right now?" Jordan asked.

"What part of 'drive me to the Jenkins's house' made you think I wasn't sure?"

The massive Jenkins estate loomed before me, its windows glowing warm against the darkness. Inside, two parents were about to have their world shattered.

"You want us to come with you?" Jordan asked, watching me like he already knew the answer.

I shook my head. "Stay out here."

Amy frowned. "Harlie—"

"I mean it." I turned, leveling them both with a look. "They're about to lose their son. They don't need an audience."

Jordan didn't argue. Amy, on the other hand, looked like she wanted to protest. But she just swallowed hard and gave a short nod.

I stepped out of the car, shutting the door with a firm click. My boots crunched against the gravel driveway and I made my way up the stone steps, each one heavier than the last.

The brass knocker felt ice-cold in my palm as I rapped it against the thick wooden door. For a moment, silence. Then—footsteps.

When the door opened, Milton Jenkins stood in the entryway, dressed in a crisp button-down, sleeves rolled to his elbows. His eyes landed on me, and for a fraction of a second, I saw something flicker across his face.

But then his expression hardened, his features smoothing into the practiced calm of a man who never let the world see him sweat.

"Detective Whitlock," he said. "What brings you here at this hour?"

I met his gaze. "Can we talk inside?"

Milton hesitated. Then, with a small nod, he stepped back, gesturing for me to enter.

The entryway was immaculate—polished floors, expensive rugs, the faintest scent of burning wood from a nearby fireplace.

Milton led me down the hall and into his study, lined with dark mahogany shelves filled with legal books and old case files. A massive desk sat in the center, pristine and orderly, like the man standing behind it.

"Nadine," Milton called, his voice carrying through the house. "Come in here."

A moment later, Nadine Jenkins appeared, a silk robe wrapped tightly around her petite frame. Her blonde hair was swept up, and her makeup was still flawless, like she had been entertaining guests rather than preparing for bed. Her face flickered with mild irritation—until she saw me.

Her lips pressed into a thin line. "Detective Whitlock."

I glanced between them, then took a steading breath. "I'm here about your son."

Milton's jaw twitched. Nadine's expression pinched with suspicion.

"What about Seth?" she demanded.

I swallowed, squaring my shoulders. "I'm so sorry," I said. "Seth is dead."

Nadine gasped, stumbling back a step as her hands flew to her mouth. "No. No, that's not—" She turned to Milton, eyes wild. "Tell her she's lying!"

Milton, however, remained silent. His face paled slightly as he slowly sank into the leather chair behind his desk.

"How?" he croaked.

I hesitated, then gave him the truth. "He died trying to run me off the road."

Nadine let out a choked sob, shaking her head violently. "No, no, no! You're lying!" she shrieked, her hands trembling as she pointed a manicured finger at me. "My son was a good boy! He wouldn't—he wouldn't—"

I said nothing.

Because I wasn't about to remind them that their son had been a drug dealer, a liar, a young man with more dirt on his hands than they probably wanted to admit.

And I wasn't about to say what I was really thinking.

That maybe—just maybe—Milton Jenkins had known exactly what his son was planning to do.

Instead, I stood there, letting Nadine sob and wail, watching as Milton finally let out a controlled breath and clasp his hands together like he was putting the pieces of his mind back into place.

His eyes flicked up to mine. "Where's Nolan?"

"I have no idea," I said. "Thought maybe you would know."

Milton's gaze bore into me. Then, he leaned back in his chair, his fingers tapping against the polished wood of his desk.

Nadine was still sobbing, rocking slightly as she clutched at her silk robe.

Milton told me, "You should go."

I nodded once. "I'm sorry for your loss."

And I was. No matter what Seth had done, no matter how close he had come to taking my life, there was no satisfaction in standing here, watching a mother shatter and a father crumble.

I turned and left the study, my boots echoing against the marble floors.

As I climbed back into the cruiser, Jordan and Amy were watching me, their expressions tense.

"Well?" Jordan asked.

"He asked about Nolan," I murmured.

Jordan frowned. "What?"

"He didn't ask how Seth lost control of the truck. He didn't ask for details. He just asked where Nolan was."

"So he already knew."

Chapter Forty-Three

Jordan pulled up to my mother's house and parked in front of the porch. The house was quiet, dark except for the porch light casting long shadows across the yard. Amy had been dropped off at the station, and now it was just the two of us.

I reached for the door handle, but Jordan placed his hand on my arm. "Wait," he said.

"Jordan, I'm exhausted."

"I don't care," he shot back. "I'm checking the house first."

I wanted to argue, but the fight in me was hanging by a thread. I let him take the lead, watching as he unholstered his gun and cautiously pushed the front door open. He stepped inside, his silhouette sharp against the dim glow from the porch.

I followed behind as he did a methodical sweep through the rooms.

Jordan secured his weapon. "All clear."

"Of course it is," I muttered, shuffling into the living room and sinking onto the couch. My body was finally acknowledging just how much it had been through. The dull ache in my neck sharpened when I shifted, and I winced.

Jordan perched on the chair across from me, tracking my every move.

"You need anything? Water? Something for the pain?"

I shook my head. "I'm fine."

"You sure? Because you look like you've been through a damn war."

"That's because I have."

Jordan leaned forward, resting his elbows on his knees. "Where do you think Nolan is?

"I don't know."

"Come on, Harlie," he pressed. "You've got some idea."

I shrugged. I had plenty of ideas. None of them good.

My phone vibrated against the coffee table. I glanced down at the screen.

Mark

Jordan's gaze flicked to the phone. "Aren't you gonna answer that?"

I leaned my head back against the couch and shook my head. "I don't feel like talking right now."

Jordan scoffed. "You don't feel like talking, or you don't feel like talking to him?"

I didn't respond.

"Harlie, he's probably worried about you."

"He doesn't need to know what happened."

Jordan shifted in his chair, his hands gripping the armrests like he was bracing himself.

He muttered, "He already does."

"What?"

Jordan was looking anywhere but at me. "I, uh, I called him."

The exhaustion vanished in a wave of cold fury. I sat up, ignoring the sharp protest from my body. "You did what?"

Jordan held up his hands. "I had to. You almost died, Harlie. Someone tried to kill you. I thought he should know."

"You had no right."

"He cares about you."

"That's not the point."

"Then what is?" Jordan demanded. "That you don't want to let him in?"

"You don't get to make that choice for me."

Jordan shook his head. "Maybe not. But you damn well should've called him yourself."

The anger simmered just beneath the surface. I wasn't mad because Jordan was wrong.

I was mad because he was right.

Jordan was still watching me.

I knew that look. And I already hated where this was going.

He leaned back in the chair, crossing his arms. "I'm staying."

"No, you're not."

"Yes, I am."

"Jordan, I don't need a babysitter."

"Never said you did," he shot back. "But someone just tried to kill you, and Nolan is missing. I'm not leaving you here alone."

"I'm fine."

"You're full of shit. You're running on fumes, your neck is stiff as hell, and you're barely keeping your eyes open. But sure, yeah—you're totally fine."

I glared at him. "You're overreacting."

"Oh yeah? Tell you what—next time someone tries to send you flying off a damn mountain, I'll be sure to underreact."

I rolled my eyes and pushed myself off the couch, ignoring the sharp pull of pain in my back. "Suit yourself," I muttered, heading for the hallway.

I yanked open the hall closet, grabbed a pillow and a thick blanket, and tossed them at him. "If you insist on being my personal security detail for the night, the couch is all yours."

Jordan caught them and grinned at me over the blanket. "Wow. You really know how to make a guy feel welcome."

I shrugged, already halfway to my bedroom. "Consider it my way of saying thanks for going behind my back and calling Mark."

"Fair enough."

I stepped into my room, closed the door behind me, and leaned against it.

Jordan was right about one thing: Nolan was still missing. I'd have to deal with that soon.

But Mark knowing what happened wasn't something I wasn't ready to deal with yet.

INTERVIEW WITH OFFICER JORDAN REYES

INTERVIEWER: Harlie was nearly killed. You were one of the first people on scene. What was going through your head when you got the call?

REYES: Panic. Even if I won't admit it out loud, that's what it was. Harlie and I — we don't exactly coddle each other, but when I heard her voice over the radio saying someone had tried to run her off the road... I knew it was bad. I could hear it in the way she said it, the way she held it together, but barely.

INTERVIEWER: And when you got there?

REYES: I saw her standing on the side of the road, staring down at the wreckage, all banged up but still standing like she wasn't feeling a damn thing. That's Whitlock for you — always acting like she's fine, even when she's not. And I knew, right then and there, she was already thinking about what came next, how she was going to spin this into a case instead of admitting that someone had just tried to put her six feet under.

INTERVIEWER: You seem to care about her a lot.

REYES: That obvious?

INTERVIEWER: It is. And I don't mean just as a partner.

REYES: Yeah. Look, I'm not gonna pretend I haven't thought about it — what it'd be like if things were different between us. Harlie's... She's something else. But I also know how she is, and that's why I never pushed it. She's got her walls up high, and I get it. I respect it. Doesn't mean I don't worry about her, though.

INTERVIEWER: So when she refused to go to the hospital after the crash, you took her home instead.

REYES: Yeah. Amy and I were both ready to drag her to the ER, but she wasn't having it. I figured if I forced the issue, she'd just dig her heels in harder, so I played it her way. But I wasn't about to leave her alone, not after what happened.

INTERVIEWER: You insisted on staying the night at her place.

REYES: 'Insisted' is a nice way of putting it. She argued, of course. Told me she didn't need protection. But let's be real — someone just tried to kill her, Nolan's missing, and we don't have any damn clue what's coming next. So, yeah. I stayed. Even if she didn't like it.

INTERVIEWER: What about Nolan?

REYES: That's the real question, isn't it? Where the hell is he? Harlie asked about him the second we got to the crash site, and no one had an answer. He left the station earlier that day and never came back. That's not like him. Even if he was drunk off his ass somewhere, he'd at least make an appearance over the death of the mayor's son. But this? Him disappearing right when someone tries to kill Harlie? That's not a coincidence.

INTERVIEWER: Do you think he was involved?

REYES: I don't know. And that scares the hell out of me.

INTERVIEWER: So what happens now?

REYES: Now? We find out who's pulling the strings. Because someone is. And if Nolan's a part of this, then we need to figure it out before Whitlock ends up in a damn grave.

INTERVIEWER: And if she keeps pushing people away?

REYES: That's the thing about Harlie Whitlock — she might think she's in this alone, but she's not. Not as long as I have something to say about it.

Chapter Forty-Four

The sound of the front door rattling jolted me upright. My neck screamed in protest, the stiffness from the crash making itself known in every muscle. I grabbed my service weapon and headed for the living room. Jordan was already on his feet, his gun half-drawn.

A heavy fist pounded against the door again.

"Whitlock! Open up."

I knew that voice.

I shot a look at Jordan, who slowly lowered his gun. I stalked to the door, sparing a glance at the clock on the wall. It was just after eight in the morning. I yanked open the door.

Chief William Nolan.

And he looked like absolute hell.

His uniform shirt was wrinkled, his tie missing, and the buttons were undone at the top. His blue jacket was ripped. I noticed a slight wobble to his stance, his usual solid presence reduced to something… off-balance. His eyes were bloodshot, and a sharp mix of stale liquor, cigarettes, and sweat rolled off him.

He'd been drinking. Hard.

He stared at me—at the bruises along my neck, at the stiff way I was holding myself—then glanced at Jordan hovering behind me.

"Jesus Christ, Whitlock. What the hell did you do?"

"What did *I* do?" I growled. "I got run off the goddamn road last night, in case you hadn't heard. And you? Where the hell have you been?"

Nolan rubbed a hand over his unshaven jaw. "I had things to take care of."

"Yeah? Like what? Taking a bath in cheap whiskey?"

Nolan's gaze cut to Jordan. "Watch your mouth, Reyes."

I crossed my arms, refusing to let him shift the conversation. "You disappeared, Nolan. Right when someone tried to kill me. That's a hell of a coincidence."

"You think I had something to do with that?"

I studied him—the way his hands flexed and unflexed, like he was barely holding it together. The way his breathing wasn't quite steady. The way his usual cool and collected demeanor was cracked.

I asked quietly, "Where were you last night?"

Nolan hesitated.

"Christ," Jordan spat. "You don't even have an alibi, do you?"

Nolan's expression hardened. "I don't answer to you, Reyes."

"You might not answer to him," I said, "but you sure as hell owe me an answer."

"I don't owe you an explanation either, Whitlock."

"That's funny, because I think you do. You're the Chief of Police. One of your detectives was nearly run off the road last night, and instead of showing up to check if I was breathing, you went AWOL. That doesn't look good."

"I didn't know."

"Bullshit."

Nolan took a step back.

"You mean to tell me," I continued, taking a step forward, "that in this town—your town—where you have ears in every damn department, where you control every damn thing that goes in and out of that station, you just missed the fact that the mayor's son died trying to murder me?"

Something flickered across his face. Regret? Guilt? I wasn't sure.

I scoffed. "Try again, Nolan."

"I wasn't at the station yesterday. I had personal business to handle."

"Where?" Jordan demanded.

Nolan's bloodshot eyes flicked toward him. "None of your damn business."

Jordan huffed. "You're right—it's Whitlock's business. Considering someone tried to kill her last night, I'd say knowing where the hell her boss was while it was happening is her business."

Nolan looked like he wanted to rip Jordan apart, but I didn't give him the chance.

"Milton Jenkins asked about you," I said, watching for a reaction.

His mouth parted like he was about to speak, then snapped shut. Whatever mask he was wearing—it was cracked.

"Yeah," I continued, "when I told him his son was dead, you know what he asked me? Not how. Not why. Not who. The first thing out of his mouth was, 'Where's Nolan?'"

Nolan was quiet.

I took another step closer, closing the space between us until we were nearly nose to nose. "Why was that, Chief?"

His eyes flickered and I could see the effort it took to keep his expression locked down. "You tell me, Detective."

"I think Jenkins already knew Seth was dead before I knocked on his door. I think the only thing he didn't know was whether I was still breathing."

Nolan was silent.

"Tell me something," I pressed. "Who sent Seth to kill me? You? Jenkins?"

Nolan shook his head. "You're walking a dangerous line, Whitlock."

I smirked. "Yeah, well, that's never stopped me before."

"You don't know what you're poking at, kid."

"Don't call me kid," I snapped.

His expression looked almost… paternal.

Jordan joined us on the porch, his patience clearly wearing thin. "You gonna tell us where the hell you were, Chief? Or do we just assume the worst?"

Nolan sighed and looked away. "I was at the old cabin."

"The cabin?" I frowned. "The one up near Cold Creek?"

He nodded.

That was his old family property—an off-the-grid place he rarely mentioned. I only knew about it because Jordan had once joked about Nolan going up there to "drink and scream at the trees" when the job got too heavy.

"What the hell were you doing up there?"

Nolan's shoulders sagged. "Thinking."

"Thinking? Or drinking yourself into oblivion?" Jordan asked.

Nolan didn't answer.

"You picked a hell of a time for a bender, Chief."

He ran a hand over his unshaven face, looking more exhausted than I'd ever seen him. "You think I planned for any of this? That I wanted any of this to happen?" He let out a rough laugh. "You think I don't know what this looks like? Hell, Whitlock. You know what I did last night?"

I didn't respond.

"I spent half the damn night wondering if I should just keep driving and never come back." Nolan held up his hands. "Seth is dead. Milton's pissed. And now you, of all people, are standing here looking at me like I pulled the damn trigger myself."

I exhaled slowly, the fire in me dimming.

But I stayed quiet. He was hiding something.

Jordan broke the silence. "So what now, Chief?"

"Now?" Nolan shrugged. "Now, I go to work."

He turned to leave but paused at the edge of the porch.

Without looking back, he said, "Watch your back, Whitlock."

Then he was gone.

INTERVIEW WITH DETECTIVE HARLIE WHITLOCK

INTERVIEWER: Harlie, let's talk about this morning. I heard Chief Nolan showed up at your door looking — well, let's just say not like himself.

WHITLOCK: That's putting it lightly. He looked like hell.

INTERVIEWER: You weren't expecting him?

WHITLOCK: Not even a little. Nolan doesn't just show up unannounced — especially not looking like that. The man is calculated. Controlled. Always. But this morning? He was a mess. Drunk, disheveled, and barely holding it together.

INTERVIEWER: That had to be unsettling.

WHITLOCK: Yeah. It was.

INTERVIEWER: And the first words out of his mouth were an accusation toward you.

WHITLOCK: Yeah. Like I was the problem. Like I was the one who disappeared while someone tried to run me off the damn road.

INTERVIEWER: Did you get the sense that he already knew what had happened to you?

WHITLOCK: Oh, he knew. No doubt about it. But he played dumb, like he was just catching up. That's the thing about

Nolan — he never reacts without thinking first. And that hesitation? That split-second delay before he answered? It told me everything I needed to know.

INTERVIEWER: Which was?

WHITLOCK: That he'd been keeping tabs on me. That he already knew about Seth Jenkins. That whatever happened last night wasn't news to him — it was something he'd been bracing for.

INTERVIEWER: That's a strong accusation.

WHITLOCK: You think I don't know that? But tell me this — if he was innocent, if he had no idea about any of this, why wasn't his first reaction shock? Why wasn't he asking if I was okay? Or why Seth did this? Instead, he went straight to 'What did you do?' Like this was my fault.

INTERVIEWER: And then he told you he was at his cabin.

WHITLOCK: Right. Convenient, isn't it? No witnesses, no alibi. Just Nolan, alone in the middle of nowhere while someone tried to kill me.

INTERVIEWER: Do you believe him?

WHITLOCK: I believe he was drinking himself into oblivion. That part checks out. But was he up there all night? That's the million-dollar question.

INTERVIEWER: Did you mention that Mayor Jenkins asked about him?

WHITLOCK: Yeah. And he reacted. A flicker. But it was there. You don't survive in Sinister Falls without learning to read people, and Nolan? He's usually damn near impossible to read.

INTERVIEWER: Are you saying Nolan and Jenkins——

WHITLOCK: I'm saying I don't believe in coincidences. Not in this town.

INTERVIEWER: How did you leave it with Nolan?

WHITLOCK: He told me to watch my back.

INTERVIEWER: What do you think he meant by that?

WHITLOCK: That's the problem. I don't know if it was a threat... or a warning.

INTERVIEWER: You don't trust him.

WHITLOCK: Trust? No. But that's not the part that keeps me up at night.

INTERVIEWER: What does?

WHITLOCK: I don't know if I should be afraid of Nolan... or for him.

The station was quieter than usual when Jordan and I walked in. Amy was the only one at her desk, tapping at her keyboard, a coffee cup balanced precariously on top of a pile of case files. She looked up as we approached, her eyes filled with concern.

"How are you feeling?" she asked.

"Like I got hit by a truck," I muttered, rubbing the ache in my neck. "Nolan here?"

Amy shook her head. "Nope. Haven't seen him."

Jordan let out a short laugh. "Well, we had the pleasure of a visit this morning. Nolan showed up at Harlie's house looking like hell."

Amy blinked. "Seriously?"

"Yeah," Jordan nodded. "Like he just crawled out of the bottom of a bottle."

"Never mind Nolan," I cut in. "I need you two to dig up everything you can find on Seth Jenkins, and I mean everything. Old reports, traffic tickets, complaints—if his name is on it, I want to see it."

Amy straightened, already reaching for her files. "Got it."

Jordan frowned. "You got a hunch, Whitlock?"

I extended my hand. "Your keys."

Jordan stared at me for a beat, then sighed and pulled them from his pocket, tossing them my way. "Okay... but where exactly are you going?"

I caught them and turned for the door. "Dylan Cross."

"Try not to wreck my car."

"No promises."

Dylan Cross's house was still barely standing under the weight of its own neglect. The music from inside was loud enough to make the walls vibrate.

I knocked on the door.

Nothing.

I pounded. "Dylan! It's Detective Whitlock. Open up."

The music shut off. I heard a shuffle, something being knocked over. Then nothing.

I wasn't in the mood for games. I banged on the door again. "You've got ten seconds before I start making this really inconvenient for you."

More shuffling. Then the door cracked open an inch. Bloodshot eyes peered out at me, Dylan's fingers twitching as he struggled to keep the door from swinging open too far.

"W-What do you want?"

I shoved the door open the rest of the way, forcing him to step back. "We need to talk."

Dylan's eyes darted around the room. "I-I don't know anything."

I shut the door behind me, keeping myself between him and the exit. "Seth Jenkins is dead."

The color drained from Dylan's face. He stumbled back and gripped the edge of a wobbly table. "No. No way."

"He drove off a cliff last night. The same cliff he tried to send me over."

Dylan blinked rapidly, his whole body trembling. "Oh God. Oh God."

I folded my arms. "So, wanna start talking? Because I have a feeling you know exactly why he came after me."

Dylan raked a hand through his greasy hair. "I-I don't—"

I stepped closer. "You're high as hell, but you're not stupid. Seth is dead. That means whatever hold he had on you. It's gone. So start talking, now."

His mouth opened and closed like a fish gasping for air.

Then his face crumpled, and suddenly, he was sobbing. He slid down to the floor, knees pulled to his chest, hands gripping his head. "Oh God, oh God, oh God—"

I crouched down, forcing him to look at me. "Dylan, tell me what happened to Leah."

He sniffled, rocking slightly, his breath hitching. "W-We partied, okay? All the time. Drugs, drinking, all of it. Me, Leah, Seth… we hung out a lot."

I nodded. "And?"

Dylan wiped his nose on his sleeve. "One night, we were all high. Leah started talking about how she found out her birth mom was Evelyn Carter. She said she'd been digging, found out Evelyn died in a car accident, but—" He let out a shaky breath. "She wasn't focused on that. She was obsessed with who her real dad was."

"Did she say anything specific?"

Dylan nodded frantically. "She said she found notes—like, old papers her adoptive mom had stashed in a drawer. Stuff about the adoption, and there was this part that said Evelyn wasn't sure who Leah's father was. She said the notes mentioned two names."

"Whose names?"

Dylan licked his lips. "Milton Jenkins… and William Nolan."

"And that's when Seth lost it."

Dylan nodded violently. "Yeah. He freaked. Started calling Leah a lying bitch, saying there was no way he was her half-brother. But she wanted answers. She wanted Seth to ask his dad. Said she wanted a DNA test."

"And Seth refused."

Dylan let out a broken laugh. "Not just refused. He snapped. Told me later he'd rather die than let that 'little whore' get her hands on his dad's money. He was terrified of his dad. Said if Leah turned out to be his half-sister, it would 'ruin everything'."

"And then what, Dylan? What did Seth do?"

Dylan shook his head violently. "H-He—" He sobbed. "He killed her. He killed her, Harlie."

And then he'd tried to kill me.

"How?" I asked.

Dylan curled in on himself again. "He told me he went to talk to her—to convince her to drop it. But she wouldn't. She told him she'd go public if she had to." He shuddered. "And he—he strangled her."

His whole body trembled. "I didn't know. I swear I didn't know he was gonna… He told me after. He was scared. Scared of his dad. He thought if Leah were really his sister, his dad would turn on him. He thought—" He buried his face in his hands.

I waited until his sobs subsided. "Where, Dylan? Where did Seth kill Leah?"

His breath hitched. "I don't—I don't know."

"Bullshit," I snapped. "You were his friend, right? You ran in the same circles, partied together. He confided in you enough to admit he killed her. You're telling me he never once mentioned where?"

Dylan shook his head rapidly. "No! I swear! He just—he just told me he handled it. That she wasn't gonna be a problem anymore. He was freaking out, pacing, saying he couldn't believe he did it."

"When did he tell you this?"

Dylan wiped at his nose again. "That night. The night Reyes stopped us and you arrested us."

"You're telling me," I said, anger rising, "that the night I pulled you out of that car and questioned you both, you already knew? You knew he killed Leah? And you said nothing?"

Dylan whimpered. "I was scared! You don't understand, Whitlock! Seth—he—he was losing it! He said if I said anything, I'd end up just like her!"

"You had a chance," I bit out. "You had a chance to tell me. You could've saved a hell of a lot of people a hell of a lot of pain. But instead, you let me walk away blind. Now, Seth is dead, and I got up close and personal with a goddamn cliff!"

Dylan flinched, his breath ragged as he rocked slightly, his fingers digging into his scalp. "I didn't know what to do! I didn't know how to stop him!"

"Does Seth's dad know what he did?"

Dylan's mouth opened, closed, then he rasped, "I don't know. I really don't know."

INTERVIEW WITH DETECTIVE HARLIE WHITLOCK

INTERVIEWER: Harlie, after your conversation with Dylan Cross, do you believe you finally have the truth about what happened to Leah Emerson?

WHITLOCK: The truth? Maybe a piece of it. But the truth is never that simple.

INTERVIEWER: Dylan admitted that Seth Jenkins killed Leah. That's a major breakthrough.

WHITLOCK: Yeah, it is. But the bigger question is: Who else knew? Did Seth act alone? Or was he just the one who got his hands dirty while someone else made sure it all stayed buried?

INTERVIEWER: Do you think Mayor Jenkins knew what his son did?

WHITLOCK: Dylan made it clear that Seth was scared. Not of getting caught — of his father. He thought if Jenkins found out Leah might be his daughter, it would ruin everything. And Seth was desperate to make sure that never happened.

INTERVIEWER: But desperate enough to kill?

WHITLOCK: Yeah. Seth wasn't exactly a mastermind, but he seemed to know how to make problems disappear. And Leah? She was getting too close. She wanted answers, a DNA test, the kind of proof that would shake up the whole damn town. So he silenced her.

INTERVIEWER: But do you think the mayor ordered it?

WHITLOCK: I don't know yet. That's what I need to figure out. Did Jenkins know about Leah before Seth killed her? Did he find out after? Or is he still in the dark? Because if Jenkins had nothing to do with it, then that means Seth was terrified of the wrong person.

INTERVIEWER: What about Chief Nolan? His name came up in Leah's search. Could he be her father?

WHITLOCK: That would explain a lot, wouldn't it? Nolan's been playing this whole thing real close to the vest. Every time I get near the truth, he throws up another wall. He either knows something, or he's protecting someone.

INTERVIEWER: Could Nolan have been involved in Leah's murder?

WHITLOCK: No. If Nolan had wanted Leah gone, she would've disappeared without a trace. And I don't think he would've let Seth handle it — Seth was too sloppy, too impulsive. But Nolan's not innocent, either. He's up to his neck in this, I just haven't figured out exactly how yet.

INTERVIEWER: Where do you go from here?

WHITLOCK: I make more people uncomfortable.

INTERVIEWER: Meaning?

WHITLOCK: Jenkins is sitting in his big house, pretending like his world isn't falling apart. I'm gonna change that. If he knew what Seth did, I'll get him to admit it.

INTERVIEWER: You're going to confront him?

WHITLOCK: Damn right I am. Jenkins is used to being in charge, to making the rules. But his son just died trying to kill me, and now he's got to answer for it. If he's hiding something, I'll find it. If he didn't know Seth killed Leah, he's about to get one hell of a wake-up call.

INTERVIEWER: And Nolan?

WHITLOCK: Nolan's running out of places to hide. I'll deal with him soon enough.

Chapter Forty-Six

I could tell the second he opened the door, Milton Jenkins hadn't slept. His shirt, the same one he had worn the night before, was wrinkled, the top buttons undone.

But the moment his gaze landed on me, whatever weight he was carrying vanished behind a practiced steel exterior.

"Detective Whitlock," he said flatly, gripping the doorframe. No pretense of civility. No invitation inside.

I returned the favor. "I need to talk to you."

He glanced past me like he expected to see a fleet of cruisers in his driveway. "I think you've done enough of that already."

I didn't budge. "I just came from Dylan Cross's house."

His fingers flexed against the doorframe, but his expression didn't crack. "I assume you have a point to make."

"Oh, I've got a hell of a point," I said, crossing my arms. "Dylan told me Seth killed Leah Emerson."

"And?"

"And? That's all you have to say?"

His entire stance shifted like he was bracing for a fight. "I assume you're here to ask if I knew."

I didn't answer.

His lips pressed into a thin line. "I didn't."

"You expect me to believe that? That your son, who was terrified of disappointing you, who spent his entire damn life trying to live up to your name, suddenly snapped, killed a girl, and never once thought to come to you?"

Milton didn't flinch. "That's exactly what I expect you to believe. Because it's the truth."

I studied him, watching for some tell, some shift in his composure. But Milton Jenkins was too good at this.

"You knew Leah was looking into her father," I said.

"Nolan mentioned it."

"Did that worry you?"

"Should it have?"

I shrugged. "Maybe. If she was about to find out something that could ruin you."

"I had nothing to do with that girl's death."

"But Seth did," I shot back. "And you're telling me you had no idea?"

"That's exactly what I'm telling you."

"Then what the hell was Seth so scared of?"

Milton hesitated.

"He told Dylan he thought you'd turn on him," I said. "That if Leah was really his sister, it would ruin everything. He was more afraid of you than he was of the police." I leaned in. "Why is that, Milton?"

Milton started to say something, but then a slight crease formed between his brows and he straightened. "What the hell are you talking about?"

"Leah Emerson. There was a chance she was your daughter."

Milton's face went blank.

I pressed on. "Evelyn Carter had an affair with you. Leah found notes in her adoptive mother's things—documents suggesting Evelyn didn't know whether you or Nolan was Leah's father." I let the words sink in. "That's what she wanted Seth to ask you. She wanted answers. A DNA test."

Milton's lips parted slightly, but no sound came out.

He looked genuinely caught off guard.

I folded my arms. "You really didn't know, did you?"

His throat worked. "No. I didn't."

If Milton was lying, he was damn good at it.

Milton glanced over his shoulder inside the house, then stepped outside and closed the door.

"Something you don't want Nadine to hear?"

"She's been through enough already."

"Did she know?"

"Know what?"

"About you and Evelyn. About the affair. About the possibility that Leah Emerson was your daughter."

"That's none of your business. That was between me and my wife."

"You're telling me," I said, "that it never crossed your mind that Evelyn's baby could've been yours?"

"Evelyn and I were over by then. We had a thing—a long time ago—but she moved on. I assumed Nolan was the one she ran to afterward."

"And if she was pregnant when she left you?"

His fingers twitched. "I never knew."

"Seth knew. Or at least, he feared it. And he snapped."

Milton was quiet for a moment as he looked out over the driveway. "And now he's dead."

"You almost sound relieved."

Milton's gaze snapped back to mine. "Watch yourself, Detective."

"You know, Seth wasn't the only one scared of you. Nolan seems to be a little jumpy these days."

"What are you implying?"

"That Evelyn Carter's accident was no accident. And I think you and Nolan killed her."

The anger came first, flashing across his features like a storm cloud ready to burst. Then, something deeper. Something that looked an awful lot like fear.

"That's a dangerous accusation, Detective," he said.

"But it's true, isn't it?" I stepped closer, my voice just above a whisper. "You and Nolan got rid of her because she was a liability. Maybe she threatened to expose your affair. Maybe she was going to tell someone who Leah's father really was. But one way or another, you made sure she never had the chance."

Milton's jaw clenched so tightly I thought his teeth might crack.

"You don't know a damn thing," he growled.

I smiled. "I know enough. And I'm going to prove the rest."

"Seth's dead, Whitlock. Leah's dead. There's nothing left to prove."

"You think that's how this works? That you can just sweep decades of dirt under the rug and hope no one notices?" I shook my head. "Not this time."

Milton's eyes burned into mine Then, his expression settled into an eerie calm.

"You're playing a dangerous game, Detective."

"Good thing I'm not afraid to lose."

INTERVIEW WITH MAYOR JENKINS

INTERVIEWER: Mr. Jenkins, I appreciate you taking the time to speak with me. I understand this is a difficult time for you and your family.

JENKINS: Difficult doesn't even begin to cover it. But something tells me you're not here to check on my well-being.

INTERVIEWER: No, I'm here because Detective Whitlock paid you a visit today. She confronted you about your son and Leah Emerson.

JENKINS: Yeah. She came here, all fire and accusations. She thinks she's got it all figured out.

INTERVIEWER: Does she?

JENKINS: She knows my son killed Leah. I won't dispute that. But what she's implying — about me, about Nolan — she's grasping at shadows.

INTERVIEWER: She told you that Leah may have been your daughter.

JENKINS: That was news to me. You think I wouldn't have done something if I knew?

INTERVIEWER: Done what?

JENKINS: You don't get it. I didn't even know Evelyn was

pregnant. We were over. She had her fun with me, had her fun with Nolan — then she was gone. If she had doubts about the father, she sure as hell didn't bring them to me.

INTERVIEWER: So, you're saying she died before she could tell you?

JENKINS: That's exactly what I'm saying. She could have told me when she was pregnant or after she had the baby. She didn't want anything from me.

INTERVIEWER: But if Leah was yours——

JENKINS: She wasn't. No DNA test, no proof — just a girl looking for answers and getting herself killed in the process.

INTERVIEWER: Killed by your son.

JENKINS: I told you, I didn't know. If I had, I would've stopped it. Seth was reckless, but he wasn't a murderer. Not until he felt like he had no other choice.

INTERVIEWER: Because he thought Leah would ruin him?

JENKINS: He thought she'd ruin everything. She wanted a DNA test. If she was mine, he thought I'd... I don't know, push him aside? Maybe he thought I'd take responsibility for her. Maybe he thought I'd care.

INTERVIEWER: Would you have?

JENKINS: Doesn't matter now, does it?

INTERVIEWER: Let's talk about Mrs. Jenkins.

JENKINS: What about her?

INTERVIEWER: Did she know about the affair?

JENKINS: That's between me and my wife.

INTERVIEWER: Fine. Did Nolan ever mention Leah's search

for her father?

JENKINS: Nolan brought it up once. He didn't seem worried. Said it was nothing. Just a girl asking the wrong questions.

INTERVIEWER: Was he really not worried? Or was he just making sure you weren't?

JENKINS: You want the truth? Nolan is never as cool as he pretends to be. He puts on that tough guy act, but back then? When it came to Evelyn? He lost his damn mind over her.

INTERVIEWER: What do you mean?

JENKINS: He wanted her to be his. Acted like he owned her. She wasn't the type to let a man claim her, though. She knew how to play the game. But Nolan? He took it personal. When she died, he drank himself stupid for months.

INTERVIEWER: Do you think he knew Evelyn was pregnant?

JENKINS: If she'd reached out to him, he wouldn't have turned her away. And if she had started causing problems, I can tell you right now, that would've been a problem for him.

INTERVIEWER: Are you saying Nolan had a reason to want her gone?

JENKINS: He had more reason than I did. Evelyn was the one who left me. I moved on. But Nolan? If he thought she was gonna embarrass him, take him down? Yeah. He would've done something about that.

INTERVIEWER: So you think Nolan——

JENKINS: I'm not saying a damn thing. I wasn't there. I don't know what happened between them. But you want my advice? If Whitlock wants to solve this, she needs to stop looking at me and start looking at Nolan.

JENKINS: I invited you here to cover our town, not to peddle accusations. Watch your line of questioning. Push much further, and you'll find that door closed.

INTERVIEWER: Because I struck a nerve?

JENKINS: This interview is over.

Chapter Forty-Seven

The station parking lot was packed with State Police cruisers. Officers moved in and out of the building, their uniforms crisp, their demeanor all business. State Police didn't just show up without reason. What the hell was going on?

Then, I saw a Portland Police Department vehicle parked off to the side.

Mark.

What the hell was he doing here? This wasn't his jurisdiction. He had no reason to be in Sinister Falls, let alone rolling up in a city-assigned vehicle like he belonged here.

I threw Jordan's cruiser into park and climbed out, slamming the door shut before marching toward the station entrance.

Amy was standing just inside, leaning against the front counter, arms crossed, talking to one of the State Police officers. The second she saw me, she straightened, her eyes flicking to the conference room.

"Harlie—"

I didn't stop.

I rounded the corner to where Jordan's desk sat. He was there, watching the scene unfold, but I barely registered him because, in the middle of the station, standing with two very official-looking men in suits, was Mark Callaway.

I froze just long enough to take in the scene.

Mark looked right at home, arms crossed, talking low to the two men like this was his case. My blood pressure spiked.

"What the hell are you doing here?" I snapped, my voice cutting through the room.

Mark turned, his expression carefully neutral. "Harlie."

"Don't 'Harlie' me," I shot back, stepping closer. "Didn't know Portland PD was so generous with their city vehicles that they let their officers take them for personal field trips."

Mark sighed, rubbing the back of his neck. "I was worried about you."

"Oh, so you called in backup?" My voice dripped with sarcasm. "Are you serious?"

One of the men in suits—a tall guy with thinning gray hair and an air of quiet authority—took a step forward and held out his hand.

"Detective Whitlock, I'm Detective Lance Walker with the State Police. Mark didn't overstep. He's part of a multi-agency task force investigating government corruption. He does have jurisdiction."

I stared at his outstretched hand but didn't take it.

Walker dropped it after a moment. "I'd appreciate if you'd come sit down and brief us on what you've uncovered."

I gritted my teeth, still staring at Mark. "You had no right to bring them into this."

"I had every right. You nearly got run off a cliff. When you didn't pick up your phone, I figured you needed all the help you could get."

I pressed my lips together, forcing myself to swallow the irritation. I didn't have time for this. I didn't have time to waste being pissed at Mark, or the State Police.

I turned to Walker. "Fine. You want a briefing? Let's go."

Walker nodded, gesturing toward the conference room. I pushed past Mark, my pulse still ticking high, and stepped inside.

Amy and Jordan filed inside and sat at the table, along with another State Police detective who had been flipping through a file. They all turned their attention to me.

I pulled out a chair but didn't sit.

"I just came from Dylan Cross's house," I said. "And I got a confession."

Jordan sat up straighter. Amy's brows shot up. Walker, leaning against the table, gave a slight nod. "Go on."

"Seth Jenkins killed Leah Emerson," I said flatly. "Dylan told me Leah was digging into her birth parents. She found out her mother was Evelyn Carter, but she wasn't sure who her father was."

Walker made a note on his notepad. "And?"

"She found notes—old documents her adoptive mother left behind. According to them, Evelyn wasn't sure either between the only two men who could be Leah's father: Milton Jenkins and William Nolan."

Walker jotted down more notes. "Go on."

"Leah wanted a DNA test. She wanted Seth to ask his father. And Seth lost his damn mind."

Jordan leaned forward, resting his elbows on the table. "So that's why he killed her?"

I nodded. "Dylan said Seth freaked out—said there was no way Leah could be his sister, that it would 'ruin everything.' And then he strangled her."

Amy pressed a hand to her mouth.

Walker jotted something down in his notebook. "Did Milton Jenkins know?"

I hesitated. "According to him, no."

Walker's brow lifted. "You believe that?"

"I don't know. I confronted him. He admitted to having an affair with Evelyn Carter twenty years ago, but he claims he never knew she was pregnant."

Mark finally spoke. "And Nolan?"

"Evelyn was with him around the same time. So either one of them could be Leah's father."

Jordan shook his head. "This is a mess."

I crossed my arms. "It was enough to send Seth over the edge. If Leah got a DNA test and it turned out they were half-siblings, he thought his dad would turn on him." I let that sink in before adding, "He panicked. He killed her."

Walker tapped his pen against the notepad. "Alright. We can work with that. But there's still a problem."

I met his gaze. "Nolan."

Jordan nodded. "We still don't know where he is. And like I said earlier, he showed up at Harlie's house this morning."

"That true?" Walker asked me.

I nodded. "Yeah. Drunk as hell. Looked like he'd crawled out of a whiskey bottle."

Walker exchanged a glance with his partner, then turned back to me. "Well, he never showed up here. No one's seen him since."

Mark swore under his breath. "So what now?"

I straightened. "We find Nolan. We keep digging into Evelyn Carter's accident. There's something there."

Walker put his notebook on the table. "I'll have my people track Nolan's last known whereabouts. Financials, phone records, anything we can pull."

"I'm going to pay the coroner a visit. I need to see what he found on Seth Jenkins's autopsy," I said.

Walker leaned back against the table, arms crossed. "Alright, Whitlock. Where's Nolan's office? We need to go through it."

"You think he left us a neat little paper trail of corruption?"

Walker smirked. "I don't expect it to be that easy, but we need to look."

Jordan stood up. "Amy and I will keep going through records, see if there's anything buried in the system that connects back to Evelyn, Leah, or Seth."

Walker turned to one of his men. "Take a couple of guys and start pulling files from Nolan's office. If he's been covering something up, there might be something worth finding."

I glanced at Jordan. "If you find anything, call me."

Mark spoke up. "I'm going with you to the coroner's office."

I turned to him, narrowing my eyes. "You are?"

Mark crossed his arms. "I want to see if there's any evidence I can push through the state crime lab."

I forced a tight smile. "Fantastic. I could use a chauffeur."

Mark smirked.

Walker ignored our exchange. "Alright, people. Let's get to work."

As the room emptied, I turned to Mark. "Try to keep up, Callaway."

He gestured toward the door with a grin. "After you, Whitlock."

INTERVIEW WITH LIEUTENANT MARK CALLAWAY

INTERVIEWER: Lieutenant Callaway, let's cut to the chase. Why didn't you tell Harlie that you were part of a statewide task force that could have helped her from the beginning?

CALLAWAY: You ever try telling Harlie Whitlock she needs help? It's like trying to put a leash on a wild dog — she bites first, asks questions later.

INTERVIEWER: So you didn't think she'd take it well?

CALLAWAY: I knew she wouldn't take it well. Harlie doesn't trust easily — especially not outside her circle. She's been fighting this battle on her own for so long, I wasn't about to waltz in and tell her she'd been outgunned from the start. She's stubborn as hell, and if I had told her, she would have pushed me away just to prove she didn't need anyone.

INTERVIEWER: But she was outgunned, wasn't she?

CALLAWAY: She is fighting corruption in a town where half the power structure is dirty, and the other half is too scared to do anything about it. That's not a battle you win alone. But try telling Harlie that. She's got this idea that if she just fights hard enough, digs deep enough, she can take on the world by herself. And I get it — I do.

INTERVIEWER: Why do you get it?

CALLAWAY: Because I've known her a long time. I know how she thinks. I know what drives her. And I know that when she feels like someone is trying to take control away from her, she digs her heels in deeper. This case? This fight? It's personal to her. I knew if I came in too early, she'd see me as an obstacle instead of an ally.

INTERVIEWER: So instead of telling her, you waited until she nearly got killed?

CALLAWAY: No. I waited until she was in so deep that I knew she couldn't afford to push me away. I waited until I had to step in — because if I told her earlier, she would've fought me on it. She would've shut me out. And that would've gotten her killed.

INTERVIEWER: So you went behind her back?

CALLAWAY: I made a call. Reyes told me she almost got run off the road. Then she ignored my call. That's all I needed to know. I knew Harlie — she'd be out there chasing leads, putting herself in more danger, refusing to slow down. And I couldn't stand by and watch that happen.

INTERVIEWER: And now the State Police are involved.

CALLAWAY: Damn right they are. This stopped being about just Leah Emerson or even Seth Jenkins the second we realized how deep the rot goes. Evelyn Carter's death? That was just the beginning. Now we're talking about a mayor with secrets, a missing police chief, and enough cover-ups to make Watergate look like a clerical error.

INTERVIEWER: I bet Harlie still isn't happy about you bringing them in.

CALLAWAY: No, she's pissed. But I'd rather her be pissed at me and alive than let her keep walking blindly into danger.

INTERVIEWER: Do you think she's capable of handling this

case?

CALLAWAY: Harlie Whitlock is the best damn detective I've ever known. She's smart, relentless, and she doesn't scare easy. But she's also human. She's exhausted. She's pushing through this on pure adrenaline and sheer will, and that won't last forever. I know she won't admit it, but she needs backup. That's why I'm here.

Chapter Forty-Eight

"I hate these places." Mark said as we walked into the morgue.

I shot him a sideways glance. "Didn't realize you were squeamish, Callaway."

"I'm not," he said, stuffing his hands in his pockets. "I just don't like talking to dead people."

"Good news," I muttered, pushing the door open. "You're talking to Dr. March, not Seth."

March was sitting behind his desk, peering over his reading glasses at us. He wore his permanent expression of mild irritation.

"Whitlock," he said, leaning back in his chair. "What, you miss me already?"

"Like a hole in the head," I shot back. "What you got for me?"

March's eyes flicked to Mark. "Who's the suit?"

I crossed my arms. "Lt. Callaway, Portland PD. Also assigned to the State Police Task Force."

"State's involved now? This case just keeps getting messier."

"You have no idea," Mark said dryly.

March sighed, opening the folder in front of him. "Alright, let's get to it. Seth Jenkins. Cause of death was, as expected, blunt force trauma from the crash. He was basically mush by the time they pulled him out of that truck."

"No surprises there," I muttered. "Anything else?"

March tapped a finger against the page. "His BAC was .25."

Mark let out a low whistle. "He was tanked."

"Drunk as hell before he even got behind the wheel," March confirmed. "No way he was making rational decisions at that point."

I frowned. "So he was drinking long before he got in that truck."

March nodded.

I exchanged a look with Mark before turning back to March. "What else?"

March flipped to another page in his report. "That's where things get interesting." He turned the folder around so we could see it. "He had marks around his neck. Subtle, but they're there."

I leaned forward to get a closer look at the photographs. "Strangulation?"

March lifted a shoulder. "Hard to say. Could be from the seatbelt tightening on impact. But I doubt it."

Mark frowned. "Why?"

March tapped the diagram of Seth's injuries. "Seatbelt injuries usually run diagonally across the chest and shoulder. This? This was different. The bruising was more uniform. Like someone with big hands had their fingers around his throat."

I sat in the guest chair. "So he got into an altercation before the crash."

"Looks that way," March said. "And that's not all." He flipped another page. "Found something under his nails. Blue synthetic fibers."

"Like from fabric?" Mark asked.

"Most likely," March confirmed. "Could be clothing. Could be upholstery. But it was wedged in deep, like he was fighting someone. We sent it to the lab for analysis."

I sat still, staring at the file.

The room faded out for a second. When Nolan had shown up at my house, he'd been on a bender. He was wearing a blue jacket.

And Nolan had big hands.

Could he have been drinking with Seth? Could they have gotten into a fight?

Mark noticed my silence. "Whitlock?"

I blinked, shaking the thought loose. "Nothing," I said.

"Bullshit. What just ran through your head?"

I exhaled slowly. "Nolan."

March frowned. "What about him?"

I looked between them. "When he showed up at my house, he was wearing a blue jacket. Said he'd been drinking at his cabin."

Mark narrowed his eyes. "And?"

"Nolan has big hands."

"Now that is interesting," March finally said.

"So what are we thinking? Nolan and Seth were drinking together? Got into it?" Mark voiced my thoughts.

March leaned back in his chair, watching me closely. "You think Nolan put him up to trying to kill you?"

"Maybe," I said.

INTERVIEW WITH DR. LIONEL MARCH

INTERVIEWER: Dr. March, you performed the autopsy on Seth Jenkins. What stood out to you the most?

MARCH: Honestly? That he was still walking around before this crash even happened.

INTERVIEWER: Was there anything in his injuries that were not consistent with the crash?

MARCH: Yeah. The bruising on his neck — it's not from the crash, and it's not from the seatbelt. The pattern suggests someone grabbed him hard. Not hard enough to choke him out, but enough to leave marks.

INTERVIEWER: So someone got their hands on him before he died?

MARCH: Sometime within 24 to 36 hours before he went off that cliff, yes.

INTERVIEWER: Could it have been Chief Nolan?

MARCH: You'd have to ask him. But I'll say this — Detective Whitlock mentioned he showed up at her house wearing a ripped blue jacket. And guess what we found under Seth's fingernails? Blue synthetic fibers. Could be nothing. Could be everything.

INTERVIEWER: Could those bruises around Seth's neck be matched to Nolan's hands?

MARCH: I don't have a perfect imprint, so no. But Nolan is a big guy. Big hands. Seth? Skinny as hell. If Nolan got his hands on him, he'd leave a mark. And Seth had marks.

INTERVIEWER: But you can't confirm it was Nolan?

MARCH: I can't confirm anything yet. Just that someone laid hands on him before he died. And that someone had blue fabric on them when Seth fought back.

INTERVIEWER: Let's talk about what was in his system. Was Seth under the influence when he crashed?

MARCH: Oh, without a doubt. His BAC was .25 — that's three times the legal limit.

INTERVIEWER: Any other substances?

MARCH: Toxicology takes a little longer. We won't have a full report for a few weeks, but let's be real — Seth was a known user. I'd be more surprised if alcohol was the only thing in his system.

INTERVIEWER: What's your gut telling you?

MARCH: My gut doesn't solve cases — evidence does. I deal in facts, not assumptions. And the facts say Seth Jenkins was heavily intoxicated, had been in an altercation before he died, and somehow ended up speeding toward a cliff with the intent to take someone else with him. Whether that earlier fight had anything to do with his final actions or not? That's for the detectives to figure out.

CHAPTER FORTY-NINE

I leaned against the doorway of Nolan's office, arms crossed, watching as Jordan rifled through a filing cabinet while Amy hunched over Nolan's computer.

Amy let out a frustrated sigh. "He doesn't have anything on here besides a cluttered desktop. Just like his actual desktop."

Jordan, crouched in front of the cabinet, flipped through a handful of files. "At least we know he's thorough," he muttered. "There's enough paperwork in here to build a second station."

Amy scoffed. "Half of it's probably useless."

"Yeah, but the other half?" Jordan shook his head. "That's what we need to find."

Mark and Walker had left twenty minutes ago to check Nolan's house, and they'd told me to stay put in case he showed up.

I hated that I wasn't the one out there hunting him down. But Walker wasn't wrong. This wasn't my investigation anymore.

That didn't mean I was going to sit around and do nothing.

Jordan let out a low whistle. "Well, this is weird."

I pushed off the door frame and stepped into the office. "What?"

Jordan didn't answer right away. He was holding a thick, well-worn file, his brows furrowed as he skimmed the pages.

"What is it?" I pressed.

"Nothing. Just… something I didn't expect to find in here."

"Let me see it."

Jordan's grip on the folder tightened.

"Jordan, let me see it." I snatched the file from his hands.

"Harlie—" Jordan started, but I wasn't listening. My eyes dropped to the name stamped across the front.

```
Wainswright, S.
```

The breath rushed from my lungs. I sank into a chair, the file suddenly a crushing weight in my hands.

"Harlie… you probably don't want to look in there."

"I'm tired of people telling me what they think I should and should not look at."

Amy and Jordan exchanged a glance but kept their mouths shut.

I slowly opened the file. I turned each page carefully, my fingers lightly tracing over the text, absorbing every word, every detail, every memory it dragged back to the surface.

And then I saw the photos.

My hand froze, hovering over them.

Jordan shifted.

I could feel his eyes on me, could sense Amy watching from across the desk. Watching as I quietly drowned in the past.

I ran my fingers over the image.

A lump rose in my throat. My vision blurred slightly, but I refused to let the tears fall. Not here. Not now.

My fingers trembled as I traced the edges of the photograph, the glossy surface cold under my fingertips. Shelby.

Her face stared back at me, frozen in time. Young. Full of life. Gone too soon.

I forced air into my lungs, but it was like breathing through smoke. The edges of the room seemed to close in, the weight of the file pressing heavier against my lap.

I barely registered Amy standing up, or Jordan moving beside me.

The world outside this file didn't exist anymore.

It was just me and the past.

I flipped to the next photo. Her body at the bottom of Devil's Backbone. The fall had been brutal, the rocks unforgiving. The Shelby I remembered had been vibrant, fierce, stubborn.

Not broken. Not—

I sucked in a sharp breath and slammed the file shut.

"Harlie," Jordan said carefully.

I held up a hand, squeezing my eyes shut and pressing my fingers into my temples. "Why did he have this?"

"I don't know," Jordan muttered.

Amy stepped over to my chair. "Harlie, maybe we should—"

I pushed up from the chair so fast it fell against the floor. "I need air."

Neither of them stopped me. They just watched as I turned and walked out of the office, the file still clutched tightly in my hands.

INTERVIEW WITH DETECTIVE HARLIE WHITLOCK

INTERVIEWER: Harlie, can you tell me what's in that file you're holding?

WHITLOCK: It's Shelby Wainswright's file. Of all the things I thought we'd find, Shelby was the last person I expected to see in that damn office.

INTERVIEWER: I remember when she died. It was ruled a suicide.

WHITLOCK: That's what they told us. That's what they wanted us to believe.

INTERVIEWER: But you never believed it, right?

WHITLOCK: Shelby wasn't the kind of girl who gave up. She was tough. She could talk circles around anyone, and she didn't scare easy. We had plans, you know? The night before she died, we were sitting on her bedroom floor, stuffing clothes into a duffel bag, planning our escape.

INTERVIEWER: Escape?

WHITLOCK: We were leaving Sinister Falls. That was the plan. We'd been saving money — cash we stashed in an old shoe box under her bed. It wasn't much, but it was enough to get us out of town, enough to start over somewhere else.

INTERVIEWER: But she never made it.

WHITLOCK: No. She never made it.

INTERVIEWER: What was the last thing she said to you?

WHITLOCK: She told me she had something to do before we left. That there was something she had to take care of. I begged her to just forget it, to just pack her bag and leave with me the next day. But she was stubborn. She told me, 'I need to do this, Harlie. Just trust me. I'll see you tomorrow.'

INTERVIEWER: But there was no tomorrow.

WHITLOCK: No. There wasn't. The next morning, I woke up to sirens. They said she jumped. That she'd been heartbroken over some stupid breakup with a guy. That she stood at the edge of Devil's Backbone and just let go. But I never bought it. Not for a damn second.

INTERVIEWER: And now, after finding that file in Nolan's office?

WHITLOCK: Now I know I was right.

INTERVIEWER: What's in the file?

WHITLOCK: Reports, notes, interviews that never made it into the official case file. And photos. Photos of her at the bottom of that cliff.

INTERVIEWER: You've seen crime scene photos before.

WHITLOCK: This was different. This was personal. Shelby wasn't just another body. She was my best friend. And now, after all these years, I have to sit here and wonder if she died because she trusted the wrong person with the wrong secret.

INTERVIEWER: What do you think happened?

WHITLOCK: I think she saw something she wasn't supposed to

see. And I think Nolan made sure she never had the chance to talk about it.

INTERVIEWER: Do you think Nolan covered it up? Or even killed her?

WHITLOCK: I don't know. I've spent my whole life thinking I'd never get answers about Shelby. That she was just gone, and there was nothing I could do to change that.

INTERVIEWER: What happens next?

WHITLOCK: Next? I put the pieces together. I find the truth. Nolan is still out there, and I'm done waiting for answers to come to me. It's time to bring this to him.

INTERVIEWER: You sound certain.

WHITLOCK: I am. I don't care what it takes — I'm going to get justice. For Shelby. For Leah. For Evelyn. For all of them.

INTERVIEWER: And if Nolan doesn't go down easy?

WHITLOCK: Then he's about to find out exactly what happens when you push me too far.

INTERVIEWER: But aren't you supposed to stay at the station? Walker and Callaway gave you a direct order to stay put.

WHITLOCK: Orders? I'm done taking orders. I'm done sitting on my hands, waiting for Walker and Mark to 'get back with me.' I've spent my whole damn life waiting for the truth to come to me. I waited for someone to tell me what really happened to Shelby. I waited for the justice system to do its damn job. And where did that get me? Nowhere.

INTERVIEWER: So what are you going to do?

WHITLOCK: I'm going to find Nolan. Right now. I don't need permission. I don't need backup. I need answers. And I'm not waiting for anyone else to find them for me.

CHAPTER FIFTY

Jordan and Amy were still buried in Nolan's files when I stepped out into the late afternoon air, the file on Shelby burning a hole in my thoughts. I hadn't told them I was leaving—didn't need the looks, the questions, or the well-meaning warnings. Jordan's keys were still in my pocket from earlier, and I wasn't about to waste time. I didn't know exactly where Nolan was… but my gut did. And I'd learned to trust it.

I headed to Nolan's cabin. I knew State Police had already checked it, but Nolan was smart—too smart to get caught that easily. It wouldn't surprise me if he'd waited for them to leave, doubled back, and holed up there, thinking no one would expect him to return. If he was desperate, if he had nowhere else to go, the cabin was his best bet. And I knew he had a couple of nearby hangout spots.

Every mile gnawed at my nerves. I white-knuckled the steering wheel, my mind flitting between Shelby, Evelyn, and the thousand unanswered questions they'd left behind. I kept seeing Shelby's face. Hearing the last thing she said to me.

"One more night, Har. Then we're gone."

We had plans to leave Sinister Falls the next day. Pack up and never look back. She was done with the secrets, the lies, the small-town judgment. So was I.

But she never got that chance.

I reached the cabin just as the sun was dipping low. The front door hung open, creaking slightly in the breeze. Bottles littered the porch, cigarette butts scattered like dead flies.

"Nolan?" I called.

No answer.

I stepped inside. The cabin was wrecked—furniture overturned, drawers yanked open, more whiskey bottles everywhere.

But he wasn't here.

I hit his hangout spots. The old ridge turnout near Lockwood Quarry, where the view stretched forever and cell service vanished. Then the clearing off Highway 9, near the abandoned ranger station. Nolan had taken his coffee there once, years ago, told me it was where he went when he couldn't breathe inside city limits. Both were empty.

I sat in the car just off the gravel shoulder, engine idling. He wasn't at the cabin. Wasn't at the quarry. Wasn't anywhere obvious.

I pressed my forehead to the steering wheel. Every second ticking past felt louder than the last.

I slammed my hand against the steering wheel.

"Damn it, Nolan, where the hell are you?"

My eyes burned, but I didn't blink.

A feeling came over me. One of those gut feelings cops get. You don't know where it came from, but you learn to go with them.

Devil's Backbone.

It was isolated. Quiet. A place where a man could think and not be found.

I threw the car into gear and turned toward the cliffs, the engine roaring as gravel kicked out behind me.

By the time I reached Devil's Backbone, the sky was a bruised purple. I saw Nolan before he saw me.

He stood near the edge, swaying slightly, his service weapon in his hand catching the last bit of light. His shirt was soaked through with sweat, his face blotchy and red. Drunk. Desperate.

I stepped out, gun drawn. "Nolan. Drop the weapon. Put your hands behind your head."

He didn't move.

"Don't do this," I said.

He laughed bitterly. "This is exactly where it ends, Whitlock. You don't get it, do you? You were never meant to find the truth."

I kept my aim steady. "I found a file in your office. Shelby Wainswright. Why did you have that, Nolan?"

His shoulders dropped, like the question deflated him.

"Because she saw too much," he murmured.

I stepped closer. "Tell me what happened. Evelyn Carter. Start there."

He didn't look at me. Just stared out over the edge.

"I loved her," he said. "God help me, I was so damn in love with Evelyn Carter. But she wanted more. Milton was giving her gifts, promising her things I couldn't. She said she was pregnant… might've been mine, might've been his, hell, maybe neither of us. But she started blackmailing him. Threatening to ruin him if he didn't pay."

"And Milton paid?"

He nodded slowly. "Until he didn't. One day, he called me. Told me he needed help. I went to his house and found her there, dead. Lying on the floor just inside the door. Head bashed in. Nadine was standing over her with a brass statue, just… staring. Blood all over it."

"Nadine killed her?"

He nodded again, a single, trembling motion. "Milton panicked. Said we had to clean it up. I helped. We put Evelyn in my cruiser. Milton took her car. We drove up Pinnacle Road. Milton rolled the car off the cliff, then we threw her body beside it, to make it look like she was ejected."

"You covered it up," I said.

"Yeah," Nolan whispered. "We did."

"Why didn't you just put Evelyn in her car before rolling it off the cliff? Would've looked more… natural."

He kept glancing between the drop and me, his eyes wild, unfocused.

"I wasn't thinking straight, okay? The whole thing happened too fast…"

"Milton was barking orders, swearing we had to move fast before anyone saw. I-I didn't stop to think. I just did what he said."

"Did you know Leah might have been your daughter?"

Nolan broke. He covered his face, sobbing. "No. God, no. I didn't know. Not until Seth came to the cabin, ranting. Said she had been digging. Said she'd wanted a DNA test. He said she was a threat—to his inheritance, to me. Tried to blackmail me. Said if I didn't help him shut you up, to keep you from finding out he'd killed her, he'd take me down with him."

I took another step closer. "Is that when he tried to kill me?"

Nolan nodded. "He said you were getting too close. Said he was going to take care of you. I tried to stop him. I grabbed him by the neck. He fought me off and left."

"What about Shelby?"

His whole body sagged like it couldn't hold the weight anymore.

"She was walking. Down Pinnacle. We didn't see her. She saw us roll Evelyn over. Saw the whole thing. She started screaming. Milton hit her, knocked her out. Then he looked at me and said, 'Get rid of her'."

My vision blurred.

"You killed her."

"I brought her here," Nolan choked out, his voice breaking between ragged sobs. "I… I told myself it would look like suicide. I thought that would make it easier."

I tightened my grip on the gun. My hands were shaking.

"It's over, Nolan. No more lies. No more running. You can still do the right thing. Come with me."

He looked at me, eyes glassy. "You know, the other day when you asked me if I ever wished I had kids?"

I nodded.

He smiled. A broken, tragic smile. "I do. And I always imagined if I had a daughter, she'd be a lot like you."

I heard footsteps behind me.

I hoped it was Mark.

I kept my eyes on Nolan. "Please, Nolan. Come with me. You have a chance to make this right."

He looked away, toward the horizon. Then back at me.

"I can't do that," he whispered.

He stepped back—just one step—and vanished over the edge.

"NOLAN!"

The scream ripped from my throat as I lunged forward, gravel sliding under my boots. I hit the ground hard, skidding to my knees, fingers clawing at the rocky ledge like I could somehow catch him.

Mark was there in an instant, arms wrapping around my waist, yanking me back just as the edge crumbled beneath my hands.

"Harlie, stop—he's gone!"

But I wasn't listening. All I could hear was the rush of blood in my ears, the echo of Nolan's final step, and the sound of my own voice, still calling his name into the void.

"I wanted him dead so many times," I whispered. "So many times. Why do I feel like this?"

Mark wrapped his arms around me, holding me against his chest.

"Because you care, Harl," he said quietly. "Because you care."

I let myself break.

INTERVIEW WITH LIEUTENANT MARK CALLAWAY

INTERVIEWER: Lieutenant Callaway, thank you for speaking with me. I know this... isn't easy.

CALLAWAY: No, it's not.

INTERVIEWER: You were there. At Devil's Backbone. You saw what happened.

CALLAWAY: I saw enough. Too much.

INTERVIEWER: Were you surprised Nolan jumped?

CALLAWAY: No. I know the type. Men like him — they build their lives on control. Power, intimidation, secrets. And they spend years thinking they're untouchable. Until the walls start closing in. Then they crack. Never all at once. It's slow. Ugly. Loud on the inside, even if they keep it quiet on the surface.

INTERVIEWER: Did you expect him to go out like that?

CALLAWAY: I hoped Harlie would reach him. But deep down... I knew what kind of ending he was chasing.

INTERVIEWER: What was she like when you got there?

CALLAWAY: Focused. Calm, but... not okay. She had her gun drawn, but it wasn't about force. It was about connection. She was trying to keep him tethered. You could hear it in her voice — she didn't want to arrest him. She wanted him to face it. Say it. Own it. And live with it.

INTERVIEWER: Do you think he was going to confess?

CALLAWAY: He already had. Not in a courtroom. But to her. She got the truth out of him, piece by piece. She held her ground and just... kept him talking. I've never seen anything like it. She didn't flinch. Didn't look away.

INTERVIEWER: But it wasn't enough?

CALLAWAY: No. It wasn't. He made his choice the second he stepped onto that cliff. All she did was delay it. Hold the weight of it with him for a few more minutes. And that's... that's the part that breaks me.

INTERVIEWER: You mean watching her try to save him?

CALLAWAY: Watching her carry it. Watching her try. Watching her hope. Even after everything she'd uncovered, everything he'd done — she still wanted to save him. And when he went over, it didn't just take him. It took something out of her too.

CALLAWAY: You ever see someone die?

INTERVIEWER: No.

CALLAWAY: It's a hell of a thing. No matter what a person's done... seeing them stop being. One second they're right there — breathing, talking, broken and flawed and human — and the next, they're just... gone. It leaves a mark on you. Doesn't matter if you thought they deserved it. It still leaves a mark.

INTERVIEWER: She cared, even though she wanted him dead before.

CALLAWAY: She did. And that's Harlie. She can want justice, she can want the truth, but she's not made of stone. People like Nolan — corrupt, dangerous — she still holds space for them in some corner of her heart because she sees the damage, not just the destruction. It doesn't excuse anything, but it explains everything about her.

INTERVIEWER: And now?

CALLAWAY: Now she has to live with all of it. The truth, the lies, the ending. And I'll be here. Whether she wants me or not. Because no one should carry this alone.

Chapter Fifty-One

I stood with my arms crossed in the dim hallway of the station, eyes locked on the one-way glass. Inside the first interview room, Milton Jenkins sat with his arms resting on the table, fingers laced, his spine straight like he thought he was sitting behind his desk in city hall. He looked calm. Composed. A man still playing the part.

Mark stood beside me. He handed me a coffee he must have picked up from the breakroom.

"I don't want this," I muttered.

"I know," he said. "But your hands are shaking, and now they have something to hold on to."

I looked down. They were.

We stood like that, shoulder to shoulder, watching.

"You holding up?" he asked softly.

I didn't answer.

He didn't push.

Inside the room, Walker leaned forward. Milton didn't flinch.

"We have your statements. We have Nolan's confession. We have physical evidence. What we need now is your truth," Walker said.

Milton tilted his chin. "Truth is a funny word, Detective. Everyone seems to have their own version."

Walker didn't bite. "Let's focus on Evelyn Carter."

Milton exhaled slowly. "She kept showing up at our house. Said the baby she'd had was mine. She wanted money. Said if I didn't give it to her, she'd destroy us."

"And your wife was there?"

He nodded once. "Nadine was pregnant at the time. Already struggling. Evelyn pushed her. Not physically, but emotionally. She kept saying that child was mine. Kept saying she'd tell the whole damn town."

"So what happened next?"

Milton stared at the table. "I wasn't there when it happened. I came home and found Evelyn on the floor. Blood pooling under her head. Nadine was standing there… shaking. Holding that brass statue. The one from the hall table."

"Did she tell you what happened?"

"No," Milton said quietly. "She just kept saying she was sorry."

Walker let the silence stretch. "So you called Nolan."

"Yes."

"You told him what?"

"That I needed him to help me fix something."

"And he did."

Milton looked up. "We both did."

I stepped away from the glass, the coffee still untouched in my hand. Mark followed me as I walked down the hallway.

"You okay?" he asked again.

I paused outside the second interrogation room. "What does 'okay' even look like anymore?" I asked.

Mark didn't answer.

I looked at him. "You ever watch someone unravel in real time?"

"Yeah," he said finally. "But not like that. Not with a gun in their hand and a lifetime of rot on their back."

I nodded slowly, staring through the glass again. "It's like watching a house burn down. You know there's no saving it, but you can't stop looking. And later, all you smell is smoke."

"And it stays in your clothes. Your hair. Your skin."

I turned to him. "But you still go back into the next fire."

He met my eyes. "Yeah," he said. "Guess I've just accepted I'll always smell a little like smoke."

We stood there in silence.

Amy stepped up beside us, looking into the room through the glass, where Nadine Jenkins sat hunched, hands clasped in her lap.

"Is she talking?" Amy asked.

I nodded. "Just started."

Nadine's voice was barely above a whisper. "I was pregnant," she said. "I was exhausted. And scared. Evelyn showed up, out of nowhere. Said she'd had Milton's child. Said she wanted money or she'd ruin us. Said she'd tell everyone in town."

"How did you respond?" the detective asked.

Nadine's face crumpled. "I told her to leave. I begged her."

"And then?"

"She wouldn't stop. She kept shouting. I didn't think. I grabbed the statue and I hit her."

Amy laid a hand gently on my arm. "Harlie…"

I shook my head, eyes fixed on the glass. "Just… listen."

Nadine's voice wavered. "I didn't mean to kill her. I didn't. I just wanted her to stop."

"What did Milton do?"

She covered her mouth, tears slipping down her cheeks. "He said we had to fix it. Said no one could know."

"And you let him?"

Nadine looked straight at the detective. "I didn't just let him. I wanted him to."

I felt Mark's hand brush mine.

I was still holding the coffee. My fingers had gone numb around the cup, like I was afraid that if I let go of it, the weight of everything might finally crush me.

INTERVIEW WITH OFFICER AMY WALSH

INTERVIEWER: Officer Walsh, thank you for making time to speak with me. I know the last few days have been... difficult.

WALSH: That's one word for it.

INTERVIEWER: You've been with Sinister Falls PD for under a year, is that right?

WALSH: Yeah. Still a rookie. At least, I thought I was getting a handle on things. Turns out, the rulebook kind of gets thrown out the window when half your town's leadership collapses.

INTERVIEWER: You've been working closely with Harlie. What has that been like?

WALSH: Intimidating. Inspiring. Honestly? Both. She's not what I expected when I got into this job. She's... sharp. Focused. Not afraid to push boundaries if it means getting to the truth. At first, I thought she was reckless. But now I think she's just... brave in a way I haven't learned to be yet.

INTERVIEWER: That's quite a statement.

WALSH: It's true. I watched her walk into every fire, every impossible situation, and never once ask for backup. She took hits no one should have to take — emotionally, physically — and she kept going. Even after Nolan... even after what happened on that cliff, she didn't break down. Not where anyone could see, anyway.

INTERVIEWER: What was it like, watching all this unfold? The chief. The mayor. Nadine Jenkins...

WALSH: I used to think everything was black or white. That good people wore the badge, and bad people got arrested. But now? Now I know it's not that clean. I watched a man I used to say 'Good morning' to walk off a cliff. I watched the mayor, a man who ran our town for years, sit behind a pane of glass and admit he buried a body. And his wife — God... I still can't get her voice out of my head.

INTERVIEWER: Has it changed how you see the job?

WALSH: Completely. I don't think it's about catching the bad guy anymore. I think it's about standing in the gray. Making sure truth has someone to speak through, even when it's ugly. Especially when it's ugly. Harlie taught me that — maybe without meaning to.

INTERVIEWER: Do you think she'll stay on the force?

WALSH: I don't know. Part of me hopes she does. God, do I hope she does. But part of me also thinks... maybe she deserves a break. To breathe. I don't know how someone carries what she's carrying.

INTERVIEWER: And what about the department? Who leads it now?

WALSH: That's the question no one wants to say out loud. Nolan's gone. Milton's behind bars. And Harlie? She's the strongest one we've got, but... is she supposed to lead us while still bleeding from the fight?

INTERVIEWER: If she does leave, how do you think that will affect the department?

WALSH: It'll be like losing the compass. She was never the

chief, but she was the one we followed. At least, I did. She was the one who reminded me this job is more than just rules and codes — it's people. Messy, hurting, complicated people.

INTERVIEWER: You've also gotten to meet Lieutenant Callaway during the investigation.

WALSH: Yeah. The famous ex-fiancé. He's sharp. And he really cares about her, you can see that. He kept his distance when he had to, but he stepped up when it mattered. It was... kind of nice, watching Harlie let someone have her back for once.

INTERVIEWER: What comes next for you?

WALSH: I keep showing up. That's what Harlie does, and that's what I'm going to do too. Even when it's hard. Even when I don't know what tomorrow looks like. I put on the badge, and I try to be better than I was the day before.

INTERVIEWER: And for her?

WALSH: I just hope she finds some peace. Even if it's just a moment. She deserves that much.

INTERVIEW WITH OFFICER JORDAN REYES

INTERVIEWER: Jordan, I appreciate you taking the time to speak with me. I know this hasn't been easy.

REYES: That's an understatement. But yeah — I'm here.

INTERVIEWER: You've worked with Harlie for a while now. Can you tell me what it's been like, watching this case unfold?

REYES: Like watching a controlled burn get out of control. You think you're containing the damage, but the fire's already in the walls. Harlie... she tried to fight it anyway. Kept coming back with more ashes on her boots.

INTERVIEWER: Was there ever a moment where you thought she wouldn't come out the other side?

REYES: The night she nearly went off that cliff? Yeah. I thought that was it. Not just because she almost died, but because she came back different. Quiet. Focused, but in that way you recognize when someone's holding too much and just waiting to collapse.

INTERVIEWER: And you just let her keep going?

REYES: You don't let Harlie do anything. She makes the call. But I tried to be there, where I could be. Sometimes that meant backing her up. Sometimes it meant shutting the hell up and staying out of her way.

INTERVIEWER: What was it like when you found the file on Shelby Wainswright?

REYES: Like my heart dropped into my shoes. I opened that drawer just like any other, expecting more junk. But when I saw her name on that file... everything stopped. And Harlie — she was right there. Watching. I didn't even have a second to think about hiding it or softening the blow.

INTERVIEWER: Did you try to stop her from looking?

REYES: I did. I told her she probably didn't want to see what was inside. But you don't tell Harlie Whitlock what to look at or what to feel. She took it, sat down, and opened it like it was her responsibility. And maybe it was. That was her best friend. Shelby wasn't just a name in a case file. She was someone Harlie had loved. Someone she'd lost. That moment — it was like watching her pick up a wound that had never really healed, and slice it open all over again.

INTERVIEWER: Did you know about Shelby Wainswright?

REYES: Yeah. I went to school with both of them. Shelby, Harlie, me — we were all in the same circle. Or as close to a circle as three kids with very different lives could be. Shelby's death... back then, we just accepted what we were told. Suicide. Small town tragedy. But Harlie never bought it. She buried the grief and kept the suspicion. Now I know she was right to.

INTERVIEWER: What was it like watching her look through that file in Nolan's office?

REYES: Gut-wrenching. She didn't say much, didn't have to. The way she held that file, like it weighed a thousand pounds. The way she looked at Shelby's photo like she was apologizing. I knew right then this case wasn't just about justice anymore. It was about ghosts. And Shelby was one of hers.

INTERVIEWER: Were you surprised when Nolan jumped?

REYES: No. I was surprised it took that long. You could see it all unraveling in him, like one thread after another was being pulled and there was no fabric left to hold. The only thing holding him up in the end was Harlie's voice — and even that couldn't pull him back.

INTERVIEWER: What about Milton and Nadine Jenkins?

REYES: People like them — they thrive in places like this. Small towns with too much pride and not enough oversight. They thought they could control the narrative forever. But time has a way of catching up. Harlie just sped it along.

INTERVIEWER: What do you think happens to the department now?

REYES: Hell if I know. We've got no chief, half our leadership's in jail or dead, and the people left standing are tired. Amy's good. She'll find her legs. Me? I'll hold the line where I can. But the one holding this whole place together was Harlie. Still is, even if she doesn't want the job.

INTERVIEWER: Do you think she'll leave?

REYES: Yeah. I do. Maybe not today, maybe not next week — but she's running on empty, and she's done more than her share. If she stays, she'll burn out completely. And no one deserves that, least of all her.

INTERVIEWER: Would you blame her if she walked away?

REYES: Not for a second. But if she does, I hope she finds something that gives her back what this job took. Peace. Sleep. Hell, even just silence. And I hope wherever she ends up, she knows she changed this place for the better.

INTERVIEWER: And you? What will you do?

REYES: Keep the lights on. Keep the coffee hot. And keep telling the truth — like she taught me.

INTERVIEW WITH MRS. NADINE JENKINS
LOCATION: COUNTY DETENTION CENTER – VISITATION
ROOM

INTERVIEWER: Mrs. Jenkins, thank you for agreeing to speak with me today.

MRS. JENKINS: I'm not sure I deserve to speak. But... I'll talk.

INTERVIEWER: Let's start with the question on everyone's mind. What was it really like being married to Milton Jenkins?

MRS. JENKINS: It was quiet. Polished. Controlled. From the outside, we looked like the perfect couple. The judge and his wife. The mayor and the mother of his child. We hosted fundraisers. Shook hands. Wore the right clothes. Said the right things. And behind closed doors... I was shrinking.

INTERVIEWER: Shrinking?

MRS. JENKINS: I stopped existing for myself. Everything was about Milton — his career, his legacy, his image. I learned early that the easiest way to survive was to become small. Agreeable. Gracious. And invisible. If I questioned him, I was 'emotional.' If I was upset, I was 'ungrateful.' He never raised a hand to me. But he didn't need to.

INTERVIEWER: Psychological control?

MRS. JENKINS: Yes. He could silence me with a glance. Make

me question my memory, my instincts, my worth. And for a long time, I let him. Because I was terrified of what would happen if I didn't.

INTERVIEWER: And what about your relationship with Nolan?

MRS. JENKINS: Nolan... he was kind to me. In quiet ways. When Milton left the room, Nolan stayed and asked if I was okay. He brought me books once, when I was on bedrest with Seth. He never crossed a line, but I think he saw me. Really saw me. And I saw him too. What Milton did to me, he did to Nolan too. Different chains, same prison.

INTERVIEWER: He called you a good woman.

MRS. JENKINS: I don't know that I am. But I think Nolan wanted to believe I was, because he needed something in that house to still be good.

INTERVIEWER: What would you say to him, if you could?

MRS. JENKINS: I'd say... I'm sorry. For my silence. For what I helped Milton make you into. For what we asked of you that night. You were a broken man trying to be loyal to someone who didn't deserve it. I don't forgive what you did, Nolan — but I understand why you thought it was your only way out.

MRS. JENKINS: I wish I'd spoken up sooner. Maybe none of us would be here.

INTERVIEWER: What about Harlie Whitlock?

MRS. JENKINS: She's everything I wasn't. Brave. Loud. Unrelenting. She kicked open every door I spent my life pretending wasn't locked. And she did it without losing herself. That girl... she carries too much, but she never drops it. I envy that. I admire it. And I hope she knows — she saved more than she knows. Not just Evelyn. Not just Shelby. She saved the truth.

INTERVIEWER: And Evelyn Carter?

MRS. JENKINS: I hated you in that moment. Because I was afraid. Because you said the things I didn't have the strength to say. But you didn't deserve what happened to you. No one does. And I am so sorry. For every time I looked the other way. For the life I helped destroy. For the child you lost. And for the girl I used to be... who might've been your friend, if the world had been different.

INTERVIEWER: Do you think people will ever forgive you?

MRS. JENKINS: I don't expect them to. But maybe, in telling the truth now... I've started to forgive myself.

INTERVIEW WITH MILTON JENKINS
LOCATION: COUNTY DETENTION CENTER – INTERVIEW ROOM B

INTERVIEWER: Thank you for sitting down with me, Mr. Jenkins.

JENKINS: I'm not sure what there is left to say, but... I suppose even broken statues cast shadows.

INTERVIEWER: That's a poetic way to start.

JENKINS: That's how I survived for so long — polish. Presentation. Keep the speeches flowing and the hands shaking, and nobody asks what's underneath.

INTERVIEWER: What is underneath?

JENKINS: Fear. Mostly. And pride. I built my whole damn life trying to outrun both.

INTERVIEWER: You were a judge. Then mayor. You had power, influence. Why wasn't that enough?

JENKINS: Power isn't about having — it's about keeping. People think success is the reward. It's not. It's the leash. Every move you make is about defending what you've built, what people expect you to be. I stopped being a man and became a symbol a long time ago. And symbols? They don't get to crack.

INTERVIEWER: But you did crack.

JENKINS: Didn't I just. The problem with secrets is they multiply. And I had too many to count. Every decision I made to protect my image only bought me more chains.

INTERVIEWER: Let's talk about Evelyn Carter.

JENKINS: She was a problem. A fire I couldn't contain. And I... I loved her. Once. But not in any way that meant anything to her. I was... convenient. Powerful. And she was angry — at everything. She wanted to burn the house down, and I was standing in the doorway.

INTERVIEWER: Did you believe the child was yours?

JENKINS: I didn't want to know. That's the honest answer. If she was, then everything I had would crumble. My marriage. My campaign. My spotless record. So I chose willful ignorance. And that made me weak. It made me dangerous.

INTERVIEWER: You let Nadine carry the burden of that night.

JENKINS: No. I handed it to her. Nadine had been unraveling for years, and I... I needed to control the narrative. I saw what that statue had done. Saw the blood. And all I could think about was how to clean it up. Not comfort my wife. Not mourn the woman on the floor. Just — damage control.

INTERVIEWER: That's what defined you, isn't it? Controlling the narrative.

JENKINS: I told myself I was protecting my family. My town. But really? I was protecting myself. And when you start calling cowardice 'strategy,' you're already lost.

INTERVIEWER: What about Shelby Wainswright?

JENKINS: She shouldn't have been there. She was just a kid. A loud, scared kid. She saw too much. And I made a call I'll regret for the rest of my life.

INTERVIEWER: You gave Nolan the order?

JENKINS: I didn't say the words. I didn't have to. He knew what I meant. He always did. That's the kind of loyalty we trafficked in. I leaned on him for everything. Every mess I made, he cleaned. I didn't have a deputy. I had a shield.

INTERVIEWER: Did you ever feel guilt?

JENKINS: Of course I did. But guilt's a quiet thing. Easy to ignore when applause is louder. I convinced myself that what I was doing was for the greater good. That I was preserving something bigger than myself. But I see now — I wasn't a pillar. I was the rot.

INTERVIEWER: What do you think your legacy is now?

JENKINS: Legacy? A fancy word for what's left of your lies. I think people will remember the headlines. The downfall. Maybe a few will remember the parks I built, the roads I fixed, the scholarships I funded. But those won't outshine what I buried.

INTERVIEWER: And what would you say to Harlie Whitlock?

JENKINS: She saw through me. From the beginning. I underestimated her — called her reckless, impulsive. But the truth is... she has something I never had. A spine made of iron and a heart that won't quit. I hated her for it. Feared her for it. And in the end... she was the only one brave enough to rip the mask off.

INTERVIEWER: Last question. What do you want people to understand about the man behind the mayor?

JENKINS: That I started out believing I could make a difference. That I let fear turn me into something unrecognizable. That I destroyed lives not because I had to — but because I chose to protect myself first. And I'll live with that. In this cell. In my silence. For however long I've got left.

INTERVIEWER: I want to ask you about your son. About Seth.

JENKINS: Yeah. I figured you would.

INTERVIEWER: What kind of relationship did you have with him?

JENKINS: Complicated. I loved him. I did. But... I don't think he ever felt it.

INTERVIEWER: Why not?

JENKINS: Because I didn't know how to show it. I thought if I gave him opportunity, structure, discipline — he'd understand. That he'd grow up to be a man who could carry the name I'd spent my whole life building.

INTERVIEWER: So it was about legacy?

JENKINS: At first. Then it became about control. Seth wasn't like me. He was... fragile in ways I didn't recognize until it was too late. I pushed him hard. Told myself I was shaping him. But really, I think I was just molding him into something he never asked to be.

INTERVIEWER: Did you know what he was capable of?

JENKINS: No. I didn't want to. That's the truth. There were signs — his drug use, the outbursts, the drinking. But I looked the other way. Told myself he'd grow out of it. That boys flail before they find their footing.

INTERVIEWER: And when you found out what he did to Leah Emerson?

JENKINS: I wanted it to be a lie. I prayed it was. But somewhere deep down... I think I always knew he was capable of something terrible. He was unraveling, and I was too busy holding up my own mask to stop it. Maybe if I'd shown him compassion instead of expectation... maybe he wouldn't have——

INTERVIEWER: Killed her?

JENKINS: Yes.

INTERVIEWER: Do you blame yourself?

JENKINS: Every day. I built a house of lies and raised my son inside it. What kind of man does that? What kind of father?

INTERVIEWER: If you could speak to him now — what would you say?

JENKINS: I'd tell him I'm sorry. Not just for what happened. But for everything I made him believe he had to be. I told him weakness was failure. That fear was shameful. I passed my own sickness onto him, and then stood back and watched it devour him.

INTERVIEWER: And Leah?

JENKINS: She didn't deserve what happened to her. None of them did — Evelyn, Shelby, Leah... they were all casualties of my choices. My silence. My cowardice. I let my son carry a burden that started with me. And I'll carry that until the day I die.

Chapter Fifty-Two

The house was quiet when we got back. I let us in through the kitchen door. The place smelled faintly like lavender dryer sheets and whatever was left in the fridge that should've been thrown out last week.

Mark stepped in behind me, looking around like he was trying to picture the younger version of me growing up here.

"Wow," he said. "You actually had a normal childhood?"

"Define 'normal'."

He shot me a grin. "Well, for starters, I didn't picture wallpaper with sunflowers."

"Mom redid that in '04. You should've seen it before—everything was mauve. Like a funeral parlor married a dollhouse."

He wandered into the kitchen and opened a few cabinets like he was looking for something.

"Make yourself at home," I muttered, setting my bag down on one of the dining chairs.

"I plan to," he said. "You got wine?"

"Somewhere. Probably bottom shelf behind the instant coffee."

He always found what he was looking for—on the job, and apparently in my mother's kitchen. He pulled out a bottle of red, sniffed the cork like a snob, then poured two glasses.

"You even have clean glasses," he said, handing me one.

"Not my house. My mom's neurotic."

We sat at the dining table, legs stretched out, wine in hand, like the day hadn't just chewed us up and spat us out.

"So," he said after a sip. "Want me to make dinner?"

"You offering or showing off?"

He smirked. "Bit of both."

"You remember the last time you cooked for me?" I asked.

His eyes lit up. "Dallas. My apartment. You accused me of trying to poison you."

I grinned. "You made chicken. It was pink in the middle."

"It was medium rare!"

"It was salmonella on a plate."

He stood up, rolled his sleeves, and headed toward the fridge. "Well, lucky for you, I've grown. I know how ovens work now."

I leaned back, sipping my wine as he rifled through the fridge.

"Jesus," he muttered. "Not a lot to work with in here."

"Cook or complain, your choice."

He grabbed eggs, butter, spinach, and a pack of pasta. "Omelet and garlic noodles. It's what I used to make after graveyard shift in Dallas."

"That was ten years ago," I said.

He shot me a look. "Muscle memory, Whitlock."

The kitchen filled with the sounds and smells of sizzling butter and garlic. Mark moved like someone who'd had to learn how to make a meal without burning the house down.

"So," he said, glancing over his shoulder. "When are you gonna admit I was your favorite partner?"

"You weren't."

"Bullshit."

"You were loud. Messy. Always late. You ate my snacks."

"You labeled your snacks. That's bait."

I laughed. It'd been a while since anything felt light.

He plated dinner like we were at some fancy five-star restaurant—folded omelet, twirled noodles, even wiped the rim with a paper towel.

"Who are you?" I asked, eyeing the dish.

"I'm a man who doesn't burn eggs anymore. You're welcome."

We ate at the table, trading stories from Dallas. Cases that had gone sideways. The time I tackled a guy into a koi pond. The night we stayed in the car during a stakeout and argued for two straight hours about which *Die Hard* was the best.

The first one. Obviously.

After dinner, I stood to clear the plates, but he stopped me. "We wash together."

"Since when do you volunteer for dishes?"

"Since I cooked. Don't make it weird."

So we did—elbows bumping, drying plates, stacking them in the cabinet like nothing about our lives was broken. It was domestic and ridiculous and a little too easy.

After the last fork hit the drawer, he leaned against the counter and crossed his arms. "So... serious question."

"Shoot."

"You still got that dartboard?"

I blinked. "In the garage, yeah. Why?"

He gave me that smug little grin that used to drive me nuts. "Loser makes breakfast."

I grabbed the wine bottle on my way to the garage. "You're gonna be up early."

The garage was cold and smelled like oil and old cardboard. The dartboard was still hanging by the far wall, a little faded but intact. I'd been using it when I needed something to take the edge off without taking it out on drywall.

Mark picked up the darts from the shelf and tossed one lazily at the board—bullseye.

"Of course," I muttered.

"What can I say? I thrive under pressure."

We played in silence for a few minutes, the thunk of darts hitting cork the only sound.

"You're different, Harl."

I didn't look at him. "Everyone's different after this much death."

"No," he said. "You've changed. But you're still standing. That's something."

I met his eyes. "So are you."

"We were good together, weren't we?"

I threw a dart. Hit the edge of the board. "We were."

He walked over, pulled out the darts, and looked back at me. "Think we still could be?"

I stared at him. Thought of Shelby. Of Nolan. Of Evelyn. Of the things I couldn't unsee. The truths I now carried like bricks in my ribs.

"I don't know," I said softly. "But maybe that's not a no."

He nodded. "That's enough," he said. "For tonight."

We played another round. And for a little while, we didn't talk about grief or guilt or ghosts.

Just darts.

And wine.

And the weight of maybe.

Chapter Fifty-Three

The meeting was held in the community room at the station, though it felt more like a courtroom by the time everyone was seated. State Police, town council members, the district attorney, Jordan, Amy, Mark, and I—all seated, all quiet, waiting for someone to start.

Detective Walker stepped up to the podium. "First and foremost," he began, "we want to thank the officers of Sinister Falls for their cooperation, and especially Detective Whitlock, whose work brought truth to light. Without it, we wouldn't be standing here with the answers we now have."

There were a few nods, and I felt every pair of eyes shift toward me. I didn't flinch, but I didn't smile either. The attention felt like light through a magnifying glass.

The town council followed, led by Councilwoman Rayne. She announced the interim mayor—Harold Dorsey, the local high school principal. A steady hand. A well-liked face. He didn't look particularly thrilled about it, but he gave a short, earnest speech about rebuilding trust, transparency, blah blah blah.

Then came the part that actually mattered.

State Police would be temporarily taking over command of the Sinister Falls Police Department.

"The department needs time to restructure," Walker said. "That

"

doesn't mean we don't recognize the good people already in place." He looked toward Jordan and Amy. "It just means they need support. A framework. Some breathing room."

Jordan nodded. Amy looked relieved.

The district attorney stood up toward the end and announced that both Milton and Nadine Jenkins had entered guilty pleas. No deal, no trial, just the sound of a gavel waiting to fall. I didn't feel relief. Not quite. But I appreciated the simplicity.

After the meeting wrapped, people milled about in hushed side conversations. Coffee refills, the occasional handshake, small talk.

I was heading for the door when I felt a hand on my shoulder.

Walker looked down at me, a smile behind the lines on his face. "You did damn good work, Whitlock."

"Thank you," I said.

"Not just good work. Smart. Intuitive. Relentless." He glanced around the room. "We could use someone like you at State."

"You're offering me a job?"

"I'm planting a seed. Think it over. You ever want to run with a bigger team, give me a call."

I gave him a tight smile. "I appreciate it. Really. But I think I need a minute before I jump into another fire."

He nodded. "Fair."

As he stepped away, Mark appeared beside me, hands in his pockets like he hadn't been hovering nearby listening to the whole thing.

"So," he said, tone casual, "Portland PD's hiring."

I gave him a side-eye. "Oh yeah?"

He shrugged, looking entirely too innocent. "Wouldn't be the worst thing. City's got some perks. Good food. Decent people. Solid detectives. One in particular could probably use a dartboard partner."

I huffed a laugh. "You just want to keep an eye on me."

He tilted his head. "Can you blame me?"

I didn't answer that.

"I've got a lot of thinking to do," I said instead.

"I figured," he replied. "That's why I came up with a plan."

I raised an eyebrow.

"There's this cabin," he said. "Near Mount Hood. Middle of nowhere, but cozy. No cell service. Big river nearby. Good for clearing your head. Or for fishing, if you're the outdoorsy type."

"You offering me a vacation?"

"I'm suggesting," he said, "that you take some time for yourself. Let your brain and body come back down to earth. You've been in survival mode for too long."

He looked so damn sincere I couldn't even make a sarcastic comment.

I sighed. "What's the catch?"

He grinned. "You have to let me drive you out there. Just to make sure you don't change your mind halfway up the mountain."

I shook my head. "You're impossible."

Mark smirked. "And yet, here you are. Still talking to me."

I crossed my arms. "What am I supposed to do, just disappear to a cabin in the mountains? What about my mom?"

"I think your mom and Ernestine are perfectly capable of terrorizing every bakery within Portland's city limits without you."

"They do have an unholy obsession with almond croissants."

"Exactly. Between the pastries and Ernestine's campaign to find your mother a proper hobby, I think they'll survive."

I shook my head, trying not to smile. "God help Portland."

Mark grinned. "City's survived worse. And besides, you deserve some quiet. Or, at the very least, a week without gunfire, emotional breakdowns, and coffee that tastes like motor oil."

I rolled my eyes. "You're starting to sound like you care, Callaway."

He leaned in. "Harlie. That ship sailed years ago."

Before I could reply, Amy and Jordan made their way over from across the room. Amy had that bright, eager energy that always made her look like she was two seconds from sprinting into the next crisis.

"I just wanted to say..." Amy glanced between us, then at Mark. "Thank you. For everything. Seriously."

Mark nodded. "You're welcome. You've got a good crew here."

She smiled, then turned to me. "Can I steal you for a second?"

I followed her a few steps away, near the vending machine.

She lowered her voice. "So… are you really going to leave the department and run off to marry Officer Blue Eyes?"

I blinked, then laughed. "Jesus, Walsh."

"Well?" She nudged me.

I shook my head, grinning. "Relax. I'm not getting married. And I haven't made any decisions yet."

"Yet," she said, wiggling her eyebrows.

I gave her a mock glare. "You're lucky I like you."

She winked. "I know."

Meanwhile, Jordan had cornered Mark near the door. I watched them talk, arms crossed, their heads bent in that casual guy-way that somehow still seemed like gossip. I walked up to hear Jordan say, "Thanks for keeping an eye on her."

Mark gave him a crooked smile. "Trust me. Full-time job."

Jordan chuckled. "Lord knows."

I elbowed Jordan in the ribs. "I'm standing right here."

He winced dramatically. "I know! That's why I said it. Accountability."

Mark laughed, his hands up like he was innocent. "I plead the fifth."

I rolled my eyes and shook my head—but this time, I was smiling for real.

For the first time in weeks, the air didn't feel like it was pressing down on my chest.

For the first time in years, maybe, I didn't feel like I was standing on a cliff edge waiting to fall.

I didn't know where I was going next. But I had people beside me—and maybe, just maybe, that was enough.

Epilogue

The cemetery on the hill was quiet. A breeze danced through the grass. The chapel ruins stood off to the side, nothing but scorched bones of what used to be. I didn't look at it. I'd looked enough times before. Today wasn't about that.

I followed the path worn by years and weather, my boots scuffing stone and dirt. I stopped and looked down at the weathered gravestone under a large pine tree.

SHELBY WAINSWRIGHT

I crouched down, fingertips brushing the cool edge of the granite, brushing away some pine needles. I laid the bouquet of forget-me-nots against the stone. Shelby always loved those flowers. She would braid them in her hair and say that was so no one forgot her.

"Hey," I murmured.

"I used to dream about you. After you died. You'd show up at the end of my bed and ask why I didn't come with you. You were mad, every time. You'd say, 'You promised'."

I sniffed, blinking quickly as tears threatened. "And I did promise, didn't I? One more night. That's all we needed. We would've been gone by morning. We could've started over."

My knees ached, but I didn't move.

"I'm sorry," I whispered. "For what happened. For not knowing. For not looking harder."

I brushed my knuckles against the edge of the stone. "But I found the truth. And I made them pay. All of them."

The breeze ruffled the petals.

I stood, brushing the dirt from my jeans. My fingers lingered on her name one more time before I walked on.

The next grave wasn't far. Tucked in a little clearing by a slope of trees.

LEAH EMERSON

Smaller stone. Cleaner space. She hadn't been here long.

I knelt again, this time with no flowers. Just myself.

"You didn't know who you were," I said. "But you were brave enough to ask."

I bowed my head. "I hope you know that matters."

I stayed there a while. Didn't speak. Just let the breeze say what I couldn't.

Then came the farthest grave. Back near the edge of the cemetery. Rough stone.

EVELYN CARTER

She wasn't buried next to anyone. No family. No one claiming her.

My voice didn't shake this time. "I don't know what kind of mother you would've been. But I know you fought. I know you tried."

She couldn't answer. But I felt the gravity of the past lift a little.

I stepped back. I didn't leave flowers. That wasn't what Evelyn needed. She needed truth. And I had found it.

As I walked the path back toward the car, I passed a newer grave. The dirt was still soft.

WILLIAM NOLAN

I stared down at the name.

"I didn't come here for you," I said quietly. "But… here we are."

The breeze answered.

"You broke a lot of things, Nolan. Hurt more people than I'll ever be able to count. But part of me… I think you wanted to be better. I just wish you'd figured out how before the end."

The sun broke through the clouds. A sliver of light hit the edge of his headstone, then vanished.

I waited for something. I didn't know what.

After a beat, I turned back toward the car.

Mark was leaning against the passenger's side, hands in his coat pockets, head down like he was giving me the space I hadn't asked for but still needed.

When I got close, he opened the door without a word.

I paused next to him, glancing up once before I slid inside. He shut the door gently behind me, then walked around to the driver's side and got in.

We didn't speak on the drive down the hill.

I stared out the window for a few minutes, watching the trees blur past, then turned to him. "You ready to lose at fishing?"

He smirked. "Only if you're ready to eat your words. I've got three rods, a cooler full of bait, and a spot near the river that'll make you forget this place ever existed."

I smiled. "Not sure that's possible."

"Doesn't mean it's not worth trying."

I nodded, settling back in my seat. Leaving Sinister Falls, even just for a little while, felt strange.

But I wasn't running. I was just… breathing. And for now, that was enough.

SINISTER FALLS LIVES UP TO ITS NAME

by the Interviewer

I came to Sinister Falls, Oregon, to write about small-town governance — how places far from major media centers manage power, policing, and public accountability.

Mayor Milton Jenkins, who was preparing for re-election, contacted me and invited me to spend time in town. He instructed both his staff and the Sinister Falls Police Department to cooperate with me, and they did. I want to thank everyone in town who spoke with me, especially the officers who shared their time and insight.

I also have personal history here. I spent summers in Sinister Falls growing up, staying with my aunt. I hadn't been back in years.

When I arrived, the story seemed routine: a look at the structure of local government, a police department working with limited resources, and a mayor managing campaign pressures in a place that hasn't changed much in decades.

Then, a murder happened.

The body of a 23-year-old waitress was found near the old power station just outside town limits. What followed was not just a criminal investigation, but the unearthing of systemic dysfunction in how the town handles justice.

The town's police chief, William Nolan, has been in the role for years. Officers I spoke with described his approach as hands-off at best and obstructive at worst. The town's only detective, Harlie Whitlock, who returned to Sinister Falls after serving in the Dallas Police Department, was assigned to the case.

Apparently, murder is not convenient during an election year. Detective Whitlock quickly encountered pressure to step back.

Interviews with police officers and other town employees painted a picture familiar to anyone who has reported from rural America: power is tightly held, oversight is minimal, and the pressure to protect reputations often outweighs the need to pursue the truth. Most people don't speak up unless they're forced to. Even then, the consequences for asking questions can be personal, professional, or both.

Small towns can be places of trust and community. But they can also be places where silence protects the wrong people. Sinister Falls proved that to be true.

As I wrote this story, I kept coming back to the same realization: When there's black in the walls and rot in the foundation, it doesn't matter how charming the exterior looks. Eventually, the damage spreads.

But so can resistance.

I witnessed firsthand that even in places long weighed down by silence, people still push back. Goodness still exists — and justice, even if incomplete, can still be fought for.

I want to express my deepest appreciation to the Town of Sinister Falls — and especially to the members of the Sinister Falls Police Department — for their cooperation, candor, and honesty during a very difficult time.

Follow for future updates as I continue reporting on power and accountability in rural America.

The making of *Sins in Black* has been a journey of years, false starts, rewrites, and total pivots—the kind that made me want to shelve the whole thing more than once. But some stories don't let you walk away. This was one of them.

When I first started writing Harlie Whitlock, she wasn't exactly who she is now. But over time, she revealed herself: sharp, relentless, bruised but never broken. Harlie is the kind of woman who doesn't ask for permission and doesn't wait for backup. She walks into the fire because someone has to—and she does it with grit, sarcasm, and a whole lot of heart. I didn't always know where she was leading me, but I trusted her to get us there. She's tough, flawed, and fiercely loyal. In other words, a survivor.

Sinister Falls, on the other hand, came easy. Maybe too easy. I think most of us have lived through a version of this town—where secrets rot beneath the surface, where power protects the wrong people, and where justice is something you have to fight for. Sinister Falls is fictional, sure, but the feelings it evokes—helplessness, anger, defiance, determination—are all too real. It's not just a setting; it's a character, one that wraps around you like fog and doesn't let go.

This book, at its core, is about facing the darkness, both in the world and within ourselves. It's about deciding who we are when things get ugly. It's about knowing the system's broken and doing the work anyway. And maybe most of all, it's about not giving up. On the truth. On the people who need us. On ourselves.

So thank you—for reading, for sticking with Harlie through the rain and the rot, for seeing the heart beneath the grit. If this story made you feel something—if it lit a fire in you, even for a moment—then I've done my job.

There's more to come. But for now, I'll leave you with this: Fight the good fight. Protect the ones who can't protect themselves. And when the world gets dark—be the one who turns on the damn light.

With all my gratitude,

Dita Dow

About the Author

Dita Dow is an award-winning author celebrated for her gripping thrillers—but her creativity doesn't stop at the page. She's also a songwriter and motivational writer, blending storytelling with rhythm and purpose. With over 30 years of experience in law enforcement and private investigations, Dita brings razor-sharp realism and deep psychological insight to every story she tells.

Born and raised in New Mexico, Dita is a lifelong adventurer with a passion for uncovering ancient ruins, hiking untamed landscapes, and exploring the mysteries of the world. Her work is driven by a love of the unknown and a desire to inspire readers to pursue the extraordinary in their own lives.

Stay up to date on new releases, music, and exclusive content by subscribing to her free newsletter at www.ditadow.com.

Sins in Black: The Album is available now on all major streaming platforms.

Love her work? Don't forget to leave a review!

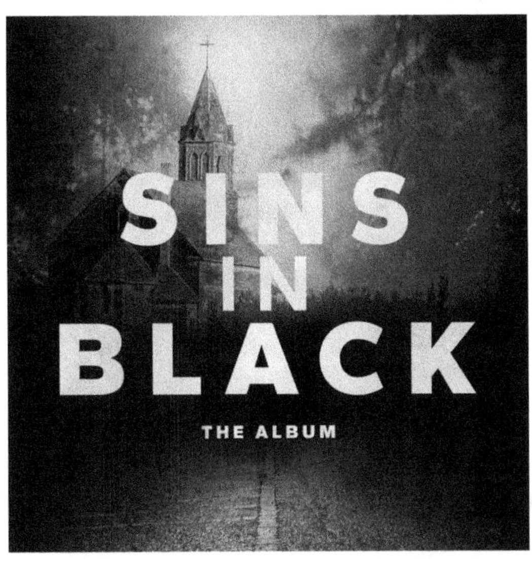

Behind the Lyrics –
Sins in Black: The Album

When I first started writing *Sins in Black*, I never imagined it would one day have its own soundtrack. Music wasn't something I was trained in. I didn't grow up writing songs or composing melodies. But this story—this world—refused to stay on the page. It had a rhythm, a pulse, a voice that needed more space to breathe. So I listened. I learned. And I wrote.

This album is the result of that leap into the unknown. Each track is a piece of the story's soul—Harlie's fight, the weight of secrets, the blurred lines between right and wrong, love and betrayal, truth and silence. These songs came from a place of vulnerability, determination, and raw emotion. I didn't always know what I was doing, but I knew what I needed to say.

No Way Back

This is Harlie's anthem of return. Coming home to Sinister Falls wasn't a choice—it was a reckoning. She didn't come back to heal. She came back to finish something. This song is about staying when running would've been easier. It's about facing the place that hurt you and daring it to try again.

She's Got a Name

If you try to break Harlie Whitlock, you'll learn real fast—she doesn't shatter. This is a defiant, driving piece about identity, survival, and owning every scar. She's not a ghost. She's not a whisper. She's a name you won't forget.

Light of Day

Chief Nolan may have buried the truth, but lies don't stay buried. This song peels back Nolan's layers—his power, his fear, and the shadows he hides in. But light has a way of finding the cracks.

Hell Won't Stay

This one belongs to Sinister Falls. A town so poisoned, even the devil wouldn't make a home here. It's gritty, heavy, and full of ghosted warnings. Some places aren't haunted—they do the haunting.

Roads We Ride

This is about all of us. The lives we live, the choices we make, the people we meet—every bit of it shapes the road we're on. It's a song about the journey, not the destination. About scars that teach, and paths that change you.

Line in the Sand

Trusting in Sinister Falls is a dangerous currency. This song is about deception, broken bonds, and how once that line is crossed, there's no going back. It's sharp, emotional, and honest in a way that stings.

Whisper in the Dark

This is the most introspective track. It's not about fighting the darkness—it's about listening to it. Finding your voice inside it. Accepting that sometimes, the quietest moments reveal the most.

Stand or Fall

My personal favorite. This song carries the weight of the entire story.

It's about that split-second choice we all face: Do we stand for what's right, even when it costs us everything? Or do we fall into silence? Harlie makes her choice. And so do we.

Where the Fire Hides

This song echoes Harlie Whitlock's search for meaning in the shadows of Sinister Falls—a fight to hold onto the fire that still burns beneath the weight of loss, guilt, and buried truths. It's about chasing the thing that keeps you alive, even when the world tries to put that fire out.

What I Couldn't See

This song was born from the idea that we all take different paths, some broken, some quiet, and often without knowing why until much later. The song mirrors Harlie's journey and the choices of those around her, showing how clarity often comes not in the moment, but in what's revealed after the damage is done. It's about the unseen purpose in detours, and the grace hidden in the mess.

Soaring Free

"Soaring Free" wasn't meant to be part of *Sins in Black*, but it found its place—much like the characters it echoes. With its imagery of a raven carving through storm and silence, the song became a symbol of defiance, survival, and the wild freedom that comes from letting go. It's about the ones who refuse to be caged by their past, who rise not because they're unbroken—but because they choose to fly anyway.

Creating this album pushed me in ways I never expected. I'm proud of the songs, not just because they exist, but because of what they represent—grit, growth, and refusing to be quiet when there's something to say.

I hope you feel this music as deeply as I felt writing it. Thank you for listening.

— Dita Dow